Billionaire Lumberjack

Gwyn McNamee

BILLIONAIRE LUMBERJACK

© 2021 Gwyn McNamee

To everyone who has ever let guilt or fear push them to run.

Chapter One

BEAU

The phone in my hand must be made really fucking damn well because as tightly as I'm clenching my fingers around it, any shoddy piece of shit would have already crumbled under the strain. My grip is hard enough that my fingers actually hurt, but it doesn't stop me from channeling my anger and frustration through them and into the plastic. "I pay you enough to buy a small country so that I don't have to deal with this shit, Nate."

After working for me for almost two decades, by now, he should understand this isn't something he should be bothering me with, especially not today with this massive storm barreling down on the mountain like an out-of-control freight train.

"I'm sorry, sir, but I just don't know if I can handle it myself this time. The board is getting...restless. We're coming up on the tenth anniversary, and I'm afraid you'll have a mutiny on your hands if you don't take care of this personally."

I groan and scrub my free hand over my face. Several months' worth of growth scrapes against my calloused palm.

Shit. When was the last time I even shaved?

My ability to not give one single fuck about my appearance is just one of the *many* reasons why what Nate's asking for is off the table. If I were to make an appearance at the annual meeting, I would have to look the part. And there's no way in hell I'm willing to clean myself up and don a ten-thousand-dollar suit just to impress a bunch of assholes who I pay to run *my* company.

One of the perks of being the boss is getting to do whatever the fuck I want, whenever the fuck I want. It's something Nate seems incapable of comprehending at this moment.

"I don't give a fuck, Nate. Handle it, or I'll find someone else who can."

It shouldn't be that hard, really. The board has managed to do just fine without my physical presence for a long fucking time. All they have to do is sign off on the plans and budget for the new year, and then, it will be back to business as usual. The fact that they're giving Nate a hard time about it is only a reflection of the current climate.

They're nervous about the potential new legislation and how it might impact their bottom line. Things have been doing so well over the last ten years that they've become accustomed to the way things are. And now, everyone wants more for doing less. They think the billions flowing into the coffers—and ultimately, their pockets—should come without lifting a damn finger and somehow think my strolling into a meeting to show my face is going to prevent the government from interfering with our way of business.

Lazy fuckers!

I've done enough heavy lifting in my lifetime to know

that sometimes a little hard work and sweat, coupled with patience and a few appropriately timed phone calls to the right people, garner even greater results, and that's all that's needed now. Their meltdown is for nothing. Everything will be handled as it always has been under my watch—and without me there.

A few calls, a few promises, a few concessions—that's all it will take to ensure any new laws that pass won't put us out of business. Whether the environmental groups like it or not, they need what we supply. The business will grow exponentially in the future, as long as we stay the course set out long before I took the helm. All while I stay here, thousands of miles from the bullshit, ass-kissing, and pomp of the boardroom.

I pay lots of people to make sure things run smoothly without my having to leave this place, and I don't plan on changing that anytime soon—something Nate is more than aware of. The fact that he's even bothered to call to raise the issue shows just how dicey things have gotten, but I also have confidence he can work it out.

Nate clears his throat nervously. "I'll see what I can do, boss. Maybe if I talk to Mr. Black and Mr. Dietrich privately, I can sway them and shift the tide on the board."

"I don't care how you fucking do it, just get it done. You know I'm not coming down there. Not now. Not ever." I end the call and slam down the phone with a little more force than I intended.

The tumbler of bourbon on my desk rattles, and I release a deep sigh and pick it up to down what's left in one gulp. Spicy, soothing warmth slides down my throat and ignites my gut. But it doesn't quell the annoyance shifting through my body at having to deal with this on top of the coming storm.

I glance out the window at the lightly falling snow—quiet, picturesque, almost calming. To anyone not familiar with the way the weather works in the Okanogan Range, it might not even be cause for alarm, but I've been here long enough to know it's a harbinger for something much bigger literally on the horizon.

I'm going to need another one of these to help keep me warm before I head out there. It's going to be a real bitch of a storm, and there isn't much time before she fully hits.

It could be days or weeks before I can get out of here for any sort of supplies, and there sure as shit isn't anyone coming up here to bring me anything—I designed it that way.

Perfect beauty in perfect isolation.

But that means I need to make sure everything is battened down and I have an extra-large stock of firewood before it's too brutal outside to do it. The roaring fire in the massive stone fireplace at the center of the living room is the only thing keeping this place warm right now. If I don't keep it burning, it's going to get really uncomfortable, really fast. And a storm like this could mean going through my usual stockpile faster than normal.

I shove my chair back from my desk and make my way to the small bar in the corner with my empty tumbler, my focus on the innocuous-looking flakes outside.

For some reason, it always seems so peaceful right before the shit hits the fan. It's true for Mother Nature and in life. A lesson I wish I never had to learn and could easily forget.

My hand shakes as I grab the decanter and pour myself another double.

Shit.

The call got me all worked up—something I avoid like

the plague. Now, my chest tightens, and old wounds flare back to life, phantom pain coursing through my body.

Blood.

Screams.

Wide, terrified eyes.

Begging for help.

I squeeze my eyes closed, toss back the drink, and grit my teeth against the burn.

No time for distractions like painful memories or problems that can handle themselves.

Chopping down a tree will serve a dual purpose today—stress relief and necessity. Nothing like hacking something to bits to help you forget about the trials and tribulations in the "real" world. The ones I left behind and had hoped would be completely gone from my life by now.

But I'm not that lucky.

I learned *that* a long fucking time ago, in the worst way possible.

There are a lot of people who believe I am lucky, that I *was* lucky. But they're wrong. Things that come easy aren't real or aren't worth having, and there's no such thing as *luck*. You *make* your own luck, or at least, I have ever since that very hard lesson turned me into who I am today.

And I don't plan on repeating any mistakes of my past.

As long as I can stay locked away here in my own little world, that just might be a possibility.

I wander from my office into the living room, past the blazing fire I need to keep going. It beckons to me, and all I want to do is drop into the plush leather chair in front of it, prop up my feet, and enjoy another drink and a cigar while the storm rages around me. But the stack of wood already piled along the side of the house certainly won't be enough if Mother Nature intends to dump what the weatherman predicted.

After one more longing look at the warm spot by the fire, I pull on my boots, grab my parka from the hook beside the front door, and step out into the freezing bite of the approaching storm. Snowflakes whip around me in the growing wind, nipping at the exposed skin on my face and hands. I tug up my hood to block as much of it as I can, pull my thick, leather work gloves from my pockets and cover my hands, then pick up the ax leaning against the cabin near the door.

Hello, my old friend...

The familiar weight in my hand serves as a soothing balm, helping ease some of the tension in my body caused by Nate's call. Getting worked up isn't good for me. It makes me do questionable things I can't take back. It's one reason living here alone is safer...for everyone.

But just knowing I'm going to be working out some of my aggression on a poor, unsuspecting fir across the clearing in the next couple of minutes is enough to almost erase the memories threatening to overtake my mind and bring me down a road I left in the rearview over a decade ago. I'm never going back there, never returning to *that* life or the person I was.

Time to destroy something.

BROOKE

Goddamn you, Mother Nature!

She's such a heartless bitch. This storm wasn't supposed to hit until tomorrow, which would have given me plenty of time to get settled into the cabin and cozy before all hell broke loose, but the flakes falling faster and thicker suggest either the weatherman sucks at his job or Mother Nature decided to fuck with me—again. Like it wasn't bad enough that my first plan to head out of the country was kiboshed due to bad weather at Sea-Tac.

She's definitely fucking with me, making me pay the price for some unknown snub—probably because I use plastic straws and Styrofoam.

Okay, I get it! I'll repent!

Anything to stop this damn storm right now. Because the weather isn't the only looming problem.

Old Blue doesn't seem to want to cooperate, either.

That tiny, asshole *check engine* light has been on for over an hour, but out here, it's not like there's anywhere I can stop to have it looked at. My only hope is to get to Colleen's cabin before it completely shits the bed. Then I can settle in and get warm while I wait for the storm to blow over. It's not like I'm going to need it for a while, anyway. And when I finally do, I can call for someone to come tow it to a garage.

"Please, Old Blue, don't die on me now." I reach out and rub the dashboard of the old Jeep. She's been on her last leg for so long, it's a wonder she even made it up this damn mountain as far as she has.

It probably would have been wise to avoid steep, slippery inclines and snow accumulation in an old beater like this, but it wasn't like I had much choice. The cabin is my only option right now. And it won't be so bad...

Sitting by a fire with not another soul for hundreds of miles...a stack of books beside me. The beauty of nature my only companion. It sounds like absolute Heaven. And I can't even imagine what beautiful photos I'll be able to take on the mountain, especially after this snowfall. I am *so* ready for it.

If I ever get there...

The drive north from Seattle has been long—and that isn't exactly a bad thing, given the circumstances—but it feels like I've been on this road forever, and everything looks the same out here. Right now—white. Everything is just fucking *white*.

Old Blue's lack of GPS and the shitty phone coverage means I've resorted to the paper map on the passenger seat, and it's been well over a decade since I've used one of those.

Crap. I hope I didn't miss the turn-off. I'd be fucked.

The engine coughs and sputters like it's taking its final breath.

"Oh, no, you don't."

Another sputter.

Another cough.

"*No! No! No!* Not now!" I smack the dashboard—like *that* is actually going to do anything to keep this piece of shit alive. But petting it nicely didn't seem to get me anywhere. Sometimes, you need to be a little aggressive to make things happen—at least, that's what I've heard. I usually leave that to someone else while I hang back and wait for everything to calm down. Avoiding confrontation is more my style, but Old Blue is asking for it today.

And one more cough sounds my doom.

Old Blue dies with my hands still clutching the old, cracked wheel.

"*Fuck!*"

I stop dead in the middle of the narrow, unplowed road and drop my forehead against the steering wheel. The horn blares, and I jerk my head up.

Shit. Scared the fuck out of myself.

8

A hard gust of wind rattles through Old Blue, and without the heat blasting from the vents, the frigid air from outside seeps in to reach me, then straight through my completely inappropriate-for-the-weather jacket and jeans.

Fuck, it's cold out there.

If I open the door, I'll freeze to death. There wasn't any time to stop and stock up on outdoor gear. I had to leave. Plus, I thought I'd be at the cabin long before the storm hit, and Colleen assured me the roads weren't bad as long as it wasn't snowing.

As long as it wasn't snowing...

That train has definitely left the station, and it may have taken my chance of survival with it.

My only hope is to get someone out here to pick me up.

I need to call for help—STAT.

I shove the useless map onto the floorboard, fumble through my bag for my phone, and yank it out. My heart sinks as the freezing air in the car sends a shiver through me.

No. No. No. No.

No signal.

Of course, there isn't any signal.

One more thing to fuck me over. I'm so far up this Godforsaken mountain, I bet there isn't even electricity or running water. This is well and truly the middle of nowhere —the area Mom and Dad always joked was only for recluses and terrorists to hole up when they didn't want to be found.

It sounded ideal at the time Colleen offered her family's place. But now...I'm rethinking that decision, along with just about every other one I've made in the last three years that led to this in the first place.

No car. No heat. No phone.

No fucking hope.

I press my face against the window to try to scan my

9

surroundings for any signs of life, but the swirling snow outside makes it practically a white-out.

SHIT!

Getting out of this Jeep is the last thing I want to do, but I'll die inside this frozen, old, blue metal coffin if I don't find help.

I tug on my thin gloves, pull my hood up over my head, shove open my door, and step out into the snow in my UGGs. At least I have something warm on my feet, but the lack of a heavy winter jacket or some sort of long underwear or snow pants makes my body want to cave in on itself in the chilly air.

Survival mode, Brooke.

Keeping my head on straight and staying focused is essential right now. This is life or death shit—it has been since the moment I pulled out of my driveway.

I turn and scan the horizon on the opposite side of the road. Nothing but white snow and tall, green trees as far as my eyes can see.

FUCK!

Go back or go forward—those are my options.

But I know what's behind me. A whole lot of *nothing* for a *very* long time. There was some sort of signage for a logging company, but that was hours ago. Nothing since. Not a single sign of life. For all I know, the same lies ahead on this barely discernable road. If it weren't for the break in the trees in front of me, I wouldn't even be sure there *was* more road.

I glance that way and stop, a tiny rush of warm hope filling my blood. A thin wisp of gray smoke trickles up from the trees in the distance—barely visible through the maelstrom of snow, but it's there.

Where there's smoke, there's fire—or whatever the

saying is. Someone has to be there. But I have no idea where *there* is or how far I'll have to walk to reach it.

Old Blue or the unknown?

It's not much of a choice, really. I may not know much about the wilderness since I've spent my entire life in the city, but I do know that sitting in a dead vehicle in a snow-storm when you know there's nothing around and no hope of rescue is a death sentence.

The only place to go is onward. I reach into Old Blue, grab my bag, slam my door shut, lock it, and start trekking toward the tendrils of smoke. Leaving behind the rest of my stuff, including all my food and supplies for the cabin, sucks, but there's no way I can carry any of it anyway. The bottle of water and protein bars in my bag will have to sustain me until I can reach that smoke...and hopefully help.

The wind doesn't seem to appreciate my decision, though. It batters me from the side, threatening to bowl me right over into the high snow all around me.

How the hell did Old Blue even make it this far up the road?

Looking around now, I don't think she would have gotten much farther since I don't have chains on the tires and the snow is piling up at a rapid pace.

Yeah, you planned this real fucking well, Brooke. Great work.

I trudge through the snow, keeping my face angled down against the sharp sting of each flake hitting my skin. The closer I move toward the smoke, the more the forest closes in around me. Wherever that fire is, it's nowhere near the road. I'll have to go *through* the trees if I'm going to find it.

Just fucking brilliant.

11

But at least the trees might block some of this wind. My fingers are already freezing, and despite the warmth my boots have provided so far, I don't think they're tall enough to keep the snow from coming in over the top and down onto my ankles.

The muscles in my legs burn with each difficult step I take—my UGGs sticking in the deepening snow. It's yet another reminder of how out of shape I am. When I can finally go back to civilization, the first thing I'm going to do is join a gym.

If I ever get back, that is.

I reach the point where the trees thicken into a dense clump and pause to take one last look back at Old Blue before I take another step.

So long, old girl. I hope I see you soon.

Turning my back on her might be signing my death warrant, but so would staying. There isn't any good choice here. So...I walk.

And walk.

And walk.

More like stumble.

My legs keep getting heavier.

My breaths shorter and harder.

Weaving my way through towering trees that offer very little by way of protection from the snow and wind like I had hoped.

Fingers go numb.

Then toes.

I can't even feel my face anymore.

And inside the trees, I've lost all sense of direction and can't even see the smoke anymore. I could be walking in circles, for all I know.

Oh, God...I'm going to die out here. Frozen and alone.

I would let the tears burning my eyes go if they wouldn't just freeze on my face and make it even colder. Humans were not designed to live and survive in this kind of weather. The fact that there is any sign of life out here at all is a goddamn miracle. Yet, it feels like I've been walking in circles for hours, with no indication I'm even heading toward the only hint at another person alive up here.

Thunk.

The noise hits my ears and stills my feet.

What was that?

Thunk.

I stand stock-still and listen to determine the sound's direction, but the blood rushing in my ears makes it almost impossible to decipher.

Thunk.

Thunk.

Up ahead. It's coming from straight in front of me. I force myself to move forward toward the noise. Thick and heavy, it echoes around the trees over the sound of them creaking in the wind.

Thunk.

Thunk.

Thunk.

What is that?

It doesn't matter. *Something* is making that sound. If it's a wild animal, so be it. Getting eaten alive out here might be a better way to go than freezing to death.

Thunk. Thunk.

The sound grows louder as I advance, and I shove past a few more trees and step out into a small clearing.

A tall, broad-shouldered person in a dark parka stands with their back to me.

Oh, my God! A person!

The joy coursing through my system dies slowly as the person turns to face me. Hard, dark, wild eyes meet mine. My heart stalls in my chest and dread wraps around my spine. The man raises a large ax, glistening with blood.

Freezing and being gorged by a wild animal apparently aren't the only ways to die out here.

I'm going to be hacked to bits by this psycho ax murderer.

Chapter Two

"**Y**ou have got to be fucking kidding me."

Where the hell did she come from?

Even while I was hacking away at this tree and then the squirrel that scurried by, I could hear her approach. The footsteps behind me were not from someone who had any idea how to remain inconspicuous, so I was prepared to face anyone who might have appeared. But when she burst from the tree line and I turned to face her, I definitely hadn't expected the tiny blonde with wide, green eyes. Or that she would collapse into the snow around her the moment her gaze met mine.

Well, shit.

I toss my ax at the base of the log pile I've made and rush over to her. The snow doesn't make it easy, but when I get there, I roll her onto her back so I can make sure she's breathing. Her chest rising and falling sends relief flooding my system.

Until I see what she's wearing.

What the hell?

Medium-weight jacket. Jeans. Boots for fashion, not function. Thin gloves. Nothing covering her ears or head except the flimsy hood. She's insane to come out here dressed like this on a good day, let alone during a storm like this.

She's literally freezing...and now unconscious.

Goddammit.

This is the last thing I need when I'm trying to prepare to hunker down for the impending blizzard. I glance back through the trees in the direction from which she came.

How the hell did she get out here, anyway?

The road—if one can even *call* it that—is two miles southeast of here, and some pretty heavy woods and terrain separate it from where we are now. It would be a wicked hike for someone prepared, let alone someone dressed like this in this weather.

Sleeping Beauty must have some serious survival instinct and drive to make it this far. And, as annoyed as I am about the intrusion, I'm not going to let the girl die on my watch. There has been too much unnecessary death already. Too much loss. She's not going out like this. Not if there's any possible thing I can do to save her.

I slide my arms under her small frame and easily lift her from the snow. Her dead weight settles against my chest, and a gust of wind batters us with a blast of icy flakes.

Memories come with it...swirling in my head the way the snow does around us.

Another body in my arms.

A hopeless struggle to survive.

The look of death staring back at me.

Clenching my jaw, I shake away the visions and concentrate on the moment. I need to get her warmed up and settled in at the cabin and get back out here for the firewood before it's too bad out here for me to come to get it. While I'm used to the unpleasant weather here, it doesn't mean I want to get stuck outside during shit like this.

And while all I may want is to disappear out here and pretend the rest of the world doesn't exist, it seems fate has other plans. There's no one else to help her.

The very real weight of the situation rests heavily on my shoulders, and I glance down at the limp body in my arms.

Christ.

It's been so long since I've seen a woman, I almost forgot how beautiful they are. Soft, pale skin, perfect bow lips, thick, dark lashes spread across her wind-reddened, high cheekbones. It almost makes me miss being part of the world.

Almost.

But the slightly blue tint to her lips and a big shake of my head bring me back to reality.

Get out of your fucking head and get moving, asshole.

The snow isn't going to let up anytime soon, and it will only get worse the longer I stand here staring at this poor woman like a fucking idiot. That's what happens when someone lives alone for as long as I have—I get lost in my own head too long with no way out.

I set out through the growing drifts toward the cabin, fighting the brutal wind and biting snow with each step. By the time it comes into view on the other side of the clearing, it's practically a white-out. There's no way she would have survived or been able to find the cabin if she hadn't stumbled upon me.

It may already be too late.

All I can do now is try to warm her up and hope the sheriff can get up the mountain to bring her to the clinic in town for real treatment before we're completely snowed in.

Juggling her dead weight in my arms, I pull open the door and beeline toward the fireplace, ignoring the snow falling from my boots and clothes to land on the pine floors I laid, sanded, and finished with my own hands.

The heat of the fire flickering in the fireplace hits me—a welcome relief from the blustering wind outside—but it only accentuates how cold the girl in my arms really is. And her soaked clothes aren't doing her any favors in that regard. If I keep them on her, she'll go hypothermic, if she isn't already.

I lower her to the rug in front of the fire, and a tiny groan slips from her still-blue lips—the first glimpse of life to come from her since she collapsed outside. It's a good sign—at least she's breathing, and she might be regaining consciousness, but it definitely doesn't mean she's out of the woods yet. Not by a longshot.

Life is fleeting and fragile, and I'm not about to let her die in my house while I sit by idly and watch. Her body begins to shake, massive shivers rolling through her limbs.

Shit.

I tug off my gloves and pull the large, heavy bag strapped to her body over her head to set it aside. My hands hover over the zipper to her jacket.

Fuck. She's passed out, and I'm undressing her...

My chest tightens, and I fist my hands to stop them from shaking. Everything Mom and Dad ever taught me about being a gentleman, about how to treat a woman, screams from somewhere deep in the recesses of my mind.

Undressing one while unconscious is certainly not at the top of that list.

This is different, Beau. An emergency.

Despite my head knowing that, my body doesn't seem to want to cooperate. My hands don't want to move for the zipper. They vibrate violently in the space between my body and hers. I shake them and clench them together again, trying to regain control of my limbs.

If anyone in that boardroom saw me like this—melting down over something so simple—they definitely wouldn't be comfortable with me still at the head of the company. If they knew what a fucking mess I am, the coup Nate is worried about would be a sure thing.

Nerves be damned. I don't have a choice.

Wet clothing means a cold body. It's as simple as that. These clothes have to come off.

I just hope she understands that when she finally wakes up.

Despite her dead weight, I manage to wrangle off the jacket and wet boots. At least the long-sleeve T-shirt stretched across her chest appears dry, but then my eyes drift down to her soaked jeans. They need to be removed.

Christ, who would have thought the first time I undress a woman in a decade would be like this?

"I'm sorry, darling."

My whispered words go unanswered. Other than soft, short puffs of breath slipping from between her lips, she's still unresponsive. I undo the button at her waistband, lower the zipper, then struggle with her legs while I work her jeans off them.

I avert my gaze from her underwear as I remove the wet clothes and toss them into a pile next to the fireplace. It's only the first step, though. Her body temp is dangerously low, her exposed skin cool to the touch and alarmingly pale. I grab the heavy blanket from the chair I usually sit in every night and wrap her in it, positioning her as close to the warmth of the flames as I can.

I need to call the sheriff.

There's no way to tell if I got her inside and warm in time. She may need serious medical treatment, something I definitely can't do on top of a damn mountain. I clamber to my feet, rush to my office, and grab my phone where I left it on the desk.

Fuck.

No service.

The storm must've knocked out the only tower that *sometimes* reaches here. It's one of the many reasons this place is perfect—in any other circumstances. I never really gave much consideration to what would happen if I truly had an emergency alone on the mountain and was anywhere away from the house. Maybe because I never cared much about what happened to me, but this girl's life is on the line. So, the only thing I can do is try to get the sheriff on the radio.

Always have a backup and be prepared.

It's one of the lessons Dad made sure I understood growing up, one that has always served me well. I just never thought I'd have to use it in a situation like this.

I grab the emergency radio, check that it's set to the proper channel, and press the talk button. "Sheriff's Department, this is Beau."

Static crackles back at me for a moment. "Okanogan County Sheriff's Department. We read you."

"I'm on the mountain and just found a woman wandering in the woods on my land. She passed out, and I brought her to my place. She might be hypothermic, and the storm has already hit us up here."

A momentary silence lingers. Normally, I embrace the quiet here, but all I want now is to hear the dispatcher telling me they're sending someone.

The line crackles again; the voice that comes through this time isn't the female dispatcher. "Beau, it's Sheriff Roberts. Unfortunately, until this storm passes, we can't get up there. The roads are already blocked down here, and even if we could get a chopper from Brewster, there's no way they can fly in this. They're saying the storm may be a couple of days. And you know getting to your place isn't exactly easy even in good weather. You're just gonna have to take care of her up there."

Shit.

Crackle. "Beau? Can you handle it?"

He knows I can. I've handled much worse in my life, and I've managed to keep myself alive alone on this mountain for over a damn decade—with blood, sweat, and tears.

I swallow thickly and tighten my hand around the radio to get my reply out through gritted teeth. "Yes."

Crackle. "Do you have an ID on her?"

"She's unconscious right now. I didn't dig through her stuff. I'll talk to her when she's awake and let you know."

Crackle. "If the storm lets up, we'll get up there as quickly as we can."

Shit. Shit. Shit.

I return the radio to its charging station and make my way back into the living room. She hasn't moved from her position in front of the fire, but even from across the room, I can still see her shivering.

She's still cold.

Swallowing back the unease, I make my way over to the

fire and lower myself onto the rug behind her. My damn hands shake again as I reach out, gather her into my arms, and bring her as close against my body as possible.

If I don't get her warm, she may never wake up.

* * *

BROOKE

Dark, heavy warmth surrounds me. Like drowning in pitch-black water, only it's not freezing like it should be. It's comforting. Safe. Somewhere I want to stay. Floating endlessly in the never-ending abyss of darkness. Cocooned in its heat and secure hold. It's such a welcome change from what the world has been—icy and terrifying. A deep, bone-chilling cold that seemed to envelop everything and numb my mind. Somehow, it's gone. Whisked away to be replaced by this...

Brief flashes of sensation work their way through the blackness.

Strong arms...

Something rough brushing against my skin...

The scent of pine, snow, and the crisp winter air...

A hint of cigar smoke...

Warmth fluttering against my neck...

Then it's gone again and I'm sucked back down into the darkness.

I surface again to a soft feather pillow pressed to the side of my face and that woodsy scent invading my every breath.

Wait...

Something isn't right.

The typical smell of greasy breakfast food being cooked

at the diner next to my apartment is missing for the first time in years. And it's too quiet. The usual boisterous sounds of the busy street three stories below have been replaced by howling winds and something creaking outside.

I roll onto my back and spread out...on a bed that's way too large. On my queen, my arms and legs can reach the sides, but this one has *far* more room.

Shit. Where the hell am I?

I jerk up on the mattress, and the heavy down comforter and stack of blankets covering me fall into a pile on my legs tucked under them.

My *bare* legs.

Where the fuck are my pants?

My focus immediately darts around the unfamiliar room. Thick logs make up the walls, ceiling, and floors and were used to build the massive bed I now lie in that is definitely not mine.

How did I get here...wherever here is?

I squeeze my eyes closed and try to clear the fog enveloping my brain.

Driving...

Flashes of bright white...

Loud, strange noises...

Old Blue sputtering out and dying...

Smoke in the distance...

Hiking through the damn snow and the endless trees...
Cold.

So much cold.

And then...

The memory doesn't surface immediately, this strange fuzziness covering it and wrapping around me, trying to prevent me from seeing what's right there. I fist my hands into the comforter and try to focus.

Hard, dark eyes.

Oh, my God!

The psycho woodsman with the bloody ax!

A gasp slips from my lips, and I clamp a hand over my mouth in case he's around and can hear me. He could be anywhere. Everything after stepping into that clearing is an absolute blank—pitch black. Not even glimpses of what happened between then and this moment come. And now, I'm half-naked in a bed.

What the hell did he do to me?

I drag the comforter back up around me like it's some sort of protective shield that will keep any harm from coming to me. If only that were true. If only it were that simple. Things would be a lot different now. But I can't spend time relishing the soft comfort of the bedding or dreaming of what might have been in some alternate world where things don't try to hurt me. Instead, I focus my attention on the closed door.

There's only one entrance to the room. Only one way he can come and go from here. He could come through it at any moment. My heart thunders against my ribcage, my breathing short and jerky.

Don't panic. Stay calm.

If I panic, I might give him an advantage and miss my chance to escape from this psycho who has already done only God knows what to me while I've been unconscious.

Here I thought I was heading somewhere safe, that Colleen's cabin would be a refuge and time for me to think and regroup.

How damn wrong that was.

But I'm not going to let whoever this monster is do whatever he wants to me. I'm not going down without a fight. Scanning the room for any weapon, my eyes land on a white and blue vase on a small table near the door.

Dainty and delicate, it looks completely out of place in this log cabin in the rugged wilderness. And it's my only real option since the rest of the room is rather sparsely decorated in dark browns and reds, with only a nightstand, a dresser, a chair, and the small table where the vase sits—and the head of some sort of bear mounted above the door.

Definitely the sleeping quarters of a gruff, classless man who rapes and murders young women who stumble upon him as he's slicing up victims in the woods.

I toss off the covers and step onto the chilly wood floors with shaky, unsteady legs. The cool air hitting the bare skin on my lower half feels like I'm being battered by an arctic blast, after being wrapped up under so many layers of blankets. It sends a full-body shiver through me, followed closely by a bone-deep ache. Whatever happened before I got here, it took a toll on me physically. Every muscle burns, and it feels as though all energy has been zapped from my body by some cataclysmic force designed to render me unable to fight back.

Maybe he gave me something that's messing with my system.

My legs wobble, and I brace my hand on the nightstand. An injection or a pill could make my brain foggy like this and inhibit my memory. The man must be a true monster to drug a helpless woman and keep her captive in his cabin.

I need to get out of here.

But there's no way I can do that half-dressed.

Where are my pants?

A thump sounds just outside the door, and I freeze where I stand, half-naked beside the bed. I can't remember a time I've felt more exposed and vulnerable, except maybe that time at the community pool when I was seven and Allan Beasley made fun of my two-piece suit.

But I was a mere girl then, shy, embarrassed, and unable to defend myself against childish attacks. I stood there, shaking, tears streaming down my face until Marisol finally grabbed me and dragged me to the bathroom to find some privacy while I tried to get control of myself. That was the last time I ever wore a two-piece suit, and that pool still makes my chest tighten and tears burn in my eyes every time I drive past it.

That was a long time ago, though. Now, I'm stronger, despite my body trying to rebel against movement. My self-preservation instinct has grown along with my ability to stand my ground. I'm ready to go on the offensive to keep that lunatic from hacking me to pieces when he's done with me.

I haven't made it through so much and gotten this far to give up now and resign myself to whatever fate he has planned for me.

Heavy footsteps move closer to the door, and I release my grip on the nightstand and lunge for the vase. My hands curl around it, and I raise it above my head and press my back against the wooden wall, holding my breath while waiting for the door to open.

One second.

Two.

Three.

Blood thunders in my ears, a steady thrum that almost drowns out the steps of the man with the ax. Familiar feelings of dread crawl up my throat. The doorknob turns slowly. I tighten my grip on the vase, its weight heavy in my hands despite its dainty appearance.

Hopefully heavy enough to do some serious damage when I smash it on the fucker's head.

The door creaks open slowly. Only a sliver of flickering light slips in, then his hand and forearm...

Finally, the moment his head breaks the plane of the jamb, I bring the vase arching down against the side of his temple.

Chapter Three

BEAU

Something hard slams against my head from the left, shattering across the floor and sending a sharp pain slicing through my temple, followed by a quick, hot gush of blood down my cheek.

"Fuck!" I jerk my arm up to press my hand against the wound and whirl toward my attacker—the woman who was practically comatose in my bed only an hour ago when I last checked on her.

She's *very much* awake now.

Those wide, green eyes, clear from whatever fog lingered from her ordeal, and are now filled with fear and determination. She tries to dart around me and out the door, but I lash out and grab her wrist with my free hand, pulling her back toward me.

I take a quick glance at the broken remains of the vase spread across the floor at my feet. Flashes of memories assault my brain, threatening to bring me back to a past I have no desire to revisit.

The flowers she kept in it.

Always fresh.

Always beautiful.

Their scent permeating the house.

My hand tightens around the girl's wrist, and she yelps and tries to pull away.

Get the fuck back in the box where I keep you, dammit.

If I let myself go down that rabbit hole now, there's no way I'll be clear-headed enough to deal with the imminent issue—who is now thrashing against my hold.

I jerk her a little harder than I should to try to stop her from fighting me. "Why the fuck did you do that?"

Her resistance stops for a second, and now that we're so close that I can feel her body heat radiating between us, the little flecks of gold in her eyes shimmer with defiance. "So I could get away."

I snort at the absurdity of her statement. "Where the hell do you think you're going? It's twenty degrees outside and a white-out. You plan on walking out of here barefoot and half-naked?"

She recoils from my hold at the mention of her lack of clothing, anger and fear flickering in her gaze. "Please let me go."

Oh, shit...

She thinks...

I quickly release her arm and step back. No wonder the girl tried to smash me to death with the vase. She was acting on survival instinct, trying to protect herself. I likely would have done the same if I had woken the way she just did.

Another step back brings me to the door, the hard wood pressing against me now, and I raise my hands—one covered in my own blood—in what I hope is an unthreatening move. "I promise, I didn't hurt you. Your clothes were soaked, and you were hypothermic. I had to get you warm."

Those glistening eyes of hers that haven't left me for a moment now narrow. She scans me from head to foot—from my unruly and unkempt hair and beard down over my long-sleeve thermal shirt, black work pants, and to my bare feet. The defensive set of her shoulders softens slightly. Her thin arms wrap around her, and she glances toward the window where outside, the storm rages on.

I return my hand to the cut on my head and wince. "What the hell are you doing out here, anyway?"

There isn't anything even remotely resembling civilization for hours, and the road that comes up this way can hardly even be called one. It's the way I like it. The very reason I chose this location. It's almost inaccessible without a massive four-wheel-drive vehicle, studded snow tires, and a lot of determination. No one has ever wandered onto my land before, not even a stray hunter.

What the hell would a beautiful woman like this be doing all the way out here?

Her gaze snaps back to meet mine, and she pulls the corner of her bottom lip between her teeth. "Um, I was trying to get to my friend's cabin. My Jeep broke down, and I didn't have cell service. I saw some smoke in the distance. It must have been from this place."

Shit.

"There aren't any other cabins around here. Where is your friend's place? Are you meeting him there?"

Surely, she wouldn't come out here all alone this time of year.

She considers my question for a moment, almost like she's planning out her answer and trying to anticipate my response, then shakes her head. "It's somewhere near Four Point Lake, and I was going alone."

I snort and groan. "That's on the other side of the mountain. You must have missed the turn back near town to wrap around to the other side."

That turn is easy to miss. The sign's old and barely visible. Plus, with the snow starting earlier than anticipated, it was likely difficult to spot it.

Her eyes start to shine with unshed tears.

Oh, fuck. I so cannot deal with this.

I turn and leave the room without a word to her, making my way to the bathroom off the small hallway that leads to the bedroom. The blood flowing from the cut near my hairline isn't too bad, but it definitely could use a couple of stitches.

At least I was able to get the rest of the firewood brought to the cabin before she maimed me.

I grab what I need to patch myself up from the medicine cabinet, and when I close it, I freeze.

After all these years, I'm not used to seeing someone reflecting back at me in this mirror—just my own face, one I sometimes don't even recognize. No one else has ever set foot in this place, let alone stayed long enough for me to get used to having them around. Her appearance throws me for a moment, sending my heart skittering in a thousand different directions.

She stands a few steps from the bathroom door, watching me curiously, her tiny arms wrapped around herself protectively. "Are you okay?"

Seriously?

A low grunt is all I manage for a reply. Her being here is definitely *not* okay. Smashing me on the head and breaking one of only a few sentimental items I actually keep here is *not* okay.

I thread the needle from the medical kit and swipe a little iodine over the cut. It's nothing, really. A scratch. I've had far worse and survived.

The drying blood on my cheek sends another flash of a memory, but I can't get the visual of the pieces of the vase on the floor out of my head...and what it looked like the last time it held anything.

A little pain will help with that. I push the needle through the ripped skin, and a tiny gasp comes from behind me.

"What are you doing?"

I let my eyes meet hers in the mirror. "What does it look like I'm doing? I'm fixing the wound *you* gave me."

"But..."

I finish with the three stitches to close it up, tie it off, and turn to face her, leaning back against the bathroom counter, the supplies still scattered on the top. "But what?"

Her pink lips open and close a few times like she's searching for her words. Their color is a good sign. Her body is likely back to normal temperature now, but it isn't the question of her health that keeps my eyes focused there.

One of her hands points toward my head. "But you just gave yourself stitches."

She says it like I just performed open-heart surgery or something. This woman clearly hasn't seen much in her life if *that* shocks her so much.

I snort and shake my head. "Yeah, well, the closest doctor is hours away. There isn't much choice out here. Just like there wasn't much choice for me when you stumbled onto my land—inappropriately dressed and almost dead. I couldn't just leave you out there to die, could I?"

"I'm so sorry. I—"

"You shouldn't have been out here in the first place." My words come out harsher than I intended them, but she deserves it. I shove off the counter and storm past her back toward the bedroom.

"What the hell is that supposed to mean?"

The indignation in her question makes my blood heat. I whirl back around toward her, faster than she expects, and she almost plows into me. She jerks to a stop just inches away, her eyes locked on mine, then steps back. That fear still lingers in her gaze.

And she probably should be afraid.

When I'm like this, no one should be near me—let alone someone who invaded my private space then attacked me. "It means that you came out here completely unprepared. You weren't wearing proper outdoor gear or clothing layers for this altitude this time of year, let alone in a storm, and leaving your car out here could have gotten you killed. *Should* have gotten you killed. You never would have made it here to the cabin in the state you were in. If I hadn't been out felling that damn tree, you would have collapsed in the snow and frozen to death in minutes."

A red flush creeps up her neck and over her pale cheeks. She fists her hands at her sides. "I was prepared to be *indoors* at a cabin. And if you were just cutting down a tree, then why was there blood all over your ax?"

Is she for fucking real right now?

"Wow." I shove my hands back through my hair and wince when I bump against the wound I momentarily forgot is there. "Just wow."

One of her pale eyebrows rises. "What?"

"I just saved your fucking life and you're asking me that?" I don't know why I care so much what she thinks, but

33

the insinuation in her statement makes me want to punch through a wall. Which I might do if these weren't made of foot-thick tree trunks. "What? Did you think I was out there hacking up one of my *victims*? That you're next?"

She shrinks back like I've slapped her, and regret automatically creeps in to tighten my chest.

Shit.

I didn't mean to *yell* at her like that. She has every reason not to trust me, especially out here.

"Fuck." I squeeze my eyes closed and rub at the tension in the back of my neck. "I'm sorry. I didn't mean to scare you. I'm...not great with people."

When I force myself to reopen my eyes, hers have softened, and she's watching me like someone might a wounded animal to see if it's going to lash out and bite again.

It's the last thing I want to see in her gaze—fucking pity. I'd rather she were afraid of me. That would be more sensible and safer for both of us.

I turn away from her and enter the bedroom to clean up the remains of the vase. Seeing what's left again has the same effect, but I force myself to squat to pick up the pieces, pushing away the feelings they threaten to bring to the surface.

She drops to her bare knees next to me. "I can do that."

"No." I hold out my free hand to stop her. "Don't."

For some reason, the thought of her touching it makes it worse. Like it will somehow tarnish it the way fingerprints do silver.

"I'm really sorry I broke it." Her soft voice wavers slightly. "Can it be fixed?"

The laugh that bubbles up my throat comes out dark and low. I glance at her and fight a smile that tries to pull at my lips. "My father would have loved that."

34

Her eyebrows fly up. "Loved what?"

I smirk at her. "That innocent question." I scoop up the rest of the pieces and rise to my feet. "No, it can't be fixed. It is...*was* priceless."

* * *

BROOKE

Priceless?

He surely can't mean *priceless* the way I use the word. He must mean sentimental value, and the fact that he rescued me and I destroyed something so important to him turns my stomach.

I press my hand against it and push to my still bare feet. "I think we should try."

Dark, hard eyes meet mine, and a shiver rolls through my body—though whether it's from being half-naked or from the intensity in their depths is something I am not going to explore. There's too much there—anger, loss, fear, and a dozen other things I can't identify.

He shakes his head slightly, like he's trying to clear something from it, and his lips twist down into a frown that only draws my attention to them. "Your clothes are by the fireplace, but I don't think they're completely dry yet." His head inclines toward the dresser along the wall. "There are some sweatpants in the bottom drawer on the right. You can probably cinch the drawstrings on them enough that they'll fit you."

Wearing some pants would definitely make this entire situation a whole lot less awkward—and chilly. I literally stumbled into this man, and he had to not only save my life but also put up with me assaulting him. And I've been walking around with only my underwear and shirt on for the last fifteen minutes.

Oh, God. How embarrassing.

"Thank you."

What else can I say to the man after what happened?

He turns without a word and disappears down the short hallway behind us, ignoring my statement that we should try to fix the vase. I make my way to the dresser and pull out a pair of black sweatpants. The soft, fuzzy material feels like Heaven against my skin, but I don't take any time to relish it. I still have no idea what's really going on or even *where* I am besides the home of some dark-haired stranger who carries an ax.

I follow my grumpy, bearded rescuer out into the main portion of the cabin. The large, open room with a vaulted ceiling and massive stone fireplace isn't exactly what I expected. I had imagined some shoddy, little place that was unkempt and looked like somewhere the Unabomber would hole up, but this is actually big, and it is definitely well-maintained. Whoever he is, he cares about this place and takes good care of it.

A noise to my left draws me toward the kitchen, which sports modern stainless-steel appliances, a coffee maker on the counter, and beautiful cabinets lining the walls. This isn't some vacation getaway spot for this guy—he lives here —and given the looks of this kitchen, he's spent a good deal of money equipping this place. It's nice but not lavish.

Comfortable.

I clear my throat to announce my approach to where he stands at the counter, staring out the window at the snow with his back to me. "Um, is there any chance of getting a tow truck to come to get my car?"

He barks out a laugh and turns slowly to face me,

resting back against the counter with his arms crossed over his chest in a way that causes the long-sleeve thermal shirt he's wearing to pull and stretch over clearly defined biceps and pec muscles. "You're stuck with me for a while, Sleeping Beauty. I talked to the sheriff when I found you. This storm is forecast to last several days, and even if it lets up, the snow isn't easy to get through. It's not like we have snow plows that come this far."

"Shit." I guess I hadn't really considered the realities of the situation before now. Seems I was too distracted with thinking my life was in danger and trying to destroy this man with porcelain.

One of his dark eyebrows rises. "You have someone who will be worried about you? I can have the sheriff get word to them. I already told him I would radio with your information once you were awake."

The truth sits at the tip of my tongue, but I swallow it back with a thick gulp and avert my gaze from his probing stare. If he contacted the sheriff like he said he did, then he can't really be much of a threat, but that doesn't mean I'm about to regurgitate my whole life story to him.

Just tell him what he needs to know to get through this storm.

"I don't have anyone waiting for me at home. My friend who was letting me use her cabin won't be worried unless she doesn't hear from me for a week or so. This was an..." I search for a word that can easily describe my purpose for coming to this remote area, "extended vacation."

He nods slowly and scrubs a hand over his beard. "Well, it could be longer than that. I'll give the sheriff your name and friend's number so he can update her."

My name...

I can't believe I haven't given him my name yet or asked

his. This entire situation has me so frazzled. It feels like I'm losing my fucking mind.

"Oh"—I step forward with my hand held out awkwardly—"I'm Brooke. Brooke Beck." The lie falls from my lips so easily, even I would believe it.

His eyes drop to my extended hand, but he doesn't make a move to take it. Instead, he turns his back to me again and reaches for a tea kettle on the stove. "You can call me Beau."

You can call me Beau? Really? That's all I'm going to get?

"No last name?"

He freezes and glances over his shoulder at me for a brief moment before he fills the kettle, sets it onto the stove, and lights the flame. "Not one you need to know."

Well, damn.

This guy really is a major grump. Though, I did just give him a fake last name. And I *am* intruding on his life. He's going to be stuck with me in his space for days or potentially longer. I guess I can see why he'd be less than pleased with that prospect.

"Uh, well, thanks for saving my life, Beau." It's the only thing I can say to try to ease some of the tension between us right now.

"You might not be thanking me soon."

"What?"

Did I hear him right?

He mumbled the words under his breath, but I'm almost positive he said I might not be thanking him soon.

What the hell does that even mean?

He ignores my question, grabs something from a cabinet above the stove, and turns back toward me. "I'm making you some tea to help you stay warm. Are you hungry?"

My stomach growls at the mention of food, and I let his avoidance of my question pass as heat spreads over my cheeks.

God, that's embarrassing.

I don't even know what time it is, but my body tells me it's been a *long* time since I last ate.

A tiny twitch at the corner of his mouth almost looks like he's fighting a smile. "I'll make you something to eat. You might not like what I have available, though."

"Oh, I'm pretty easy."

His jaw hardens, any amusement playing on his lips only a moment ago gone instantly, and he gives me his back again to mess with something in the fridge.

Oh, God, that sounded bad!

Somehow, I've developed verbal diarrhea since waking in this stranger's bed. It isn't something I'm normally prone to, but it seems today is chock full of new adventures.

He turns around and holds up a container of something brown that looks like it might be some sort of soup. "Go sit by the fire. I'll bring you some tea and stew."

I scurry away before I embarrass myself any further.

Jesus, Brooke, get a grip!

In general, men don't usually rattle me like this. But the last two days have been about as far from my normal as is possible. When I first woke up, things were confusing. I clearly didn't understand the situation, but now that things have been resolved—in some way, at least—I should be settling down. Yet my heart thunders in my chest.

It might have something to do with the ordeal I've been through. Perhaps my body is simply trying to cope with the trauma of hypothermia and the emotional upheaval of our little misunderstanding—not to mention everything that got me up this mountain in the first place.

I'm absolutely *sure* it has nothing to do with the gruff mountain man currently making me *tea* and dinner in his kitchen while I sit wrapped in a blanket on a couch in front of a fireplace that has to be fifteen or twenty feet tall. He's done nothing to suggest he's a danger to me—other than his attitude—and he literally saved my life.

But that doesn't stop me from watching his every move from here.

The way his shirt stretches across his strong back. The bulge of his biceps threatening to almost rip open the sleeves.

It would be a lie to say he isn't handsome.

Now that I've gotten the idea that he's a murderer out of my head, I can admit that to myself even if I don't want to. In fact, if Colleen saw him and knew where I was, she'd probably be begging me to snap photos to help support her beard fetish.

"I hope you like squirrel."

"Wait. What?"

Shit.

I've been so busy ogling him that I didn't even notice he's staring right at me and approaching with a tray in his hands.

"Did you say *squirrel?*"

He flashes me a mischievous grin, one that lights his russet brown eyes for a moment, softening them slightly for the first time since I smashed his damn head. "What did you think the blood on my ax was from?"

"Oh, shit. You're serious?"

A low, deep chuckle rumbles in his chest, and he leans down and sets the tray on the wooden coffee table in front of me. When he stands back up, a crisp, woodsy scent wafts

40

over me, sending a whole different type of shiver through my body.

My brain struggles to process something—a fleeting memory. Something just beneath the surface of my consciousness. Something that happened while I was out.

He takes a seat in the chair to the left of the couch and releases a deep groan, dropping his head back against it and letting his eyes drift closed.

"Are you all right?"

"Yes, just tired. And I need to go out and chop up some more firewood. I got the larger logs brought back while you were out, but it needs to be broken down more. I'm just waiting for the storm to die down a bit."

I glance toward the windows on the far wall where the white flakes fall rapidly and batter the window with each gust of wind. "You're going back out there?"

He raises his head and looks at me. "Are you going to go out and chop it to make sure we have enough firewood to keep this place heated?"

"Uh..." I shrink back into the couch and avoid his gaze. "Nope."

"Didn't think so." His statement isn't made with any malice, but sheer exhaustion drips off every word.

I hadn't even considered how bringing me here and taking care of me might have affected him. It probably messed with his entire plan for the day and preparations for the storm.

"Are you going to eat that?" He motions toward the stew.

My stomach gurgles, and I lean forward and take a tentative whiff. The aroma of roasted meat and vegetables literally makes my mouth water, and a low moan slips from my lips. "God, it smells good."

"Try it. I promise it's tasty. Just try not to think about what you're eating."

Excellent advice.

If I pictured it, there's no way it would be going into my mouth. As it is, my hand shakes as I pick up the spoon and bring up the first bite. He watches me with the tiniest grin on his lips. The bastard is taking pleasure from watching me squirm with this. I should be pissed about that, but I'm so hungry and exhausted at this point that I can't even muster up any annoyance.

But something is niggling at the back of my mind now. I can't shake that scent. And it's not just from waking up in that man's bed. There's something else connected to the memory.

A feeling.

A touch...

I pause with the spoon halfway to my mouth and focus on him. "Did you...get into bed with me when I was unconscious?"

His entire body stiffens, and the grin on his lips falters. He shifts forward in his chair, resting his elbows on his knees and staring into the fire. "I had to get your body temperature up. Body heat is one of the best ways to do that."

Shit.

"So...we were in bed together?"

He rubs at the back of his neck, continuing to avert his gaze. "Uh, no, I warmed you up out here by the fire first, then moved you in there."

I glance toward the fireplace where my pants, jacket, and boots lay drying. "Were you...uh...undressed, too?"

His head whips up, and a muscle in his clenched jaw

tics, but he doesn't look away from the flames. He fists his hands and shoves to his feet. "Body heat."

Body heat.

Two simple words—and the way he says them is definitely designed to make him sound indifferent and detached from whatever happened. But the memory still lingering around the edges of my brain and his reaction right now certainly make it clear he isn't unaffected.

And I can't say I wasn't, either. The feeling the memory sends through my body proves that. Despite his gruff reaction to my presence, there's more to this guy's story.

What's he hiding from up here?

It seems like I'm going to have a lot of time to find out.

Chapter Four

BROOKE

Beau wasn't joking about the stew.

As long as I didn't think about what I was putting in my mouth, the savory chunks of meat and soft, delicious vegetables practically melted on my tongue and filled my stomach, heating me from the inside out—along with the surprisingly good cup of tea he made.

I definitely needed the meal and the opportunity to continue to warm up.

No matter how hard I try, I can't shake the shivers that continue to roll through my body—even in his sweatpants and my long sleeve T-shirt, wrapped in a blanket, a pair of Beau's thick wool socks that he brought me now covering my feet.

The last spoonful of the stew tastes just as good as the first, and I set the empty bowl with my spoon back on the tray as Beau finishes lacing up his boots near the front door.

At least he didn't sit and watch me eat. That might have

brought a constant reminder of what was going into my mouth. Instead, he disappeared into the kitchen and cleaned up—or at least pretended that's what he was doing.

I appreciated the moment alone, to eat and to think. So much has happened so quickly. My entire life changed in only a matter of a few days. The last place I thought I'd find myself is holed up in a cabin with a total stranger—though it definitely has some benefits.

Like the view...

Beau pulls his parka off the hook beside the door and slides it on while an uncomfortable silence lingers between us. He grabs his hat and jerks it on his head with a little too much force before reaching for the doorknob.

A vicious blast of wind shakes the house, rattling all the windows and howling down the chimney. It brings with it the sharp memory of the freezing trudge through the wilderness that almost killed me, and I glance toward the window. "You're really going to go back out there?"

The annoyed look he tosses my way makes me wilt back into the couch. "Like I said..." He tugs on his gloves and points toward the door. "Unless you plan on swinging the ax, I don't have a choice. I have a decent stockpile of wood always on hand, but with a storm like this, it's always smart to have extras beyond the extras. I would have been done with it all before the worst of the storm hit, but someone changed my plans. Plus, I'm going to have to keep the house warmer than I normally would so *you're* comfortable."

Shit.

"I'm so sorry."

There might not be enough apologies in the world to make up for what I've already put this guy through, and I'm starting to sound like a broken record. But I want him to realize that I understand how much this imposes on him and how thankful I am that he saved my life when I couldn't do it myself.

Beau grasps the door handle and issues a heavy sigh I can feel across the small room. "If you don't stop apologizing, the next week or so is going to get really annoying."

I shrink back under the blanket and pull it tighter around me. "Okay, I'm sorry..."

He barks out a laugh and shakes his head, glancing over his shoulder at me, amusement mixing with the aggravation in his eyes. "You just can't stop yourself, can you?"

Apparently not.

That's what they say about learned habits, though. You don't even realize you're doing something until someone else points it out to you. The behavior has become so engrained in your psyche that you lose all control over it.

His dark gaze rakes over me one last time before he jerks open the door.

A cold wind whips in, sending snowflakes scattering across the rough-hewn floor, and a chill through the air that even the massive fireplace can't fight off.

"Stay in here by the fire. You need to be as warm as possible. Hypothermia can cause lasting effects, and I don't need you passing out again when I have no way of getting you medical care up here."

Crap, I really fucked this up for myself and this poor guy.

Now, not only is he worrying about battening down the hatches for this storm—and doing prep he should have completed hours ago—but he also has to keep an eye on me.

He steps out and yanks the door closed behind him with a definitive slam that reverberates through the high rafters.

Even though his anger makes me wince, I can't seem to drag my gaze away from where he just disappeared. Worry over a man I don't even know begins to make my leg bounce, and a gust of wind rattles the window to the right of the door, finally tearing my attention from where he just stood.

The vision of him holding that ax when I stumbled into the clearing flashes in my mind, and my curiosity gets the better of me. Wrapping the blanket tightly around myself, I push to my sock-clad feet and pad over to peek out at the blizzard.

Yeah, definitely looking at the storm. Not the burly man with a bad attitude whose life I'm imposing upon.

The world outside the pane of glass is almost invisible. Only a small floodlight affixed to the front of the cabin offers any illumination into the yard, and the snow rushing down reflects the light off it, creating an almost blinding white luminescence as far as I can see. Which isn't that far; a dozen yards, at most.

Beau is nothing more than a dark spot in the sea of white, moving across the yard to a small barn-like building on the far side, probably where he stores the wood and whatever vehicles he has up here.

Guilt over making the man go back out into that mess gnaws at my freshly-filled gut, and I press a palm over it and squeeze my eyes closed.

It's a feeling I should be well acquainted with, one I've lived with longer than I can remember, one that has only strengthened over the last two days. Yet, tonight it feels different somehow. Harsher. More real than it ever has.

Tears burn in my eyes, and a sob climbs up my throat. Biting it back, I try to suck in deep breaths.

In through the nose. Out through the mouth.

I need something to ground me. Something to remind me of where I am—and why—so I don't lose my damn mind.

My hands shake as I place them against the glass. The

cool, smooth texture calms my nerves but only for a moment before flashes of red fill my vision.

I force my eyes open. The simple beauty and purity of what's happening outside desperately tries to wash away the memory but it never can. Nothing ever will.

Another shiver wracks my body, and I turn away from the window and return to the heat radiating from the stone fireplace. The soft crackles and pops it emits fill the silence of the cabin, and if I hadn't almost died earlier today and weren't stuck here for the foreseeable future with the handsome, irritable, annoyed man outside, I might even think this is the perfect place to do what I need to.

Heal, Brooke.

Give yourself time to think.

To figure out your future.

If you have one...

I climb back into my spot in the corner of the couch and huddle down under the blanket again, absorbing every ounce of warmth it and the flames can offer. My eyelids droop, and the calming sound of the fire and the howling winds make me sink even deeper into the couch.

The door slamming open jerks me awake, and my scream pierces the air. I blink rapidly, scanning the room to try to get my bearings.

"Brooke, you okay?" Beau stands just inside the door, firewood in his arms, the exposed skin on his face reddened by the nasty weather and his wet boots dripping onto the mat beneath his feet.

Shit.

My heart thunders violently against my ribcage, and I suck in a few deep breaths, pressing my hand against my chest to try to calm myself before I have a coronary. "I'm sorry. I must have fallen asleep."

His brow draws low, and his jaw tightens, visible even under his beard. "Stop apologizing. Can you come grab this firewood so I can go out for another load without having to take off my boots?"

"Of course."

It's the least I can do after I've intruded on this man's life and fucked up his rhythm.

I toss off the blanket and despite the warmth the fire puts out, a chill immediately breaks out across my body. Beau was right about hypothermia. It's going to take a while for my body to recover from it, and this storm certainly isn't going to help the process. I pad across the floor and pause in front of him, tilting my head up to meet his gaze.

God, he really is big.

Living out here and having to do all this manual labor for yourself kind of requires a strength of character and physical muscle you don't need in Seattle. Or, at least, no man I ever knew there looked like this.

He raises a dark eyebrow at me like he's waiting for something.

Crap. I was staring.

I hold out my arms, and he reaches to lay the wood on them but pauses.

"Are you sure you can handle this?"

A few days ago, I might've said no, that it looks too heavy for me, but now, after I walked miles through the woods in a damn blizzard, I'm confident. "I got this."

He lowers the pile into my arms.

"Oomph."

Damn. That is heavy.

But I curl my arms around the logs, refusing to let Beau see just how much of a struggle this actually is. I turn away from him and hustle across to the fireplace.

49

"I'll go get another stack. We will probably need at least three to get through the night if we keep it going this hard."

Get through the night.

He makes it sound like that isn't certain, but it's likely just my hypothermia-fogged brain seeing danger where there is none. Beau wouldn't live out here alone if he weren't perfectly capable of handling things. The man stitched up his own head wound, so "making it through" a storm like this should be nothing.

Right?

I turn back to him and brush the bits of dirt and bark from the front of my shirt. At least the wood was dry, likely from his stores, not the new wood he cut today. "I'll be here."

His jaw hardens again as he takes me in, then he shakes his head. "You sure as hell will be."

The door slams shut behind him, and I wince.

He really is annoyed.

I have to try to interfere as little as possible with his daily routine and be as helpful as I can be with things around the house.

Nobody would call me Suzy Homemaker—and certain people would even laugh at the idea to my face—but I can handle myself in the kitchen well enough and I can clean.

I'll figure out a way to make myself useful while he's stuck with me, and then, as soon as I can, I'll hightail it out of here and leave him to get back to his secluded, solitary life.

One he clearly loves.

* * *

BEAU

A wicked northerly blast slams into me as I cross toward the cabin with another pile, one even larger than last. The fewer trips I have to make out here in this, the better. If I hadn't needed to keep the fire going at full-blast to help warm her and the cabin up, what I already had in there would have lasted at least until tomorrow night, but we're burning through this far faster than I would alone.

All I want is a stiff drink and a good night's sleep, but something tells me that won't be happening as long as Brooke Beck is around.

Something about that woman rubs at something deep inside me. A need to help her. To ensure she's cared for. And her constantly apologizing for being here and needing my help is getting on my last nerve.

She has nothing to apologize for.

Not really.

Whatever brought her up this mountain, she never intended to end up in the middle of that clearing, totally unprepared, near death. She didn't plan to have to spend the length of this storm and then some holed up with me here.

We've both been thrust into this impossible situation unexpectedly, and we need to make the best of it, the best we can. That means tolerating each other and trying not to completely lose my cool.

Easier said than done.

I feel her gaze on me from the window as I approach the cabin, and this time, she pulls open the door for me. The wave of warm air from inside almost makes me sigh in relief.

She eyes the logs in my arms warily and bites the inside of her cheek.

It may be too big a load for her. I probably should have considered that before I grabbed so much this time. "You think you can handle all this?"

Brooke straightens her shoulders and nods with determination blazing in her evergreen gaze. "I can handle as much wood as you have."

Holy hell.

I fight a grin at her words, and her eyes widen slightly, a red flush spreading across her pale skin.

"Shit. Sorry. I didn't mean to say that."

The chuckle slips from my lips before I can stop it. "You didn't mean to say that or you didn't mean the innuendo it created?"

She points a finger at me. "That. The second one. Now, give me that wood."

I bark out a laugh, the sound so foreign to my own ears that it makes me freeze for a second until I catch her staring at me with raised, blond brows. It's been so long since something made me laugh that I forgot what it sounds like.

Shit. I must look like a fucking lunatic.

She holds out her arms, her focus on the wood, not my face, and I lower the stack into them, a tiny grunt the only hint she offers at how heavy it really is for her.

But she'll never admit that. I saw it in her eyes the second she said the words she wishes she could take back. She's mentally strong—maybe more so than physically—and she would never admit defeat to me. Especially not when she feels like she isn't wanted here—which is completely my fault.

Faking my way through things used to just be part of everyday, but it's been far too long since I've had to pretend to be okay with an uncomfortable situation.

I duck outside for the final stack before she finishes unloading the second one, the thought of watching her brush dirt off her breasts again too much for me to handle.

That coupled with the little joke I just threw at her is going to make for a very long night.

Way to go, Beau. Smooth.

I grab the logs, fighting the gusts that threaten to knock me over into a pile of snow and the flakes stinging my face, and push back into the house, kicking the door shut behind me. "It's really coming down out there. The forecast said we might get two feet but it could be more."

Brooke frowns and stops in front of me to collect the wood. "Shit. That doesn't bode well for me getting out of here anytime soon, does it?"

"Sorry."

I don't miss the irony of *me* apologizing to her, but it seemed like the right response for the circumstances. She doesn't want to be here any more than I want her here—something I will keep reminding myself of even if we exchange a little playful banter.

She finishes unloading the wood while I remove my outdoor gear and kick off my boots. I turn back toward her to find her standing in front of the fire, arms wrapped protectively around herself.

"Um, I'm pretty tired."

I wince. "Shit. I'm sorry. You need sleep. Your body is still recovering."

And I'm the asshole who just asked her to carry three heavy loads of logs into the damn house.

She runs a hand back through her hair and focuses on the raging flames, worrying her bottom lip between her teeth. "What exactly are the sleeping arrangements?" She motions toward my room. "That's obviously your room." Then she points toward the office door to the left. "Is that a guest room?"

"No." My response comes clipped and low, harsh, but the thought of her digging into things in my office and what she might find there makes me fist my hands at my sides. "No guestroom. You'll take my bed, and I'll take the couch."

Brooke gapes at the couch. "What? No. You can't do that. This is your house. I'm the interloper. I'll sleep on the couch."

I cross over to the fireplace and stop in front of her. "Don't worry about me. I've survived worse than a night on a couch."

The words come out calm and steady, far steadier than I thought I could ever say them, but still, she looks at me as if she can see right through them to the things I'm not saying. To what brought me running up this mountain. To what keeps me here.

"Really, Beau, I appreciate the offer. But you must be exhausted after chopping all that wood and sleeping on a couch won't be comfortable for a big guy like you." She presses a hand to her chest, and I fight not to let my gaze follow it. "I'm small. I'll be fine."

Fisting my hands at my sides, I take several deep breaths but can't completely dispel the anger the thought of her being miserable out here on the couch while I'm happily tucked away in my bed brings. It might be warm in front of the fire, but this couch isn't meant to be slept on, and she's just been through an ordeal that has left her weak and in need of restful sleep. "You're sleeping in the bed. End of discussion."

"Excuse me?" Her brow furrows and shoulders square up like she's ready for a fight. "Is this a dictatorship?"

"This is *my* fucking house, and you're a guest in it. And if I tell you to sleep in the bed, you will."

She crosses her arms over her chest defensively, tipping her chin up. "You may be trying to do something noble and gentlemanly, but you're coming across as a real fucking dick right now. I don't appreciate people telling me what to do."

"And I don't appreciate people showing up unannounced and telling me what to do in my own house." The words just seem to fall out of my mouth as I take a step toward her, my voice rising despite how close we are to each other.

She shrinks away from me, fear flashing in her eyes again the same way it did when she first saw me in the woods and then again when she woke.

Fuck.

I freeze and hold up my hands, taking a step back, my mistake readily apparent. "I'm sorry. I didn't mean to scare you." Scrubbing my hands over my face, I release a heavy sigh. "I'm not used to sharing my space with people, with having anyone around me or having to control my reactions."

And I was being a fucking asshole.

She was right to call me out. I used to know how to talk to people, how to handle any situation—in business and personally. Women used to be easy for me. *Everything* used to be easy.

Christ, so much has changed.

I open my eyes and meet her terrified ones. "I would *never* hurt you."

But someone certainly has at some point in her life.

Brooke's reaction isn't normal—even though I *am* a stranger. It's the knee-jerk response of someone who has been through something terrible and paid a price for it in the past. And I'm only making things worse for her in an uncomfortable situation by being a total jerk.

"Please, Brooke, just take the bed. I'm still worried about you...and the lingering effects of the hypothermia. It'll be much warmer in there under the down quilt and on the mattress than out here, even by the fire. And *far* more comfortable."

She releases a long breath, like she's been holding it the entire time and is finally allowing herself to breathe again, and blinks away the fear that was clouding her gaze. "Okay, if that's what you want."

"I do."

"Thank you."

"And again, I'm sorry."

She shrugs slightly, attempting to brush off my overreaction and her response. "Don't worry about it."

But I do.

This woman is a guest in my house—whether invited or forced—and two things Mom and Dad always taught me were manners and how to be a gracious host.

I shouldn't have snapped at her and gotten angry like that. Now that I've seen her reaction, I have to be more careful around her—think about what I do and say and not let myself lose control.

The last thing I want to do is scare her into running off into the woods where she'll either get lost, eaten by a damn wild animal, or succumb to the hypothermia that almost took her the first time.

"Do you need anything else?"

She glances toward the bedroom and shifts on her feet awkwardly. My gaze travels over her long-sleeve T-shirt hugging her torso and the baggy sweatpants and heavy wool socks from my dresser. My heart does a little leap in my chest.

What the hell was that?

Something about seeing her in my clothes sends a little rush through my blood. One I shouldn't be feeling. An almost possessiveness.

"I know where the bathroom is, and I can just sleep in this, so I think I'm good."

"Sure...yeah."

"Thank you, Beau."

"Don't thank me. I'm just doing what anyone would do."

"No, you're not." She shakes her head and tears shimmer in her eyes as she stares at the fire. "There are a lot of bad people in this world, Beau. A lot of people who would take this situation and use it to their advantage."

That she knows that makes a knife twist in my chest. "How do you know I won't?"

She turns her head slowly and meets my gaze, and a single tear trickles down her cheek. "I just do." Her shoulders rise and fall again. "I don't know how. But I do."

Her words paralyze me, and before I can begin to process a response, she closes the three or four steps between us and leans up to press a kiss on my cheek. One of her small hands flattens against my chest, searing my skin even through the fabric of my T-shirt.

"Thank you, Beau."

Those whispered words near my ear send that same damn flutter through me again.

It's been far too long since I've had a woman around. Far too long since I had anyone in my space, anyone to talk to or answer to. And as soon as the storm is over—in a few days, maybe a week—she'll be out of here and I can get back to living the life I was intended to.

She brushes past me and ducks into the bathroom, closing the door behind her with a finality that makes me stagger to the fireplace and grip the mantle.

Shit. Shit. Shit.

I drop my head and let the heat melt away the chill from being outside and my own reaction to her.

Yes, she's beautiful. Yes, she's sweet. Yes, we had a little moment earlier. But that's all it was. All it can be.

The bathroom door opens again, freezing me in place. I wait to see if she's coming back out, but the bedroom door closes next and I release a heavy sigh of relief.

What I really need right now is a drink.

I make my way over to the office door and push it open. With every step I take over to the bar, my energy seems to deplete more and more. It's been a long fucking day, full of unexpected surprises and injuries. I reach up and carefully touch where Brooke smashed open my head with the vase and grimace.

That's going to hurt for a while, but it could have been worse—at least physically to my head. Mom's vase, on the other hand, that's long gone. Nothing but pieces at the bottom of a trash can.

I pour myself a drink and down half of it in one gulp. The warm, smoky Scotch sears down my throat, but it's a feeling and a burn I welcome—the kind of pain that reminds me of why I'm here doing this.

Something I obviously need a reminder of with Brooke around.

Maybe more than one reminder.

I refill the glass with more than I probably should be drinking tonight, then wander back out into the living room.

The roaring fire will keep both of us warm tonight, but it won't do anything about the chilling reality Brooke has brought with her.

There's a world outside here, one that could find me just as easily as she did accidentally. One I'm not prepared to handle.

I stop in front of the fireplace, grip the mantle with one hand, and lean against it as I take another sip of my drink.

This day sure didn't end up the way I thought it would.

Now I have a houseguest, a throbbing headache and new scar, plus a very real problem.

How am I going to keep her from finding out the truth?

We're going to be living practically on top of each other while she's here.

I'll just need to make sure I don't let anything slip that could make her ask the questions I can't answer.

Easy enough.

In theory...

I take a pull from my glass and move to the couch, sprawling out as much of my body as it can take. My feet dangle off the arm of the far side, and I groan at the ever-present twinge in my lower back.

This is going to be an uncomfortable night—the first of many—but there was no way I was going to let that girl sleep out here after everything she's been through.

Not when I know what it's like to survive a trauma and need somewhere soft to land.

I never had that, but it's the least I can give Brooke, even if she is a complete stranger who's thrown a wrench into my life.

The wind rattles the glass window panes again, and I let my eyes drift closed.

With any luck, the storm won't be as bad as forecasted

and she'll be out of here in a day or two. Worst case scenario, maybe a week. I can handle a week with her here and keep my sanity intact.

At least, that's what I'm going to tell myself.

Chapter Five

BROOKE

The familiar smell of bacon rouses me from a sleep so deep, I might as well have been dead. Based on the wind rattling the cabin, the storm hasn't abated much overnight, nor has the chill that seems to have permanently permeated my body. Even snuggled down deep under the covers of Beau's bed with a heavy down comforter covering me, I still shudder every time the wind picks up and reminds me of how I got here.

Memories I can't escape during the day the way I managed to last night come rushing back, threatening to completely unravel me before the day even gets started.

No. Not going to happen.

I take a deep breath—one filled with the woodsy, manly scent that helps push away those bad memories and bring more recent ones to the forefront.

The few tense moments Beau and I had yesterday are in the past. I'm safe here. If he was going to harm me, he would have already. God knows he's had plenty of opportunity and has proven himself trustworthy. In that regard, at least. The fact that he's so closed off still leaves me with too many questions to count, and I plan to get the answers today.

But that means climbing out of this warm bed and subjecting myself to whatever Mother Nature is throwing at us today. That isn't a pleasant prospect, but I still reluctantly drag myself out of the comfort, shivering immediately at the change in temperature.

I tiptoe to the window and behold the vast expanse of white. Cold air seeps in from outside, and I wrap my arms around myself and stare out at the winter wonderland. Even with the flakes whipping around, violently driven by a force that seems intent on destruction, the beauty of the scene takes my breath away.

Seattle rarely offers anything but rain. While that can certainly hold its own charm, this is the kind of view that reminds a person there is a higher power out there somewhere.

One that apparently wants me dead.

It's a good reminder that even the most beautiful things can be deadly. That they can lull you into a false sense of security, then try to destroy you the way the storm did.

I never imagined coming up to Colleen's cabin would be anything other than a way to escape what I left behind in Seattle, a place to decompress, to think, to find my center and face the uncertain future. Instead, the blizzard killed Old Blue, almost killed me, and left me at the mercy of a man who just wants to be left alone.

"Just my fucking luck..." My words bounce back to me off the glass pane, and I shake my head and force myself away from the window.

My stomach rumbles at the smell wafting in through the crack at the bottom of the door, and I walk over and slowly twist the knob. A slight creak makes me wince, and I pause to listen for the sounds of Beau up and moving around.

But all that greets me is absolute silence. The kind of silence you never get in a city like Seattle. The kind that makes unease crawl up my spine and wrap around my heart even though there isn't any inherent reason to be afraid of it.

I tiptoe out into the living room, but the couch is empty. No sign of Beau or that he even slept here last night. The fire still roars, though, and the stack of wood we brought in last night appears untouched.

Impossible.

This fireplace is the only heat source for the entire cabin. There are no air ducts, no vents in the floor or ceiling pushing out warm air. It would have taken all the wood in here to keep it heated all night. Which means Beau must have been up for hours already, replenishing the stack from his supply outside while I slept away instead of doing my part.

Doesn't that make me feel like an asshole.

The front door opening jerks me around to face it. Beau steps in, brushing snow off his shoulders, and closes the door behind him. He stomps the snow from his boots onto a mat, tugs off his gloves and hat, and undoes his jacket, all without so much as glancing my way. After living alone for God only knows how long, he isn't used to anyone else being here.

He turns to hang his jacket and spots me, freezing for a moment. "Oh, you're up."

I offer him a little half-smile. "I am."

"There's bacon. I can reheat it in the oven. And I could make you eggs or toast. Whatever you want."

"No, no, no." I take a step toward him, then think better of it after what happened last night and hold my ground.

"Please, you don't have to cook for me. The least I can do is handle things in the kitchen since you're letting me stay here."

He snorts and shakes his head as he bends down to untie his boots. "*Letting you* isn't exactly the right word, is it?"

The little half-grin he gives me while kicking off his boots brings a smile to my face, too, and breaks some of the tension.

"Okay, so you're being forced to deal with me? How about that?"

A smirk turns his lips, and he makes his way into the kitchen. "A little bit more accurate, don't you think?"

Completely accurate.

I sigh and follow him into the tight space. No need for the sprawling, too-big kitchens the homes in Seattle all have when you live alone and are only cooking for one.

He grabs a tray of bacon off the small slice of counter, cranks on a gas stove, and slips it in. "Shouldn't take more than a minute or two to warm up."

"Great." I peek over his shoulder at the fridge. "I'll just make myself some eggs."

Beau watches me approach him and shifts back as much as he can to allow me to pass and get to the refrigerator. But as my ass brushes against him in the tight space, the smell of pine and crisp, fresh winter air rolls off him in a way that makes me inhale deeply.

Oh, God. I hope he didn't just see me sniff him.

Fucking embarrassing.

Avoiding meeting his gaze, I pull open the refrigerator door and freeze. "Ummm."

"Yes?" He raises an eyebrow at me and leans against the counter. "Need something?"

"I don't see any eggs."

He grins and inclines his head toward the front door. "They're out in the chicken coop."

I jerk upright. "You're joking, right?"

"Sorry, Sleeping Beauty, I wish I could say I was."

The slightly smug tilt to his lips makes me momentarily forget feeling bad for intruding on his life.

But only for a minute.

My stomach grumbles as the smell of the bacon reheating fills the kitchen, and Beau's focus drifts down my body to where the sound is emanating from.

"I'll go get the eggs for you, Sleeping Beauty."

"No." I reach out and grab his arm without even thinking, tightening my hand around the hard muscle, and we both freeze, staring down at where our bodies are connected. I jerk my hand away. "Sorry, I—shit. I keep apologizing, don't I? But you don't need to go out in that again just to get the eggs. I'll go do it."

Beau runs his hand along his bearded jaw and chuckles. "Good luck with that. I don't think Betty Sue or Joanne would appreciate the intrusion from a stranger."

"Betty Sue and Joanne?"

He hooks a finger over his shoulder toward the door. "My hens. They aren't used to anyone else being here. Really, it's not a problem for me to go get them. I have to do it every day anyway, and I haven't been out there yet this morning because I was busy bringing in more dry wood and trying to fix the door on the barn."

"What happened to the door?"

"Wind pulled it straight off the hinges last night."

"Oh, damn. Were you able to fix it?"

He nods. "At least temporarily. I'll probably have to go into town once the road is passable to get some supplies in order to do a more permanent repair. I'll go grab the eggs."

"You're sure?"

No matter how many times he offers, I can't help but feel guilty that he's spending his time taking care of me when he clearly has other things to worry about and do around here.

"I'll tell you what...when I get back in here, I'll let you make me a big breakfast." He glances at a clock on the wall. "Well, I guess more like brunch. But only if that'll stop you from apologizing and constantly asking me if I'm sure about things."

I drop my face in my hands and groan. "I'm—" I manage to stop myself before I say it again and instead take a breath and square my shoulders before I meet his gaze. "Okay, deal."

With a smirk, he points to the oven. "Keep an eye on that bacon so it doesn't burn while I'm gone."

"You got it."

He watches me for a second too long before he pushes off the counter and makes his way to the door to get bundled up again.

Who the hell is this guy?

Out here all alone. Raising chickens. Fixing shed doors. Rescuing damsels in distress all in the middle of a massive snowstorm.

What would possess someone to want to live like this?

I know why *I* came up here, which makes me all the more curious what potential reason he might have for wanting to hide out in the middle of nowhere.

Beau pulls on his hat and gloves, and I work my way over to the front door as he tugs it open to step outside.

"Where'd you learn to do all this, anyway? Did you grow up on a homestead or something?"

He freezes, his body stiffening almost instantly. "Something like that."

The door slamming behind him offers a finality to the conversation that makes me jump back slightly. That man isn't interested in sharing anything about himself with me, and I suppose it's just as well since I won't be offering him much about myself, either.

While his words often come out harsh, they hold an air of truth. Solitude can be a necessity. Whether it be because you're running from the world outside or from something deep within yourself.

You just have to hope whatever it is doesn't catch up with you.

BEAU

The wooden chair underneath me suddenly seems harder than it has before, more rigid, unforgiving. I shift in it for what must be the hundredth time since I sat down and started watching Brooke bustle around the kitchen making brunch.

Having someone—anyone—in my space makes me fidgety, but her...she's making it damn near impossible for me to sit still and relax. Not that I have a lot of time for either with the way the storm continues to batter the world outside. Given the looks of what Mother Nature is throwing at us when I was out there grabbing the eggs, things won't die down anytime soon.

It's one of the worst storms I've seen since I moved up

here. Which means the beautiful, frustrating girl making scrambled eggs on my stove will be here longer than either of us want.

It would be better for all parties if she got on her way, either back to wherever it is she came from or off to her friend's cabin; though, I would hope she would stop and get some proper gear before she tried to do that.

Her trip didn't seem too well planned. Almost as if she's running from something and just needed to get away.

A feeling I know all too well.

Only, there are some things you can't run from. Some things that will chase you to the ends of the Earth. Or the top of a mountain...

She turns off the burner on the stove and approaches with the pan in hand. Even though I ate early this morning, my stomach rumbles at the scent wafting up from it.

It smells better than anything I've ever cooked before.

Or maybe it's just who cooked it that makes the difference.

She spoons eggs onto my waiting plate with the reheated bacon. "Hope they're okay. You have a decent pantry, but I didn't have a lot of what I would normally add to them to spruce them up."

I raise an eyebrow. "Spruce them up?"

She loads some onto her plate and returns the pan to the stove before she takes her seat across from me at the tiny table pushed in the corner of the kitchen. One of her shoulders rises and falls. "Yeah. You know, some fresh onions, bell peppers, tomatoes or something. Spruce it up."

I fight a grin as I push my fork into the pile of eggs. "Up here, when I hear the word 'spruce,' I think of something else."

Her brow furrows. "What do you mean?

68

"You know...the trees?"

"Oh...yeah." She offers a little laugh. "I hadn't thought about that."

"And actually, the term 'spruce it up' refers to Prussia. Pruce was an adjective used for things from Prussia, and like with most language, it got twisted over the centuries and became 'spruce.' Since things from Prussia were highly valued, it eventually came to mean to tidy up or make something better."

Brooke stares at me with wide eyes. "Um... that's...random."

Shit.

All the useless knowledge crammed into my brain by years of attending the best private schools in the country and Dad being obsessed with world history seems to have stayed solidly implanted. Though, I can't seem to keep it there. Which means I'm opening myself up for Brooke to ask a lot of fucking questions.

I shift again and shovel a forkful of eggs into my mouth to buy myself a moment to think of a reason I would know that and almost groan at how good they are. "My Dad was kind of a history buff." The flavors dancing across my taste buds give me a diversion from my slip of the tongue. "What the hell did you put in this?"

She freezes with her fork halfway up to her mouth, and her hand starts shaking slightly. "Why? Is it terrible?"

Holy shit. She's actually afraid because I might not like it?

I lean toward her and hold up a hand. "No, quite the opposite. I've been cooking eggs here for ten years, and I've never made them taste this good before."

Her breath rushes out in a whoosh, and her shoulders relax slightly. "A little milk—"

"Goat's milk."

"Huh?"

"It's goat's milk, from my two does."

Brooke's jaw falls open. "You have goats?"

I nod and take another bite. "Mmm hmm. As you can imagine, getting supplies up here isn't always easy. Having my own goats and chickens at least gives me those essentials."

She glances down at the eggs on her plate again, like she's seeing them in a whole new light. "Oh, okay. Well, I used goat's milk, butter, salt, pepper, garlic powder, and onion powder I found in your pantry. Oh, and a hint of cayenne."

"Cayenne." I take another bite and the slight heat hits the back of my throat. "I never would have thought of that. It's delicious."

She shrugs as if it's nothing and digs into her plate of food, seemingly less thrown by the goat milk than she was the squirrel stew. I eat far slower, taking the time to really examine the woman who is throwing my life for a loop.

Her pale blond hair hangs loose around her face, perfectly framing the pale, freckled skin and soft pink cheeks. I'm transfixed watching her soft bow lips open and close as she eats, and how long and elegant her neck looks when she swallows.

The woman is truly stunning. She should be on the cover of a magazine, not sitting at the rickety table in my small cabin up an abandoned mountain.

But something brought her here, just like it did me.

Something that has made her jumpy and on-edge.

"You're staring at me."

Shit.

I tear my gaze off her and return it to the almost-empty

70

plate I hadn't even realized I was so close to finishing. "Sorry."

"Do I have food on my face or something?"

"No." I shake my head and push around the tiny bits of egg still left on my plate before glancing up to catch her reaction. "Just wondering what really brought you up here."

She stiffens and sets down her fork on her now-empty plate before she pushes away from the table and brings her dishes over to the sink. "I told you, I'm staying at my friend's cabin for a little bit."

I lean back in my chair, crossing my arms behind my head. "Yes, you told me that. But it's a long drive up this mountain from basically anywhere and not exactly the best time of year to be coming up here, especially alone when you didn't seem all that prepared. Kind of like this trip was a little unplanned?"

While I phrase it like a question, I already know the answer.

And I know she's going to lie.

With her back to me at the sink, she shrugs and cranks on the faucet to wash her plate and fork along with the dishes she used to make the eggs. "I grew up in Seattle and I've never been up in the mountains before. You're right. I was woefully unprepared. I won't make that mistake again."

"I would hope not."

But she avoided answering my question, just like I knew she would.

"How do you have running water and power up here?"

Nice attempt to change the subject.

"Dozens of solar panels set up on various parts of my property that basically continuously collect energy and store it in a massive battery bank in the barn. It powers the cabin and an on-demand water heater that pulls water from an underground well."

"Sounds expensive."

It's an off-hand observation that isn't wrong, and it makes me wince at the second slip of the tongue I've made in only a few minutes. I can't let her derail my mission to get information from her.

Brooke sets the dishes on the small drying rack on the counter and walks over to the table to grab mine without making eye contact with me.

"So, do you have a job you need to get back to?"

"Self-employed."

She viciously scrubs at my plate far harder than she needs to. This conversation is upsetting her, getting her off-balance, the same way her questions got to me earlier.

"Well, I need to radio the sheriff today with your name and friend's number so he can get that message to her."

Her body stiffens again, and she peeks over her shoulder at me. "Um, how about we wait until we know how long we'll be stuck here. Like I said, she won't be worried about me for at least a week."

Something tickles at the back of my mind, an unease I haven't felt in a long time. Brooke doesn't want anyone contacting her friend...if there even is one.

Why is she really up here?

A huge part of me wants to push her, wants to demand to know what's really going on, but the woman is jumpy and scared. That much is obvious. There doesn't seem to be any point in forcing the issue when she clearly isn't going to offer me any information.

I glance out the window. "The storm is still going full force today, but I'll check the updated forecast and see how things look. Then, we can call and figure it out."

Her shoulders relax slightly, and she slides the cleaned plate on the drying rack. "Okay. What else do you have to do today? Anything I can help with?"

I scan the cabin that's been my home for the last decade, the place that—until yesterday—no one else had ever set foot in. There are a hundred little projects I could do around here while it's so nasty outside, but the last twenty-four hours—between felling the tree, chopping the extra wood, rescuing a damsel in distress, and sleeping on the shitty couch—have left me exhausted and lacking in motivation to get anything done that isn't urgent.

"Other than the necessary things I already took care of this morning, nothing else is pressing."

Especially since I told Nate to handle things with the board. If I had to be dealing with all the drama there right now on top of handling this woman who has been dropped into my lap, I'd likely be at the bottom of a bottle instead of stuffed full of one of the best meals I've had in a long time.

Brooke leans back against the edge of the sink. "Okay. I guess I'll take a shower, then."

A vision of her naked body—all pale, perfect skin, this time pink and warm instead of cold and pale like she was when I had to undress her to save her life—flashes through my head, and a part of my body that has not gotten attention for a very long time stirs to life.

I clear my throat and shift in my chair again, for a different reason this time. "You go ahead and do that."

"I'll make some more coffee, and I have some books if you want to borrow one and sit by the fire."

A tiny smile curls her lips. "Thank you, Beau, for everything. Truly."

"You're quite welcome."

It might actually be good for me to have a little human

73

companionship for a while. To help *keep* me human. The only problem is that I *am* human. A human man who sees how beautiful Brooke is and also how broken she is by whatever hides in her past.

We appear to be kindred spirits.

That should be a warning to stay far away from her—for both our sakes.

Chapter Six

BEAU

The scream jolts me awake, and I jerk straight up on the couch and wince at the jab of discomfort in my back.

What was that?

Most people would complain about the eerie quiet out here, about a silence that's almost deafening. It took some getting used to, but now that I have, any loud or new sounds tend to send my heart racing.

Another scream echoes through the cabin.

"What the hell?" I rub at my eyes, and it takes my sleep-fogged brain a moment to process what's happening. "Brooke!"

I toss off the blanket, race down the short hallway to my room, and throw open the door. The snow finally starting to taper off allows a hint of moonlight to filter in through the window and across my bed where Brooke lies thrashing back and forth.

"No!" She cries out again and swings at some unknown threat, her movements frantic. "No! Stop!"

"Brooke!" I rush into the room and scramble onto the bed, placing a hand on her shoulder. "Brooke, wake up."

She lashes out and makes contact with the side of my head, the same spot she split open when she hit me with the vase.

Pain shoots through my temple. "Fuck."

"No, get away."

Her frantic movements increase, tears pouring from her closed eyes, soaking the pillowcase beneath her.

"Wake up, Brooke." I grab her shoulders and shake her, trying to snap her out of whatever nightmare has her in its grips. "It's a dream."

She continues to thrash wildly, stuck in a violent loop of terror in her own head. I shake her again and drag her up across my lap and into my arms.

"Brooke!" I yell as loud as I can and grip her chin. The time for being gentle in trying to stop this is long gone. "Wake up!"

Her eyes fly open, tears streaming down her face. She gasps and drags in several ragged inhales, like she can't catch her breath.

"Brooke, it's me—Beau."

"Oh, God..." She sags slightly and finally manages to suck in several deep breaths as her eyes frantically search the dark room then come back to me. They zero in on the cut on my head and any lingering confusion seems to clear almost instantly. She reaches up a hand to my head. "You're bleeding."

Jesus...

She's worried about me?

"I'm fine. Are *you* okay?"

She brings her hand back down, the fingertips red with my blood, but I'm not worried about a little cut. It isn't bleeding badly enough to drip, so it won't kill me.

I'm more worried about her.

"You were having a nightmare."

"Yeah..." She brushes her sweaty hair back from her face and chokes slightly on her words, squeezing her eyes closed as her body continues to vibrate with the rush of adrenaline. "I-I'm fine."

"Are you?"

"Yes."

That word may have left her quivering lips, but she appears anything *but* fine. She's in shock. Whatever just went on in her unconscious mind felt very real to her, real enough to leave her incredibly shaken.

My chest tightens watching her struggle to regain her footing. It reminds me too much of a time that I moved out here to forget.

"Where were you?"

"Huh?" She glances at me, her brow furrowing, and swipes away the tears from her cheeks.

"In your dream. Where were you? What made you so afraid?"

Her body stiffens in my arms, and she shifts slightly away from me. "I don't remember."

Lie.

"Does this have anything to do with why you're up here?"

I don't know where this question comes from. It just seemed like an obvious leap to make, given how she showed up here and how she's reacted since she's arrived.

"No." Her answer comes too fast—like if she rushes it

out, I'll be more likely to believe her. "I'm fine. I told you. I just needed a little vacation."

"In the middle of nowhere. Completely unprepared."

She narrows her eyes on me, anger flashing deep in their green depths, and I'm almost relieved to see it back rather than the panic that was there only a moment ago. I adjust my position to take a little stress off my back, and it seems to register for her that we're in bed together and that my arms are wrapped around her.

Almost instantly, she pulls away and shifts back under the covers, her entire body shaking so badly it practically vibrates the mattress.

Her distress tugs at parts of me I didn't think were still alive. Ones I thought had died and desiccated a decade ago. Ones I don't *want* to revive.

"Can I get you anything? A glass of water? Some tea?"

She shakes her head, her focus on the window and the storm still going outside in the dark of night.

"Something stronger?"

That seems to get her attention because she shifts her gaze to me, lifts her head, and gives me a sharp nod.

Alcohol isn't the healthiest way to cope with trauma—at least, that's what I've been told. But it feels right in this situation. Something to calm her nerves a little bit.

Being in an unfamiliar place with a total stranger can't be easy under the best of circumstances, and whatever brought her up here was clearly not that. Even without her being willing to discuss what went down with me, she definitely needs something.

Something I am woefully unable to give her, but maybe alcohol will be a good temporary substitute.

I slip from the bed and pause to examine her before I step out the door—so small and vulnerable in my bed. A vise tightens around my chest, and old demons I've fought so hard against for so long threaten to rear their ugly heads and come back biting.

"I'll be right back."

Why the hell did I tell her that?

It's not like I can go anywhere—even if I wanted to. The storm might be slowing down a bit, but that doesn't mean it's over. Even if it were and the roads weren't blocked, I wouldn't leave her like this.

I couldn't.

For better or worse, we're stuck here together for a while. The least I can do is try to make her as comfortable as possible—which isn't much.

I rub at the stiffness in the back of my neck and plod into the living room. The heat radiating from the burned down fire reminds me to throw a few more logs on before I head into the office and fill two tumblers with generous amounts of bourbon.

Brooke strikes me as more of a "sweet" drink type of girl, rather than the heavily smoked scotches I usually prefer. This may be a bit strong for her, but strength is what she needs now—in her booze and to find it in herself.

I return to the room and find her in the exact same fetal position, her face buried against the pillow, body shaking; though, at least it seems her tears have stopped.

Only a few steps separate me from the bed, but I pause to inhale a steadying breath before I walk over and slide onto it next to her. She flinches and recoils slightly.

"Sorry, I should have told you I was back." I hold out one of the glasses. "Here."

She slowly opens her eyes and focuses on it, then pushes herself up until she's sitting back against the headboard next to me.

"I'll just give you some space and let you get back to sleep." I shift toward the edge of the bed to stand, but a small hand wraps around my bicep. Even with the long sleeve shirt I slept in separating us, the heat of her touch scalds me in a way that makes me squeeze my eyes closed.

"Please...don't leave."

Her whispered words strike at me like blows delivered by a four-hundred-pound man rather than the small, defenseless woman at my back. The same words I heard that day. The ones I never wanted to hear again, laced with the same pain. The same anguish. The same desperation.

Sitting on the edge of the bed, my back still to Brooke, I down half my drink, letting the burn sear away the memory, then turn and settle back in next to her. But her hand doesn't leave its place clinging to my arm.

Something tells me it won't tonight.

* * *

BROOKE

An almost-blinding sunlight hits my eyelids, dragging me from what feels like the heaviest, deepest sleep I've ever had, and I groan and try to roll away from it. But instead of the cool pillow or mattress, my face connects with something warm and hard—that smells like wood, fire, smoke, hard work, and all man.

Oh no...

I blink open my eyes and stare up at Beau's chest. With his head dropped back against the headboard, his neck elongated and breaths coming in and out steadily in his sleep, he looks more at peace than I've seen him since I got here.

Oh, my God.

I fell asleep with my head on Beau's lap?

Everything from last night comes back in slow flashes—some violent and terrifying, others soft and comforting.

I shift slightly and spot dried blood at Beau's temple. The nightmare that brought him in here in the first place rushes back in vivid detail. My heart thunders against my ribs, my head swimming and breaths coming harder and faster.

It felt so real. The danger so immediate.

It didn't come the first night I was here, likely because I was too exhausted, my body too depleted to even dream. But it sure raged with a vengeance last night, attacking my psyche while I slept and driving fear into my heart again.

And I made a fucking fool of myself in front of this man.

It isn't bad enough I screamed like a psycho, smacked him hard enough to make him bleed—*again*—and clung to him like a terrified child, I had to go and pass out with my goddamn head in his lap.

So fucking awkward.

I try to surreptitiously move away from his warm, hard body, hopefully before he wakes and realizes what an idiot I am, but his rough hand lands on my shoulder and gives it a gentle squeeze.

"You okay?" His gravelly voice freezes me on the spot, and I slowly turn my head to look back at him and find his gaze locked directly on me, soaked in concern.

"Yeah. I'm—"

He presses a finger over my lips before I can get it out. "You're not going to apologize."

Well, yeah, if you won't let me...

But he isn't wrong. I was about to apologize. And I should. This man absolutely did not sign on for my crazy. Just because I got lost and stumbled into his life doesn't mean he should have to deal with all the fallout of my issues.

"You didn't have to sleep in here last night, Beau."

A little half grin pulls up the corner of his lips. "Yeah, I kind of did. You were upset and asked me to stay. I wasn't going to say no."

As sweet and as unexpected as that is, it also stiffens my spine. I don't want Beau to think he needs to take care of me. "I would have been fine. I'm a big girl."

"And you had a pretty bad nightmare and didn't want to be alone in what is still a strange place." He shrugs slightly. "I can understand that."

"You can?"

What could this burly, solitary mountain man possibly know about nightmares and not wanting to be alone?

He nods slowly and runs the hand not resting on my shoulder through his disheveled hair, letting his chestnut eyes focus on something suddenly very interesting on the high ceiling. "I have some pretty wicked nightmares myself. Though, I tend to go in the opposite direction in terms of how I react to them—away from people rather than wanting someone with me."

That certainly explains this place and the way he lives. Whatever happened in his past to haunt his dreams must have been just as bad, if not worse, than my sob story to send him running up here, so far away from civilization.

"Well..." I release a long breath and bite back the apology again. "Thank you."

His gaze returns to mine, one eyebrow raised. "Is that what we're doing now? Going from apologizing all the time to thanking me all the time?"

I can't fight the smile that pulls my lips up despite really wanting to crawl under the covers and never have to look at this man again after how badly I embarrassed myself. He lifts his hand from my shoulder and runs it along my cheek slowly, his calloused fingertips against my smooth skin sending a shiver through me that has nothing to do with how cold it is outside.

He tilts my face up with his hand at my jaw. "Are you cold?"

"No."

Far from it.

I feel truly warm for the first time in days. Truly safe for the first time in forever. Which is equally as comforting as it is terrifying.

He drags his eyes off me and focuses on the window. "It's still snowing, though it appears the worst of it has passed."

If only that were true in life...

I turn my head to look for myself and find the bright morning sunlight shining and reflecting off a few flakes fluttering in front of the wavy glass pane. Mother Nature has finally broken her stranglehold on the mountain.

"That's good, right?"

Somehow, the words don't feel true even though it's what we've both been waiting for.

Beau slowly nods and lightly brushes his thumb across my cheek. "Yeah, it is." He swallows thickly, his Adam's apple bobbing under whiskered skin. "You'll be able to get out of here in a couple days, assuming the sun stays out and some of the snow melts off."

A lead weight settles in the pit of my stomach, making it hard to speak. "Yeah, I-I guess I can get out of your hair, then."

He slowly twists his head back to look at me. "You're not in my hair." He leisurely runs his fingers through the long, flowing blond strands splayed out on his lap, then reaches up and rubs it across his shorter, messy dark locks. "In case you haven't noticed, it's relatively short."

A joke?

A giggle bursts from my lips, and I reach up to drag my fingers over his beard. "This is kind of nice, though."

One of his dark eyebrows wings up. "Oh, really?"

"The girls back home would love this whole rugged mountain man look."

Especially Colleen.

He barks out a laugh so hard that it bounces me on his lap, his chest shaking. "Yeah, suuuure. Women love the Unabomber look."

"Really...it's a whole *thing* now. You could be on the cover of *GQ*, and I bet you look completely different without a beard..."

His body stiffens and his hand stops on my cheek before he pulls it away roughly, his hooded eyes darkening. "I should probably get up and go check on the rest of the damage the storm did. Plus, that fire is going to need some logs thrown on it."

"Shit. The fire." I lean up and rub my eyes, tugging the comforter around me against the chill both from the air and the sudden shift in the energy in the room. "You weren't out there to feed it all night."

He shakes his head but averts his gaze, looking at the window, the wall, the floor, anything but at me. "No. That's why it's a little chilly in here right now. It's probably down to just embers, but the house retains heat fairly well. The back of the chimney is the wall of this room to keep it warmer, but I've been keeping it going harder than usual for you."

"It's my fault."

All of it is.

And the comment I made about *GQ* and the beard shut him down faster than Old Blue died on me out on that road.

Way to make things super awkward, Brooke.

"I'll take care of the logs while you do whatever else you need to."

Sitting stock-still, Beau finally returns his eyes to me. For a moment, it looks like he wants to say something, perhaps offer an objection to my help, but instead, he just nods and watches me as I reluctantly drag myself up fully to free him from underneath me.

I tug the comforter even tighter around me. "You really slept sitting up like that all night?"

He slides off the side of the bed and groans, rubbing at his lower back. "Yeah." His hand moves up to his neck, and he tips his head side to side, a loud crack coming from it making me wince. "But don't worry about it. I've slept in worse places."

Somehow, I don't doubt that.

Something happened to Beau that brought him here to lock himself away, and whatever it was left him angry at the world in general and intent on keeping it out. The glimpses he gives me of how kind he can be, at how his laugh and smile light up his face—that's the real Beau. He just doesn't want to ever show it or acknowledge its existence. And now I've gone and made things fucking worse by clinging to him last night like some needy child.

He walks out of the room without a look back at me, sucking all the warmth in the air with him.

Today should be fun.

I bury my face in the pillow and issue a little frustrated scream that gets muffled by the down filling. Staying buried under the covers and pretending last night—and this morning—never happened sounds like an absolute dream, but after I fucked up his sleep and his back, I really should get out of bed and help him with whatever I can.

Yet, the scent of Beau and the last little bit of lingering body heat on the sheets where he served as my pillow all night keeps me under the comforter longer than I should be.

You can't hide forever.

That's one harsh reality I wish weren't true for a million different reasons.

I slowly drag myself out from under the covers and hustle to get dressed in my own clothes, which have finally dried—all but my underwear, which I need to either ditch or figure out a way to wash. After swimming in Beau's soft, oversized shirts and sweatpants, mine feel restrictive and rough against my skin in a way I've never noticed before—almost suffocatingly tight.

Or maybe the feeling of suffocating is more about knowing the storm has subsided and I have to face the real world soon.

This was the last place I expected to feel safe. But once I leave here, I don't know where I'll end up. If I can get Old Blue running again, I might be able to head to Colleen's cabin as planned and stay for a while, or hit the road and head even farther away from the problems and complications I've created.

But I can't hide forever.

No one can.

Chapter Seven

BEAU

The frigid post-blizzard bite in the air slapping me in the face the moment I step out from the cabin jolts away any lingering warmth I felt while sitting with Brooke in my arms.

You're so fucking stupid, Beau.

Climbing into bed with that woman was the last thing I should have done. Make her some tea. Sit her out by the warm fire. Let her talk it out if she needed to. *Anything* but pull her into my arms and let her fall asleep on my damn crotch.

The flames of attraction with Brooke need to be extinguished, not stoked. Letting her believe, even for one damn second, that anything can ever happen between us is more than stupid—it's downright dangerous.

To her.

To me.

To what I'm doing here.

To why I need to be here.

A gust of wind blasts icy snowflakes in my face, and I pull my hat down tighter over my ears and blink against the bright sunlight trickling through the last remaining wisps of clouds overhead. Flurries still trickle down—the final lingering traces of the storm that brought Brooke to me—but the tempest is far from over.

Last night proved that.

As long as she's here, further disturbances to my life seem inevitable. Ones that will continue to throw me off balance and make me think about things I left behind a decade ago and can't go back to.

I can't let down my guard.

Be prepared.

It's the way I've lived my life since coming to the mountain. I just never thought I'd have to apply my mantra to a member of the opposite sex.

The only way I'm going to get through this is by ensuring I don't get myself into another compromising situation with Brooke.

That means avoidance.

Avoid. Avoid. Avoid.

My new mantra...

Thank God there are enough things to do around the property to keep me occupied by something other than her soft blond hair and pale, freckled skin...

I make my way across the open area in front of the cabin and down toward the outbuildings. As long as these winds die down and stay relatively calm and another front doesn't come through, Brooke will be gone in a few days. The moment Sheriff Roberts can get some heavy machinery up here to pull out her car and get her from the cabin. In the meantime, I just have to keep my cool and ensure she doesn't leave with anything she shouldn't have.

Like information I've worked hard to keep hidden...
Or my fucking heart.
"You could be on the cover of GQ..."

"Jesus, fuck!" My words float away in the crisp wind as I unlatch the door to the barn and shove it open. She has no fucking clue how close she was to the truth or how badly I want to ensure it doesn't come out.

I've managed to remain anonymous up here for the last decade, without anyone except the sheriff knowing the truth. It hasn't been easy to stay hidden in a small town when everyone gossips and knows everything about everyone, but I've managed to stay under the radar and away from the people who would jump at a chance to locate me, clamber over each other to make me front-page news.

Alone is safe, and I don't have any plans on changing just because a beautiful broken woman showed up on my doorstep. Not even one who reminds me what it feels like to be a man again, to feel attracted and drawn to someone, to feel *human*.

But humans are the problem.

They expect things from you. Make demands. Hold you to standards so insanely lofty that they can never be met.

And humans make mistakes.

Bad ones.

Ones with very real consequences.

Animals are so much easier to deal with...

I squat in front of the chicken coop inside the small barn that houses the livestock and hold out a hand to Betty Sue. "You never do that, though, do you, girl?"

She clucks and struts over toward me to give me her usual morning greeting. It may seem silly, or even insane to some people, to talk to a chicken, but when you're out here, you sometimes need an excuse just to practice and make sure you remember how to talk at all.

I can still speak, but carrying a normal conversation or otherwise interacting with people is an art I've apparently lost over the years. Since the minute Brooke showed up, I've done and said things that only make things worse.

And falling asleep with her was a final nail in the I-fucked-up coffin.

Stop remembering how beautiful she looks in her sleep.

Stop imagining how her touch makes my heart thunder against my chest.

Stop thinking about what will happen when she's gone.

None of that matters, and the absolute last thing I should be doing is touching that woman. It won't happen again. Not if I have any form of willpower left.

I pet Betty Sue's silky soft feathers. "Don't worry, girl. Nobody's replacing you."

She clucks and pecks lightly at my hand, almost like she's calling me out on my lie. After the years she's been with me, dutifully providing me with eggs and companion-ship, she knows me better than anyone else on this planet, and she would be the one to really get jealous.

I push to my feet and spread out the feed, which brings Joanne and Daryl, the rooster, over—both anxious for some attention and food.

Joanne approaches, pushing her beak toward me, almost like she's sniffing me like a dog and smells something she doesn't like.

"Can you smell her on me?"

I sure as hell can.

A soft, feminine scent she manages to hold, even though she showered with my body wash and my shampoo, still fills every breath I take, even out here. It doesn't make any sense, but it's still true. The woman is weaseling her way under my skin and literally into my lungs, and I can't let it keep happening.

The list of a half-dozen things I need to do out here suddenly doesn't seem long enough. Even if I take my time and move slowly, these chores will only last a few hours—tops. And I'll end up right back inside, trapped in close quarters with the woman who is driving me absolutely mad.

Just keep as much space between us as possible for the next couple of days. That's all.

It's easier said than done, but I have to do my best. Otherwise, I'll drive myself crazier than I already am. A few days, then she'll be gone, and it will be as if she were never here.

I stop next to the pen where Muriel and Jezebel wait for me, bleating and stomping their hooves, impatient for my attention. "Hey, girls. You two aren't jealous, too, are you?"

Muriel pushes her head against my palm, desperate for my touch—the same way Brooke was last night.

It's been a hell of a long time since someone *needed* me like that...since I needed anyone like that.

When my world went to shit, I ran. I hid. I locked myself away from everything. It was the only way I knew how to handle it.

Now, Brooke is here, clinging to me like a lifeline, running from something that I can't see or even comprehend since she doesn't want to tell me. And she shouldn't. I'm not the person to be her rock. Not when I've been crumbling for years, slowly falling apart, pieces of me and what I used to be floating away on the mountain winds.

There isn't anything left.

Nothing worth saving.

I rescued Brooke, but it's too late for anything to be done about me.

She needs to leave so I can get back to being alone—where I should be.

* * *

BROOKE

My third cup of hot tea does nothing to warm the chill that's permeated the air in the cabin since Beau left the bedroom this morning. Even with the fire now back to roaring in the fireplace and the warm liquid in my belly, goosebumps still pebble on my skin.

I grab the blanket from the couch and wrap it around me with a shiver.

Where is he?

For what feels like the hundredth time in the last couple of hours, I step over to the window at the front of the cabin and scan the vast, endless white for him, but there still isn't any sign of him aside from the footprints he left in the snow when he basically ran away from me before I even got out of bed.

This has gone beyond avoiding me at this point. It's starting to feel like he might never come back. He didn't even stop to eat breakfast before he barreled out of here as fast as humanly possible, and now that we're nearing lunch, there isn't any sign he's changed his mind and might head back this way.

I turn away from the fruitless watch at the window and survey the main living area of the cabin. The space never felt cramped before. In fact, that first night, I thought it was big, but now the thought of having Beau come in and share it with me makes butterflies flutter in my stomach.

We'll basically be on top of each other in here, the same way I was on him last night. There isn't anywhere to really hide here, nowhere to get away from him, from whatever *this* feeling is.

After cleaning the cabin twice, there isn't another speck of dust hiding anywhere for me to find it. I have nowhere else to go, nothing else to do to pass the time until I can head to bed and try to avoid facing the embarrassment of what I did. But even in there, it's all *Beau*.

Everywhere I look, I see him. His scent permeates everything. Even the air smells like the man I am beginning to see in a whole different way.

What the hell do I do now?

My fingers itch for something familiar, something that once brought me joy and helped me through some of the darkest times of my life, but I can't bring myself to pull out my camera from my bag. Just thinking about having it in my hands again makes a cold sweat break out across my skin to join the goosebumps.

The nightmare...

The one thing I love now brings anxiety all because of one act. One mistake. One nightmare that still isn't over. I need to find something to occupy my mind so I don't relive it over and over again and feel the same terror I did last night.

And don't relive what happened between Beau and me this morning...

I release a heavy sigh and make my way toward the fire-place, but my eyes drift to the door to the left that has remained closed the entire time I've been here. He said it wasn't another bedroom, but it might be where he keeps his books.

Reading by the fire last night before bed helped pass the time, but I need a different book. Beau's pick for me of *Sense and Sensibility* just didn't drag me in the way it used to when I read it and reread it in college. Maybe because my life is different now than it was then, because *I* am so different because of what's happened.

But getting lost in another world, one on the page instead of this one where a man with dark brown eyes that see right to my very core will be trapped in here with me, sounds divine in the moment.

With one last glance toward the front door that remains closed, without a sign of Beau returning anytime soon, I slowly make my way over to the mysterious closed door to my left, tugging the blanket tighter around me. Unease slowly moves down my spine, making my steps falter slightly.

Calm down, Brooke. It's just a closed door.

I turn the knob and take a deep breath before I push it open into the small room. Almost identical in shape and size to the bedroom, sunlight streams through the window on the opposing wall , across a large wooden desk and over a wall of floor-to-ceiling bookcases.

What would Beau need an office for?

Or a desk this large and ornate?

I approach it and run my fingertips over the smooth, well-worn wooden surface. Though bearing the scuffs and marks of years of use, it's clearly well-loved, well-cared for. Someone has kept it in good shape, and it definitely wasn't made by Beau like so many of the other things in this cabin.

This is old, well-crafted, expensive. Something he must have had brought up here whenever he built this cabin.

Why?

The mountain man I've been living with doesn't seem like the type who would need a desk, let alone have one like this. He spends his time chopping wood, taking care of his animals, and maintaining his cabin and land.

Why the hell does he have this?

It's a question I probably will never get the answer to. Whenever we even remotely delve into anything personal, Beau clams right up or gets so annoyed he avoids me and the conversation. I can't really blame the man. Not when I literally crashed into his life and have no desire to tell him anything about my life, either.

Just keep your mouth shut, Brooke. Find a book to read and stop wondering what makes Beau tick.

I should have learned by now that trying to figure out what makes men do what they do is an effort in futility. One that leads to pain and destruction.

Instead of dwelling on the unknown mind of the man I'm stuck in here with, I focus on bookshelves. They tower over me far higher than I can reach, filled with beautiful, old leather-bound copies of all the classics as well as modern hardcovers and paperbacks.

Without much to do up here—no television, no one else to talk to—it shouldn't be surprising that he has a collection like this. The way he speaks, the things he said about his father, it's clear he's well educated. Before I showed up, Beau likely spent his evenings in front of the fire reading peacefully with a drink. Now, the man spends his nights taking care of me.

Brushing my fingers over the old leather bindings, I pause at a familiar title—*Wuthering Heights*. Seeing my favorite book on Beau's shelf sends a little thrill of excitement through me, and I pull it from between two other Brontë sister novels.

I could use a little Heathcliff right now.

"What the hell are you doing in here?"

I jerk away from the shelves, and the book tumbles from my hand and slams against the wood floor, making me jump.

Beau stands just inside the door jamb, his cheeks red from the cold and wind, his lips twisted into a scowl visible through his beard.

I press my hand against my racing heart, trying to catch my breath. "Oh, God, you scared the crap out of me."

He clenches his fists at his sides, his body tense, jaw tight. "What the hell are you doing in here?"

"Oh"—I motion to the bookcase—"I just wanted to try to find something to read."

His eyes flicker from the shelf to the book on the floor, then back up to my face. "Get the fuck out."

"Excuse me?"

He takes two steps toward me, clenching and unclenching his fists in a way that makes me take a little half-step back until my ass hits the bookcases, stopping my retreat.

"I said...get the fuck out. This room is off limits."

Off limits?

I replay our earlier conversation when I asked him about the sleeping arrangements, but I can't remember him telling me to stay out of this room. Clearly, given his reaction, he thinks it was implied.

"Beau, I didn't mean any harm. I—"

"Get. Out."

Anxiety tightens my throat, stealing any other words I

might offer by way of explanation or apology, which is just as well, as it seems he doesn't want either.

I rush past him, hot tears stinging my eyes.

All I wanted was to read the story of the dark anti-hero who fell for the woman he couldn't have. Instead, I got my own dark beast willing to rip my head off for some minor perceived transgression.

Chapter Eight

BEAU

"**D**ammit!"

My roar echoes around the office, off the wooden walls and ceiling, the window panes, and vibrates in my own ears, carrying all the weight of the anger and frustration it was meant to release.

I drop into the leather office chair and slam my fists against the desk, rattling the few items I actually have on it. The door to the bedroom slams, the sound reverberating through the cabin and straight into my chest, tightening it uncomfortably.

Brooke no doubt wants to get as far away from me as possible after I just screamed at her like a fucking psychopath when I found her in here.

Real fucking nice.

I lower my face into my palms and scrub them across it. "What the fuck are you doing?"

If only I knew the answer to that question...

For the past decade, I thought I did know. I was confident I had figured out a way to go on living without the world affecting me, pretending it didn't exist anymore, pushing the hard memories to the dark recesses of my mind where they couldn't come back to haunt me—none of the love or the joy or the pain—but all it's taken is three days and one infuriating woman to completely throw that belief out the proverbial window.

I just tore off Brooke's head for no reason.

That kind of anger isn't me. It isn't how I used to be. It isn't how I *want* to be. Yet, even all this time up here hasn't helped me when it comes to dealing with the way what happened changed me.

Brooke didn't know she wasn't supposed to be in here, had no idea why I want to keep her out, why I *have* to. But when I walked in the front door and noticed the door to the office open, all I could see was red—the same red that invades my nightmares when they come.

All I wanted was to stop her from seeing it all, from finding out what I hide. If she knew, it would change every-thing—not just between us, but everything. But she didn't deserve that, and I never meant to scare the shit out of her after she already had a very rough night last night.

Brooke wanted to get away, to come up to the mountain for the same reason I did—to find peace in solitude. At least, that's what I've managed to piece together from what very little she's been willing to share with me. Instead, she's found an angry man with no social skills anymore who keeps yelling at her for no fucking reason.

Real fucking smooth, Beau. Mother and Father would be so proud.

I reach out and grab the framed picture on the desk and brush my fingers over their smiling faces but avoid looking at my own. It was the last time we were all together, the last time I remember smiling...until Brooke showed up here.

Since she arrived, I've smiled, I've *laughed*, I've felt my heart race and my body stir to life in a way I barely remember and never anticipated feeling again.

That woman drags the best and the worst out of me.

And that's a major problem.

There's only one solution: I need to get her out of here.

Fast.

I set down the picture and reach for my only lifeline to the outside world. "Okanogan County Sheriff's Department, come in. This is Beau."

Static drifts through the line before I finally get a response.

"Beau, this is Sheriff Roberts. You're breaking up, I could barely hear you."

Rubbing my eyes, I lean back in the chair. "Just reaching out to see how things looked down there. I still have that visitor up here who's going to need a way out as soon as possible."

"Is she doing okay?"

Shit. I never did radio him with her name and the number.

"Physically, yes, but I'm sure she has a life and people she wants to get back to."

And I want to get back to my life—as basic and miserable as it may seem to her.

"I don't think we can get within twenty miles of there on the roads, Beau."

Shit.

"Her car broke down somewhere maybe three miles from my place."

"It'll be a couple more days before we can clean them

up that far, and the chopper from Brewster has been tied up with a lot of emergencies due to the storm. If your visitor up there is okay medically, I can't justify borrowing it just to come get her."

I tighten my hand around the radio and sigh, fighting the urge to chuck it across the room. As much as I may hate what Sheriff Roberts is telling me, it isn't his fault Brooke is going to stay here longer than I hoped. "I figured as much."

"Did you ever get a name, birthdate, phone number for her friend?"

"Brooke Beck, but I don't have a birthdate or a phone number. She said her friend wouldn't be expecting to hear from her for at least a week."

"Any idea where she's from?"

"Seattle, I think, based on what she's told me. She's actually *from* there, but I don't know if that's where she was last before coming here."

"And you say she was coming up to stay at a friend's cabin on the other side of the mountain?"

"Yep, must have missed the turnoff."

He's quiet for a moment, maybe checking something or answering a question from one of his deputies at the station. "Yeah, must have. I'll keep you posted with any updates. Meanwhile, sit tight. I know you'll be just fine."

That's kind of an odd thing to say.

After all the years Jim Roberts and I have known each other, he knows I can survive up here alone, without any contact from the outside world, for months and months at a time and only come into town for supplies when absolutely necessary.

So why the comment?

Maybe he's worried about damage I sustained in the

blizzard, but I'm more than competent to patch things up well enough to get me through 'til help arrives.

I push it to the back of my mind and return the radio to its cradle as I push the chair back. It bumps into something on the floor.

Oh, hell...

The book Brooke was holding when I came in.

Why couldn't she have just finished Sense and Sensibility?

It would have avoided that confrontation and the resulting strain that's sure to come with it around here.

Wuthering Heights sits heavy in my hand and heavy on my heart. I flip open the front cover to see the familiar stamp that still makes tears come to my eyes every time I brush my finger over it.

Brooke likely won't recognize it, not the way she would some of the other things in my office like the photo with Mom and Dad and some of the paperwork on company letterhead.

She just wanted a damn book.

There isn't anything for her to do here. No way for her to keep her mind occupied and away from whatever propelled her to drive up a mountain in the middle of a blizzard. I know what that's like—to be stuck in my own head, searching for a way out. Looking for another world to escape to, even if it's only on the page.

These books are the one *true* distraction I have up here. Because at the end of the day, no matter how exhausted I am from working outside all day, from chopping wood, from feeding and tending to the animals, from hiking and fishing and hunting...I'm still left with my memories.

The least I can do is give her a book to try to help her escape hers...

And offer one massive apology.

* * *

BROOKE

The knock on the bedroom door is so soft that I almost don't hear it. I wouldn't have if I were back home, with the other constant sounds of the city to drown it out. But out here, with nothing but the wind and silence, I stiffen immediately and swallow through the lump in my throat.

My heart races, the adrenaline of the confrontation and the possibility of another one making my blood rush in my ears. But if Beau were still upset, he wouldn't even knock.

The door doesn't have a lock, and it *is* his house. He would be well within his rights to charge in here and give me another tongue-lashing for invading his privacy—albeit accidentally.

"Come in."

Despite my best efforts to sound confident and unaffected by what happened a few moments ago, my voice sounds uncertain, even to my own ears.

Beau pushes open the door slightly, and at least he has the good sense to appear regretful about what he just did. He reaches back and rubs at his neck with one hand while he holds out a book in the other. "I, uh, brought a peace offering."

"What's that?"

His eyes finally meet mine, hooded and heavy with concern and apology. "*Wuthering Heights*."

"Oh..." I shrug slightly and offer him a smile I don't really feel.

He's trying. He's making an effort to apologize for what

he just did, but it doesn't undo it. It doesn't remove the fear that raged through me at his anger.

"Thank you."

He takes a step toward me and stops before he reaches the bed, perhaps sensing my unease. "Sorry I acted like a dick."

"Yeah, you did."

"I wasn't really asking for confirmation."

"I know."

But he needs it.

After living alone for so long, he's lost any ability to communicate with someone, completely forgotten that having someone in his personal space is going to mean personal things will be seen and touched—though, I still don't know what the hell his issue was with me being in the office.

He releases a heavy sigh, his shoulders sagging. "Like I told you before, I'm not used to having someone else in my space where I have private things. It's a shitty excuse for how I behaved, but it's the only one I have. I swear, I was never like this before..."

Before what?

The question is on the tip of my tongue, but he won't answer it if I ask, so I focus on something else he said.

"Your book collection is private?" I raise an eyebrow at him.

It's an odd thing to get upset over, especially after sharing another book with me earlier last night.

Beau offers me a little half shrug. "Sort of."

"What do you mean?"

He releases a heavy sigh and slowly lowers himself to the edge of the bed, keeping his distance, holding the book almost reverently between his hands. "It belonged to my parents."

"Oh..." That still doesn't explain anything. It doesn't offer any enlightenment as to why he would flip out at me being in there and touching one of the books. "And the desk? I noticed it looked old, like an antique."

"It was my father's. The only thing of his I brought up here." His whiskey-colored eyes finally flick up to meet mine. "The vase was the only thing from my mother."

"Shit." Bile churns in my stomach, leaving the bitter taste of regret in my mouth. "The vase I smashed you over the head with?"

The corner of his mouth crooks up. "That would be the one."

"Oh, God..." I bury my face in my hands. "I know you're going to yell at me again for saying it but I am *so* sorry."

I've been fucking up things left and right since the day I got here. No wonder he's on edge and snapping at me about everything. I literally destroyed the *only* thing he had from his mother, and then he found me in his office with the book collection from them and his dad's desk.

His large, warm hand wraps around my ankle, calloused fingertips brushing against the bare skin just above the thick socks encasing my feet. I drag my head up slowly and stare at where his touch raises goosebumps up my leg.

He squeezes softly. "It's okay. Really. It was an accident...kind of."

"Yeah, kind of." I smile at him even though the weight of the conversation threatens to crush me. "I *did* mean to smash you in the head with it."

"Exactly." He offers me a little half-grin.

"Speaking of which, how's your head? It was bleeding again last night."

Again, because of me.

This poor man just wanted to be left alone to live a quiet life, and I stormed into it and smashed him on the head...twice.

He reaches up and touches the wound at his temple just below the hairline. "It's fine. Stopped bleeding on its own before we even woke up this morning."

Woke up together...

He pulls his hand off my ankle abruptly, almost as if he just realized it was still there and looks at the book. "Well..."

I bounce my gaze around the room as an awkward silence settles over us. He apologized, but nothing has really been resolved. I'm still stuck here—at least for a little while —and I'm still in his personal space, messing up his routine and plans, sticking my nose places where it doesn't belong.

And here we sit on his bed, the bed *I've* been sleeping in as if it's my own while he stays out on the horrible couch. Unless he's sleeping sitting up in the bed because of my breakdown.

I clear my throat and shift slightly. "I'm happy to just stay in here, out of your way completely until I can leave." I motion toward the door. "Or my offer still stands for you to take back your bed and I'll sleep on the couch. It will be more comfortable for you."

"No." Beau shakes his head vehemently. "I would just worry about how uncomfortable you were out on the couch if I were in here. I wouldn't get any sleep, anyway." He rubs the back of his neck again. "I, uh, talked to the sheriff."

I freeze, my throat going dry almost instantly. Doing my best to appear unconcerned, I force a smile. "Oh yeah? About what?"

"About when we might be able to get you out of here. He says it will be at least a couple more days before they can get anyone up to look at your car, and there isn't any other way out of here." He motions in the general direction of the outbuildings. "I have a truck and a snowmobile, but we'd never make it all the way down the mountain, and it wouldn't do you much good even if we could since there's no car rental and yours is dead, anyway."

"True." I nod slowly. "I hadn't thought about that."

When I left Seattle, I hadn't planned much at all. All I knew was I needed to get out, and when the weather coming in cancelled my last-minute flight, I just took off. The thought of Old Blue breaking down, leaving me stranded somewhere for an indefinite period of time, hadn't even crossed my mind.

It sounds like even if I could get out of here and down the mountain, I'm not going much of anywhere without the car running. If they need to order parts or can't fix her at all, I'll be fucked.

"What's wrong?"

"Huh?"

He squeezes my leg again. "You look upset. Because you're going to be stuck up here with me for a few more days? I promise I'll try not to be such a huge asshole."

I chuckle and shake my head. "No, not that. I was just thinking that I hadn't really intended to stay around here very long. A week tops at Colleen's place."

"And then to where? Back home?"

I offer him a shrug, wrapping my arms around myself tightly as emotion clogs my throat and I fight back the tears. "I'm not sure where that is anymore."

Something flickers in the depths of his dark eyes, a flash

107

of understanding and compassion, and something else I can't place.

I shouldn't have said that to him.

All the drama and turmoil in my own life isn't Beau's problem, nor is where I'll go when I finally get down this mountain. The only thing that matters to him is that he'll get his cabin and his solitude back.

He pushes to his feet abruptly, hand extended with the book. "Well, here. Sorry again for being a dick."

I lean forward to accept it from him, and my fingertips brush his on the cover, a little zing of electricity shooting up my arm and through my body. Beau pulls his hand away quickly and shakes it, glancing away from me and toward the door.

He felt it, too.

The heavy leather-bound novel in my hands brings more comfort than I thought it would. "This is one of my favorites."

Beau turns back to me, and the tiniest smile pulls at the corner of his lips. "My mother's, too."

"Oh, yeah? Did she have a thing for bad boys like Katherine did for Heathcliff?"

He barks out a laugh and shakes his head. "Mom? Oh, no. My dad was one of the most straight-laced, non-bad boys I've ever met. I think the Heathcliff thing was more the fantasy of what she would never have."

I press my hand over the title. "And it's a lot safer to read about it in a book and fantasize than to go out seeking it to try to experience it on your own."

He raises a dark eyebrow at me. "It sounds like you're speaking from personal experience."

Which means I've said too much.

I shake my head. "No. Just an observation."

He nods and looks around the room absently. "Well, if there are any other books you want, let me know, and I'll be happy to get them from the office for you if I have it. But otherwise—"

"I should stay out of there."

"It's not that I—"

I hold up a hand to stop him. "It's okay. Really. This is your house. Your personal space. And I'm all kinds of up in it, including your bed."

Beau shifts uneasily, and I have to avert my eyes from his heated gaze. Instead, focusing on the darkness outside the window.

"I respect that you don't want me in there, Beau, and I promise I won't go back in."

"I appreciate that."

"Of course. I appreciate all that you're doing for me."

"Even when I yell at you like a total psycho."

A smile pulls at my lips, and I finally turn back toward him. "Yeah, even then."

Because somehow, even though he lashed out at me again, even though he clearly isn't fully in control of himself, I still know he would never actually hurt me. All the frustration and harsh words come from his inability to relate, the fact that he hasn't had to answer to anyone for so long that he's forgotten how. But he wouldn't ever lay a hand on me. That's been evident almost since the moment I woke up safe in his cabin.

He may wield that ax with precision and skill to kill what he needs to survive out here, but that violence would never be directed toward me. He doesn't have it in him.

If only all the men on this planet were like him.

Chapter Nine

BROOKE

"*If you ever looked at me once with what I know is in you, I would be your slave.*"

I close *Wuthering Heights* and set it on the wooden nightstand beside the bed that Beau undoubtedly built himself and stare at the cracked door, letting Emily Brontë's exquisite words seep into my head and tear apart what's left of my heart.

Such magnificent writing.

Such a dark, deceptively beautiful story.

Every single time I read it, it strikes at the places deep inside me I keep hidden, the truths I refuse to acknowledge.

Tonight is no different, especially being here with Beau. Despite his apology—or maybe because of it—I've been avoiding him as much as he's avoided me the rest of the day.

While I ate what was left of the stew he made the other night, he spent what little sunlight remained after our confrontation outside, holed up in the barn with the animals

—aside from bringing in another load of wood, conveniently while I was showering.

The question of whether he was actually taking care of something essential or just looking for any excuse to not be in the cabin with me has bounced around my head endlessly.

As has the question of what will happen when he returns.

Things feel different between us somehow, the tension of two people being thrust together unexpectedly morphing into another kind of tension. One of things left unsaid.

I would love to be able to just go to sleep and wake up with it all back to "normal" tomorrow so I can spend whatever time I have left here in a relative peace with the man whose life I've completely fucked up almost as badly as I've fucked up my own, but I don't think there *is* a normal with Beau.

He's angry and volatile at times, unable or unwilling to control himself. Yet as much as he is those things, he's also always lost, even in the home he built for himself.

After seeing the way he talked about his parents today, the anguish in his voice was enough to suggest that they're at least part of the reason why he came up here. But there's something more there—a darker truth he doesn't want to talk about, and I'm not the one to try to pry it out of him, not when I'm running from the pain of my past, too. Not when nightmares threaten to invade my dreams again tonight with memories I want to keep buried yet are so fresh that they're still seared into my brain.

As the afternoon sunlight fades away to darkness, unease begins to creep over me almost immediately. Reading for hours and hours—when I should have closed my eyes and tried to get some sleep a long time ago—has only delayed the inevitable and given me more time to dread it.

Images of the nightmare from last night keep playing in my head, over and over, more vivid each time. But I don't know how much longer I can keep forcing my eyes open every time they try to drift closed.

I don't want that nightmare to come back for a hundred different reasons. The least of which is now lying out on the couch right now, probably sleeping like a damn baby.

Beau has no intention of letting us get any closer or of revealing anything more than he did when he brought me that book, which is probably for the best given that I'll be leaving soon and God only knows where I'll end up. Why he chooses to stay here locked away from the world is for Beau alone to know.

He clearly wants to stay hidden, and I'm now confident it had nothing to do with my initial fear when I saw him holding that ax. Last night, his arms brought me such peace and comfort. It was his strength that kept the demons at bay.

How am I supposed to sleep without him tonight?

The mere thought causes my chest to tighten and lungs to seize. Darkness creeps in from the window, the small light on the nightstand not enough to truly keep it out.

I can't stay here.

Soon, the night will draw me into sleep, and sleep will drag me into the horror I can't outrun.

I climb from the bed, wrap the blanket around me, and make my way toward the door with soft, careful steps, pausing to listen. The absolute silence of being out in the middle of nowhere greets me, broken by the occasional crack and pop coming from the fire in the living room.

The light and warmth it provides will act as a shield

against the darkness and truths that haunt me.

Hopefully...

I tiptoe out, tugging the blanket around me, and make my way into the living room. Beau sits on the couch staring into the fire, a glass of amber liquid in his hand.

A second passes where I almost consider turning back around and leaving him be, but then he looks up.

His eyes, filled with a dozen different emotions, meet mine. "You okay?"

I consider lying even as the truth slips through my lips. "Not really. I can't sleep."

His brow drops low. "What's wrong?"

My entire life is in shambles.

I pause for a second, part of me desperately wanting to reveal more than I can, more than it's safe for me to. "I'm worried about the nightmare coming back."

He blows out a long, heavy breath and pats the side of the couch beside him. "Take a seat. I can't sleep, either."

Probably because I forced him out of his own bed and onto this couch.

I slowly make my way over and settle onto the leather next to him, pulling the blanket tighter around me.

"You want a drink?" He holds up the glass and tilts it toward me.

Drinking away your problems has never worked well for anyone in the long-run, but in the moment, it seems as good a way as any to deal with my anxiety.

I accept the glass from him and take a sip of the warm, spicy liquid. "That's nice. I've never been much of a bourbon drinker, but even I can tell that's the good stuff."

He offers me a little half-smile. "This is definitely the good stuff. One of the few luxuries I ensure I have available up here."

"How do you get it?"

There isn't any way the local liquor store in the tiny town at the base of the mountain would carry stuff like this. It isn't some tourism hub and doesn't have billionaires buying up the land around it, so there wouldn't be any reason to keep it in stock.

"An old friend ships a box into town every year for me."

"He must be a good friend to do that for you."

Beau nods slowly and takes the drink from me. "After working with me or for me for just shy of twenty years, he definitely knows what I like and want to have available to me."

"Working for you?"

Why would he possibly have anyone working for him?

During my time here, I haven't seen another soul or any evidence anyone else has ever been here to help Beau on his land.

His shoulders stiffen, like he realizes he just said something he shouldn't have, and he returns his focus to the fire. "Want to tell me about the dream? Supposedly, talking about it helps."

I snort and shake my head. While it's a smooth attempt to change the subject, I don't have any plan to delve into the things that prevent me from sleeping. "You want to tell me about yours?"

The admission he made the other day that he has nightmares, too, was one of the few times he let anything personal slip, and it was enough to let me know he's been through something terrible. But he will want to talk about it about as much as I do—which is not at all.

He gives me a *yeah right* look.

I chuckle, and it brings a tiny bit of relief to the tension I've been carrying around. "That's what I thought."

Playing with the ends of the blanket, twisting the fringe around my fingers, I aimlessly stare into the fire, watching the flames dance so beautifully.

He might be right, though.

The whole reason people go to psychiatrists is because discussing what's troubling you is supposed to help you sort through your thoughts and feelings and maybe help you come to a conclusion that could help your anxiety.

Maybe there's a way of telling him without really telling him.

I peek at him over my shoulder. "Did you ever have something bad happen in your life that left this mark, this stain on you that you can't seem to rid yourself of?"

His hand tightens around the glass, and he downs half of it while keeping his gaze locked on the flames. "You could say that."

After a moment, he glances over at me. I wait for him to expand but know he won't. The man won't even tell me his last name. No way in hell he's going to open up to me about the things that terrorize him.

"Well..." I pull up my legs and wrap my arms around my knees. "I didn't just want to get away for a while. I had to because something happened."

That's all I can ever tell Beau. Anything more would put us both at risk, and I'm not about to drag him into my mess. Not when all he's done is save me and open his home to me. He doesn't deserve to have to bear the burden of my mistakes. That's a weight I have to carry alone.

"That's what your nightmare was about? Whatever happened?"

I nod. "Yes, and truthfully, I don't know if I can ever go back even if I wanted to."

"What about your friends?"

Sighing, I drag a hand through my hair, then pull the blanket around me again even tighter—an armor against the reality of the situation I've now found myself in. "Colleen is my best friend. The one whose cabin I was supposed to come up to. We've been friends since we were ten and lived in the same apartment building on the same floor. She would definitely miss me, but she would understand why I didn't come back."

"Why *wouldn't* you go back?"

"I can't..."

Not with what's waiting for me.

* * *

BEAU

I consider her for a moment, watching the way the fire waltzes across her face and lights up her eyes despite them being so heavy with sadness. The pain in her voice when she talks about Colleen cuts to the heart of the one regret I have about coming up here—leaving Nate behind. Figuratively and literally.

Handing the glass back to Brooke, I try to offer her what reassurances I can, though I think running away isn't the answer for her even if it was for me. "Any good friend would understand."

Her soft brow furrows. "Do your friends understand why you're out here?"

I've already said too much, offered her more than I should have, but something tells me she won't reveal any of it, anyway. She doesn't seem like one to spill the secrets of others when she won't even reveal her own.

"Some of them do. A lot of them don't. There are people

hung up on obligations and who think I ran away from them."

As far as I'm concerned, the past is better left in the past, but Nate wanted to be there for me, wanted to bend over backward to help me in any way he could. Yet, I walked away from his efforts as if he weren't making them. Like they meant nothing, when really, they meant the world to me and I just wasn't in any place to actually tell him or show him that.

It hurt him more than I ever want to admit to myself. Because if I did, I might actually consider going back for a split-second to try to make it up to him any way I can.

"Obligations?" Her eyebrows rise. "Like what?"

I shrug as nonchalantly as I can and stare at the fire. This conversation could go down a very dangerous road very fast if I let it. "I kind of abandoned my family business when I came up here. I'm still involved somewhat, but I mostly leave things in other people's very capable hands. There are some who aren't too happy with that decision, but they've had to learn to live with it the last ten years."

A silence lingers between us, and I turn back to find her still huddled under the blanket, her bottom lip pulled between her teeth. She clearly wants to delve into this more, wants me to come clean with my own secrets so we won't have to concentrate on hers.

The dark circles ringing her eyes prove the stresses—both physical and emotional—of the last few days have definitely taken their toll on her.

"You should really try to get some sleep."

"Yeah." She takes a sip of the bourbon and hands me the glass, then slowly pushes to her feet, pulling the blanket tighter around her before she turns to face me. "Would you..." She trails off and glances at the fire, avoiding meeting my gaze and shifting on her bare feet. "Would you come sleep with me again?"

Goddammit...

I grasp the glass in an iron grip and raise it slowly to my lips to down the rest of it.

How do I say this without hurting her feelings or making her think the wrong thing?

Shifting on the couch, I lean forward and roll the empty glass between my palms. "Last night and this morning were...not good."

Not good for me.

Not good for her.

Not good for anyone in the end.

She continues to watch me, her eyes wet with unshed tears.

Well, fuck.

"I just don't think it's a good idea, Brooke."

Her damn bottom lip disappears under her teeth, like she's biting it to try to prevent herself from crying.

My chest tightens uncomfortably, and I shake my head, trying to dispel the nagging voice in the back of my mind. "If you need me, just call out and I'll come."

God willing, she'll sleep like a fucking baby tonight and I'll stay out here on this damn couch.

Brooke gives me a sharp nod, and a single tear slips from her eye down her cheek.

Fuck.

My gut tenses, the warm, delicious bourbon suddenly sour in my stomach. She's terrified of being alone, of closing her eyes, of what she'll see, of what will come for her in the dark.

And I'm a fucking selfish prick for not offering her what I can to make it better.

She pulls in a shaky breath, her tear-soaked gaze locked on me, pleading with me for something more. When I don't offer it, she turns and slowly walks back to the bedroom without another word.

I slam the empty glass down on the coffee table.

"Fuck!"

Running my hands back through my hair, I climb to my feet and throw a few more logs on the fire a little too hard, sending sparks and ash flying, and pace in front of the inferno.

The bedroom door clicks shut, sealing her in there.

Away.

Safe from me.

But not from the dangers that come to her with sleep.

Whatever sent her up here is bad. Bad enough that she doesn't even want to go back or thinks she can't. All she needs is someone to be there for her, somewhere to turn when the terrors return.

I can do that. Can't I?

It feels like I don't fucking know anything anymore. The pain I've wallowed in for a decade threatens to overwhelm me at times, yet I'm willing to let someone else suffer to make things easier on me.

What does that say about me?

Nothing good.

It's not the kind of person I want to be. Even up here, humanity found me. Found a way in to force me to face the realities of living with other people who have feelings and wants and fears.

Staring into the fire, I blow out a heavy breath, attempting to release some of the reluctancy holding me in this room when Brooke is in the other, terrified and alone.

I'm a fucking coward.

119

It wasn't how I was raised, not how I used to be, and I fucking hate it.

Man the fuck up, Beau.

All it takes is a few steps to bring me down the hallway to the door. Pausing with my hand on the knob, I drop my forehead against the wood panel and take several deep breaths. They do absolutely nothing to calm my racing heart or to deaden the thundering of my blood rushing in my ears.

I turn the knob and ease open the door. Brooke turns her head toward the noise, but she stays under the covers, her back toward the center of the bed, not acknowledging my presence at all.

If she didn't want me here, she would tell me. She hasn't been afraid to let me know exactly what she wants or needs since she arrived here. Tonight should be no different.

I close the door behind me and walk slowly around the bed I never thought I'd be sharing with anyone, lift the quilt and sheets, and slide in behind her.

That damn light, slightly floral scent she carries around her invades my next breath, and I squeeze my eyes closed and grit my teeth against my body's response.

Brooke glances over her shoulder at me. "Thank you."

Despite my better judgment, I reach out and place a hand at the curve of her hip and squeeze gently, but I don't dare shift closer, let my body press against hers. That would spell absolute disaster.

"I'll be here to fight off any demons that come for you tonight."

What she doesn't know is that what I bring with me could be so much worse.

Chapter Ten

BEAU

For the first time in ten years, I wake to the feel of a curvy warm body pressed against mine. Her soft ass pushed up against my hard cock makes me freeze and squeeze my eyes closed.

Fuck.

It's been a long fucking time since I've been hard for anything other than my own hand, and even that doesn't happen very often. I can't even remember the last time I needed that kind of relief.

Up here, there aren't a whole lot of things to stimulate my sex drive, and after what happened to send me running in the first place, getting off just doesn't seem so important anymore.

Sex is nothing but memories—so old and distant that I can barely even drag them up from the back of my mind when I try to. But *this* is not distant. This is very up close and personal and *very* real. Brooke shifts slightly in her sleep, pushing back against me to snuggle in even closer in that way that women do in their sleep without even real-izing it.

Fuck. Fuck. Fuck.

My cock twitches, and I roll away from her but can't get very far, my arm trapped under her. Though it fell asleep a long time ago with her weight pressed on it for so long, I'm very aware of where my hand rests, brushing the underside of her breast.

Fuck. Fuck. Fuck.

Last night was as good and as bad as it gets.

Nothing happened—aside from her shifting back into my arms so I could hold her until she fell asleep and throughout the night. But the tension building between us and in me has only ratcheted higher the longer we've lain together.

Every little moan in her sleep.

Every little move that brushed her body against mine.

It all only wound me tighter.

Yet, I somehow managed to have one of the best nights of sleep I've ever had—and not just since I came up here. No memories plagued me. No old wounds were reopened. No regrets.

I just *slept*.

But now my body is yearning for something it abso-lutely cannot have.

Brooke needed comfort last night. She didn't need a perverted, reclusive weirdo groping her in her sleep. I touched her as little as possible, as little as she would *let* me, but she needed the contact, the arms around her, the comfort I could offer. But she certainly doesn't need to wake up to find this very obvious evidence of my arousal.

I slowly pull my arm out from under her and shift my body back, giving me much-needed space and breathing room, though I almost immediately miss the heat and soft-ness of her against me.

Rolling onto my back, I suck in a deep breath.

Bad idea.

Her scent invades my lungs, making my dick ache. I scrub my hands over my face and shove back the covers from my side of the bed. Brooke shifts behind me, and I hold my breath and glance over my shoulder.

Please be asleep. Please be asleep. Please, for the love of God, be asleep.

Her back still to me, Brooke lies completely still again, her shoulder rising and falling rhythmically, giving no indi-cation that she's awake.

Thank God.

I need a little alone time, or I might explode. That would be embarrassing for everyone. Most of all...me.

Climbing to my feet, I pause for a moment and wait for her to move, but her breathing remains even and low. I grab some clean clothes from the dresser and pad out of the bedroom, pulling the door closed behind me as quietly as I can. The slight creak of the hinge and the click of the latch falling into place make me wince. I pause and listen for any sign that it woke her, but all that greets me is the absolute stillness and silence of the cabin, how it usually is.

Though things are definitely *not* how they usually are. They're as far from normal as is humanly possible. My entire existence here has been inextricably altered, my world thrown off its axis in such a way that it can't ever get back to its usual rotation again.

Things are so damn fucked.

My aching cock reminds me of that as I tip-toe to the bathroom and pull the door closed behind me before quickly stepping over to crank on the shower as hot as it gets.

Wow.

Examining myself in the mirror, I find a man staring back at me who I can barely recognize anymore. The beard covering my face has started to grow out beyond what is socially "acceptable," and dark lines have started to form under my eyes, making me look even older than I feel.

The small cut at my temple stopped bleeding long ago and likely wouldn't even leave a scar, but something tells me that having Brooke here, even for such a short time, has left an indelible mark on my heart and soul that won't be so easily forgotten.

She's awoken something I thought died years ago.

Something that should have stayed dead.

I shove down my sweatpants and let my cock spring free. A groan of relief slips from my lips, and I take myself in my hand and stroke slowly as steam finally starts to fill the bathroom.

It might obscure my reflection, but it can't hide the anguish twisting my face despite how damn incredible it feels to touch my throbbing flesh. I shouldn't be doing this. Shouldn't be giving in to the need, but I'm past the point of no return here.

I release myself to yank off my shirt, slide back the glass door, and step under the hard spray.

Fuck, does that feel good.

Dropping my head forward, I let the water strike my neck, shoulders, and back as I take my cock in hand once again and tighten my fist around it.

Fuck.

Somehow, I forgot how good it feels. How good and frustrating at the same time. How pent up and desperate men can get when we ignore our basic urges. They've been so far pushed to the furthest corners of my mind, I didn't even know how badly I needed this until Brooke stumbled into my world, until I felt *attraction* for the first time in a damn decade.

I drag my palm along my cock and groan at the pleasure coursing through my system. Visions of Brooke pulling her bottom lip between her teeth flash in my head and suddenly morph to her on her knees in front of me. Those beautiful lips wrapped around my hard flesh.

Sucking.

Licking.

Working me over.

"*Fuck!*" The word echoes around the tight bathroom, sounding every bit as needy and frantic as I feel.

I stroke harder, faster.

"Brooke..." Her name tumbles from my lips like a desperate plea, and I increase my pace, stroking and tugging at my cock, picturing Brooke in every damn position I can imagine.

Everything we could do together fills my head, and I imagine the final hold of her lips tightening around me while she grips the base of my cock with her small fist and she swallows, her throat undulating around me.

My entire body vibrates, and I unleash what feels like years of pent-up sexual need in one hot release. A low groan rumbles from my lips, long and satisfied, something I so badly needed yet didn't even realize it until I lifted that small blond woman into my arms out there in the storm.

A tiny feminine gasp comes from my right, and I jerk my eyes open. Through the steamed glass, a very wide-eyed Brooke stands at the cracked bathroom door, her gaze locked directly on me.

Fuck.

* * *

BROOKE

Holy shit.

That might be the hottest thing I've ever seen in my entire life.

But did I really just watch Beau jerk off in the shower like some creepy voyeur?

The throb between my legs and the heat spreading through my limbs proves just how much I liked what I saw, but his curse and hard eyes meeting mine send me scrambling back out the door and into the bedroom as fast as my feet will carry me.

Oh, God. Oh, God...

I slam the door closed and drop my forehead against it, relishing the relief the cool wood offers against the too-hot feeling overtaking my entire body. Such a juxtaposition from the constant chill I've felt since I almost died out in the snow.

A brand new feeling, but one I definitely should not be having for Beau.

I fumble on the door handle to secure the door and keep him from confronting me about what I just saw.

Fuck. No lock. Damn you, Beau.

But Beau wouldn't need a lock. He can do whatever he wants. Come and go whenever he pleases. Or at least he could...before I crash-landed in his life.

What if he comes in here?

What would I say?

What would I do?

As much as I wish I could deny it, I'd probably jump on that big, beautiful cock he had in his hand. Let it fill me and give me the relief I so badly need in this moment.

I swallow through my suddenly dry throat and squeeze my thighs together against the throb between my legs, but all closing my eyes does is bring the vision of what I just saw to the forefront of my mind.

Loud and clear. Vivid. Like it's directly in front of me again. So close I can reach out and touch him; drag my fingers over his hard, lean body, perfectly built by the hard work and determination it takes to live up here alone; watch the water trickling down over his chest and that *V* thing; his muscles bunching and flexing as he drags his hand over his cock, twisting when he reaches the head; the way his lips fell open on a silent cry just as he was about to come.

Fuck is right.

I slide my hand into Beau's sweatpants I slept in and find what I knew would be true—I'm already wet. My body ready and waiting for something it hasn't had in so long, hasn't even wanted. I glide my finger through my arousal and up over my clit, jerking at how sensitive it is even to my light touch.

God...

It's been so long since I touched myself like this, since anything made me want to. Since anything that was supposed to be pleasurable actually *was*.

A shudder of anticipation rolls through me, and I swirl my middle finger tip around the sensitive bud, the visual of Beau with his head dropped forward, muscles in his neck straining as he stroked harder and faster, my name on his lips as he came helps build me up and tense my body.

If I didn't still have one hand against the door, I might collapse to the damn floor on my shaky legs.

127

My orgasm builds, coiling inside me, tighter and tighter. I roll my finger harder. Faster. Pushing. Frantic to find the relief Beau just did. Picturing what it would be like to have him inside me, what it would *feel* like. Hot and fast and frantic.

And finally, *finally,* it crashes over me like the waves on the ocean I might never see again, rolling and cresting, pulling everything from deep down inside me I need to release.

I jerk on my feet and gasp, what would normally be quiet and unnoticed sounding loud in the utter silence of the cabin.

God, I hope he didn't hear that.

It's embarrassing enough he caught me watching him, but if he knew I came in here and rubbed one out after I intruded on his very personal moment in the shower, I don't think I could ever look him in the eye again. I'm not even sure I can now.

Christ...what a damn mess.

My heavy breaths against the door finally return to normal, and the click of the bathroom door opening makes me freeze in place. He must have closed it after I ran, maybe to hide from me, maybe so he could calm down before he confronts me.

Oh God, if he comes in here, I'll die. I swear to God, I'll die.

I rush back to the bed and scramble under the covers, pulling them up tightly around my face and burying myself as deeply in them as I can to wait for the inevitable confrontation, for him to come in and accuse me of spying on him, of watching something I absolutely shouldn't have.

But the door doesn't open.

And as the minutes tick by, I start to relax slightly. Until the sound of the front door opening and slamming shut makes me jackknife up.

He left.

Does that make me feel worse or better about the entire situation?

Oh, God...

I rub the heels of my hands into my eyes and wince.

You're such an idiot, Brooke.

Dropping back in the bed, I stare at the ceiling, trying to concentrate on the stark wood above me instead of what I saw.

But Beau's almost perfect form keeps appearing in my head. His cock heavy in his big, calloused hand. Which only makes me imagine what those rough fingertips would feel like on my smooth skin.

I squirm again and press my legs together. My clit throbs for more attention, and the memory of what I just saw clears even more to reveal the details I was too preoccupied to notice initially.

Scars...

On his chest and abdomen.

Some pale pink, some red and angry.

The clarity of what I saw and somehow managed to initially overlook in favor of getting my own release is like ice water being dumped over my libido, and guilt over what I just did washes over me so fast, I almost drown in it. That man has suffered. Something horrific. Something that makes tears roll down my cheeks.

What the hell happened to you, Beau?

Chapter Eleven

BEAU

An icy wind blasts snowflakes against the exposed parts of my face, and a shiver rolls through me for the first time all day. One nice thing about keeping myself busy so I can avoid going in and having to look Brooke in the eye is that I've been busting my ass and never once felt the chill in the air. But now that the sun has gone down and darkness has settled over the mountain, it's another story completely.

The few lightly falling flakes that were beautiful only an hour or two ago have become stinging little barbs against the skin I don't have covered with whiskers.

It was inevitable. I have to go inside at some point. As much as I may want to, I can't avoid Brooke forever. Unless I wanted to sleep out here with the girls. I glance back at the small building that houses them.

That actually doesn't sound like that bad an idea.

Definitely preferable to having to apologize for being such a fucking creep.

The woman was distraught, scared, afraid to do something as simple as closing her eyes. She needed safety in my arms, not for me to rub my hard cock and jerk off like some horny teenager to get rid of my morning wood simply from her snuggling against me.

Hell.

That had to have been one of the best and worst orgasms I've ever had. Though, it's been so long that maybe I'm just not remembering how incredible they really can be. But after so many years of not being with a woman and having almost no sex drive, that release was a long time coming.

I just wish she hadn't witnessed it.

It's going to make an already awkward and tense situation all that much worse.

I glance toward where the gravel drive leading up to my place still lies buried under at least a foot of snow. While the sun we've had the last two days helped melt some of it, especially down the mountain, there's still a fuck-load to get through before any help will be arriving to get Brooke out of here. But at least if Sheriff Roberts can get to wherever her car stopped, I can get her down to him on the snowmobile.

Tomorrow or the next day. Three, tops. Then that poor woman can leave without having to worry about me doing something assholeish or creepy again.

She woke up after almost freezing to death, worried I had done something to her. Now that she's seen me touching myself, that's probably back to the forefront of her mind. And I can't blame her for thinking that way.

No one would.

I shiver again—as much because of the weather as how much I don't want to do this—and start my walk back toward the cabin. Even with eight hours of sunlight out here to do nothing but think about what I was gonna say to her, I still have no idea what will come out of my mouth when I open that door and see her.

Probably something completely wrong for the situation. Just like everything I seem to be saying to her since she got here.

You really fucked things up, Beau.

That shouldn't surprise me, though. Story of my fucking life. Here I thought it couldn't get much worse. After last night, I know I couldn't have been more wrong.

I pause at the bottom of the steps and stare up at the door waiting, though for what, I'm not entirely sure.

For it to open. For her to smile and welcome me back and pretend it never happened. For her to ream me out and tell me what a disgusting creep I am. For her beautiful face to appear in the window like it did yesterday, when she stood there often and I caught a few glimpses of her watching me work.

There hasn't been any sign of her today. Likely because she doesn't want to see me, and I can't blame her.

Who would after that performance?

I shake my head, turn the knob, and push open the door to the welcome heat from the roaring fireplace and a delicious scent filling the warm air. It hits me square in the face, and I release a sigh. Apparently, I hadn't even realized how cold I got out there all day.

Brooke kept the fire going all day. I probably should have checked on her and made sure she was all right in that regard, but as long as I saw smoke coming from the chimney, I convinced myself it was better to stay away. Better for her, for me. Both of us.

All that occupied my mind was my utter and complete

embarrassment for what that woman saw this morning, for how it made her run.

I scan the cabin for her. The door to my office remains closed. Exactly how I left it when I went out. She promised me she wouldn't go in there, and for some reason, I trust her and believe that her word means something.

Unlike mine apparently because I told her I'd stopped being an asshole, then went ahead and did the ultimate asshole thing this morning.

I pull off my gear, hang it to dry, and follow the mouth-watering smell coming from the kitchen, expecting to find her there and face what I've been dreading all day.

Man up, Beau. Face the consequences of your actions for once in your life.

But it's empty, save for a pot on the stove. The closer I move toward it, the more my stomach rumbles. I lift the lid, and the spicy scent of chili hits my nose. Skipping breakfast and lunch wasn't wise, given how many calories I burned out there today, but it beat having to see her and deal with the judgment in her green eyes.

"I hope you like chili."

Shit.

Jerking away from the pot, I almost drop the lid and whirl toward Brooke's voice behind me.

She stands just inside the kitchen near the small table. Her hands wrapped around the back of one of the chairs. "I figured you'd be hungry since you didn't come in all day." Her gaze darts to the pot, avoiding meeting mine. "I dug around to see what you had. I hope you don't mind."

"No. Of course, I don't mind. Thank you. This smells amazing." I drop the lid back into place and clear my throat. "You didn't have to do that. I could have made something."

"I know."

A silence so heavy it threatens to break my shoulder settles over us, and I glance around the kitchen at anything but Brooke, hoping that I can hold off with the awkward apology.

Maybe if she doesn't mention it, we can pretend it never happened. Denial is a very real, very *legitimate* way of handling things. At least, that's what I've been telling myself for the past ten years. Denial and running, not facing your demons...all good ways to go.

If you want to live like a fucking hermit and scare off women with your behavior.

"So..." Brooke shrugs and motions toward the table where two bowls are set out. "Should we eat?"

"Let me just spray off real quick, if that's okay."

Her eyes widen slightly, and internally, I cringe.

Real fucking nice, Beau.

The last time she saw me "just spraying off" I was also just *jerking off*.

"Um, sure"—her unsteady voice matches her restless shift on her feet—"it can stay on as long as we need it to."

"Okay, I'll be right back." I brush past her, holding my breath to avoid sucking that sweet scent of hers into my lungs, and make my way straight back to the bathroom.

Normally, I wouldn't care about eating dinner or climbing into bed smelling like smoke, diesel, my cigar, and sweat from working the property all day, but I don't want to sit across the dinner table from her and make her suffer through that.

And God knows I won't be stupid enough to do what I did in the shower again, even though my body seems to think it's a great idea after seeing the red flush that spread over Brooke's cheeks when I mentioned it.

* * *

BROOKE

The clank of Beau's spoon landing in his empty bowl finally breaks the unbearable silence that's hung between us since the moment he reappeared after his shower, after I spent ten minutes picturing what he was doing in there, re-examining every detail in my mind despite trying *so hard* not to.

I knew things might be tense after what happened this morning, but I hadn't anticipated him giving me the cold shoulder this way.

Awkward, yes.

Icy and aloof, no.

Maybe I should have expected it, given how badly I violated his privacy by spying on him in his most intimate moment. This is just the way it's going to be between us from now on. I have to get used to it until I can get down the mountain.

"That was amazing." Beau leans back in his chair and motions at the tiny kitchen while he rubs his flat stomach. "Thank you. I don't know how you managed to throw that together with what you were able to find here."

I shrug and poke at the remains at the bottom of my bowl. "It's just some canned beans, canned tomatoes, some seasoning, and whatever that frozen meat was."

He opens his mouth, but I hold up my hand to stop him.

"I don't want to know what it was."

The tiniest of smiles curls at the corner of his lips—the first break in the freezeout. "I actually think you'd be okay on that one."

"I think you give me too much credit. I'll have nightmares about the squirrel we ate until the day I die."

Beau chuckles and absently toys with the crumpled-up paper napkin on the table in front of him, watching it like it's the most interesting thing he's ever seen. "Look...I'm sorry."

I freeze and let my spoon fall into my bowl. "For what? Killing the squirrel?"

He smirks at me. "No."

His gaze shifts away from mine, toward the dark window, and he studies it for a moment before sitting forward in the chair and finally locking his focus on me again. "About this morning."

"I-I shouldn't have been in the bathroom. It's completely my fault. I woke up and you were gone. And I heard a noise and—"

He holds up a hand. "And we all know what happened after that."

Except you have no idea that I raced back to your bedroom and rubbed one out thinking about how hot you looked while doing it.

I clear my throat and try to appear unaffected by this conversation even though I can feel the heat rushing to my cheeks.

Goddamn being so fair-skinned.

"I shouldn't have intruded. I should have left right away. And—"

"You didn't leave right away?"

Shit. Shit. Shit.

His dark eyebrows rise, and the vein in his neck throbs with his rapid heartbeat.

I push back my chair, grab my bowl, and round the table for his, snatching it from in front of him before he can object. "Never mind."

The sound of his chair scraping back across the wood

planks makes me wince, and I set the bowls in the sink and turn on the water to wash them.

"How much did you see?" His voice comes low and husky and from directly behind me.

It makes me jump slightly as I scrub out one of the bowls and set it on the drying rack. "Stuff I shouldn't have."

He really wants me to say it. Now he knows I didn't just walk in and see him and leave. He knows I *watched*. That I stood there like a pervert and relished in seeing him touch himself. That I didn't immediately turn away like I should have, like *anyone* should have.

Christ.

If I thought I could walk out into that snow right now, crawl into a bank, and die without Beau coming after me, I just might try.

I scrub at the other bowl, his presence looming close behind me, the heat of his gaze on me the entire time. With only two bowls, I've quickly run out of reasons to avoid having this conversation. I set the second one in the drying rack and turn back to the sink to find Beau setting the now empty pot into it.

"I put the leftovers in the fridge already."

Which I was too preoccupied to even notice. "Thanks."

For changing the subject.

If someone would have told me yesterday that I would beg to talk about leftovers and to clean dishes, I would have laughed in their face. But today, I'm wishing I had just cooked for twenty people instead of two so this would take me longer.

I didn't think it was possible to die of embarrassment, but I was wrong.

So. Damn. Wrong.

His dark eyes follow my every move as I scrub the pot,

set it to dry, and step away from the sink—and, more importantly, *him*—with the dish towel, drying my hands and scanning the kitchen for anything else I can use to occupy my time rather than risk returning to the uncomfortable topic.

"Well"—I release an exaggerated sigh—"I'm tired. I think I'm just going to go read in the bedroom."

I set the dish towel on the counter, but he reaches out and grabs my bicep gently, stopping me from rushing away like I so badly want to.

The warmth of his body radiates into me this close, and my entire being instinctively wants to lean toward it, but I force myself to do the opposite.

"Don't run and hide in the bedroom, Brooke. I'm sorry if I made things awkward. The last thing I want to do is make your time here uncomfortable. Please"—he squeezes my arm gently—"grab your book and sit out by the fire with me tonight. We can have a drink, if you want." He shrugs. "Or not."

As tempting as the offer is, to have the heat of the fire seeping through my body and the soft crackle and pop of the dry wood filling the silence that's so heavy in this cabin, the idea of sitting there with him while the visions of his solo session dance through my head makes climbing into bed by myself all that more much more appealing.

I'm going to be sleeping alone tonight. After this morning, there's no way Beau is going to allow a repeat of last night—even if it did prevent me from reliving the horrific nightmare.

Something tells me another kind of dream will plague me tonight. One that's going to leave me hot and sweaty and needy in a way I haven't been in an awfully long time.

All because of this man—and the way he had the strong

hand that's now wrapped around my arm wrapped around his cock this morning.

Shit.

I squeeze my eyes closed for a second and shake my head. Against my better judgment, I offer him a small smile, my will power to resist battling with the knowledge of what trying to sleep will bring. "Okay."

"Good." He releases my arm and runs a shaky hand through his hair. "I'm going to throw a few more logs on the fire and pour drinks. Do you want one?"

God yes.

I'm definitely going to need alcohol to deal with the few remaining nights I'm going to have here with Beau.

A lot of alcohol.

Chapter Twelve

BROOKE

Flames leap in the fireplace, dancing and dipping to the sound of their own music.

I snuggle into the corner of the couch closest to the warmth and try to concentrate on the page in front of me that I've probably read a thousand times already.

"Be with me always—take any form—drive me mad! Only do not leave me in this abyss, where I cannot find you! Oh, God! It is unutterable! I cannot live without my life! I cannot live without my soul!"

The familiar words blur in front of my eyes, any ability to process them seemingly lost.

Who am I kidding?

I'm not going to be able to concentrate on this book. Not while Beau is sitting only a foot away from me, so close I can feel every shift he makes on the cushions, every time he flips another page in his book, or takes a sip of the scotch he has resting on the end table.

Whatever the tension was when I arrived—me crash-landing into his life and being wary of him—has morphed into something else, similar but notably different in a few key ways. Mainly that it now makes me squirm constantly and glance at him out of the corner of my eye. Watching the way his big hand tightens around his glass when he takes a drink. The way his Adam's apple bobs when he swallows.

Hell.

I grab my drink and take a sip, letting the liquid burn down my throat and warm my belly. It feels like hours have passed since we finished eating and came to sit in here and read, but it's impossible to tell how long we've really been here without a clock. And since I haven't advanced more than a few pages since I sat down, that isn't helping me figure it out, either.

"You okay?" Beau's question comes heavy with concern.

I glance over at him and raise an eyebrow. "What do you mean?"

He motions toward my book. "You've been on the same page for almost half an hour."

Dammit.

I've never been particularly good at hiding my feelings, and Beau is far too observant for something like me being spaced out for so long to pass his notice.

I close the book and set it on a small table next to me. "I'm having trouble concentrating."

He closes his book and sets it down, too. "I know what you mean." His fingers drum on the cover of his book, and he glances over at me. "I know I already apologized for before...but I can't stop thinking about what you said about watching me."

Oh, hell...

I drop my face into my hands. "Shit. I am so embarrassed."

"How long were you watching?" His already deep voice drops even more. "Tell me, Brooke. How long?"

The air thickens between us, and the memory of gaping at him as he stroked his hard length completely fills my mind, pushing out all of my best attempts to keep it locked away. "Long enough."

"Why didn't you leave right away?"

Good God, he's going to make me say it?

I lower my hands and look over to find him watching me closely, waiting for an answer. And while I could lie, I could make an excuse for what I did, staring at the man who saved my life, the man who comforted me through that horrific nightmare, who has clothed me and fed me and let me invade his personal space, I can't bring myself to.

"Because I liked what I saw."

Heat floods my body. It has nothing to do with the fire beside us and everything to do with the way his hooded russet eyes assess me after my confession.

"You liked watching me stroke my cock?"

Liked *isn't a strong enough word.*

The vivid image flashes in my head again, and I nod slowly, biting my lip to prevent a little moan from escaping. "Yes."

Dammit.

The word comes soft and breathy—almost desperate in a way I hate.

Beau doesn't react, just sits stick straight, his heated gaze raking over me in a way that makes it impossible to look at him. I avert my eyes down to his lap and the obvious bulge forming there.

"I...heard you, too."

Hell. Why did I just admit that?

"What did you hear?"

142

The way he asks the question, like my answer will somehow change everything, has me lifting my focus back to him and shifting toward him slightly when I should really be moving away, closing myself off from him and where I think this might lead. "You, say my name."

His eyes burn even brighter now, searing my skin as if he were pressing a flame directly against it, marking me somehow with just a look. "You're the first woman who has ever slept in that bed. The first woman I've lain in any bed with for ten years, Brooke. But even if it hadn't been that long, I still would have woken up with my dick hard. You're a beautiful woman, Brooke." He swallows thickly. "I'm sorry that I couldn't control myself. I'm sorry if it offended you. Sorry it's going to complicate your stay here."

"Beau, I assure you, I wasn't offended..."

The admission slips from my lips before I can stop it, and his jaw hardens, like he's fighting the urge to say or do something he thinks would lead to something neither of us should want.

"It turned you on?" He asks it so low, his voice so rough, that it almost doesn't even sound like the question came from the man I've spent the last few days with.

And it's the understatement of the year...

It had been so long since I'd felt like that, since my body had responded so fully to a man in that way that it felt foreign and new. Almost magical. Another truth I should keep from him but that I, somehow, can't withhold.

"Watching you touch yourself while thinking about me was probably the hottest thing I've ever seen in my life."

His eyes widen slightly, hands tensing on his thighs. "Really?"

How does Beau not know how hot he is?

I would tell him—after all, I've already revealed *way* too

much as it is—but I can't seem to find any words. Instead, I just nod.

One of Beau's eyebrows rises slowly. "Then why did you run back in the bedroom? Why did you run away?"

When he puts it that way, I can see how he might think I was appalled or angry or offended by what I had seen. But running away was for my own good, not because he did anything wrong.

"Because I-I was embarrassed about spying, about watching you do something so private that you never intended for me to see."

I was embarrassed by how badly I wanted to join you in that shower.

"You're right, Brooke. I never intended for you to see that. But you did."

"I sure did."

He watches me for another moment, analyzing my face as if it will reveal something he longs to learn, as if he's searching for some truth. "What did you do when you went back in that room, Brooke?"

Oh, God, he knows.

He fucking knows.

The heat flooding my cheeks now isn't from the fire, or even the embarrassment of Beau knowing what I did. It's the way he's looking at me, like a starved man who sees a meal in front of him. One he's ready to devour.

Only, I'm not afraid of him.

Not even a little.

I should be. God knows I should be, but fear isn't what fills me under his scorching assessment.

There isn't any point in lying now. If I did, he would just call me out on it.

I swallow and shift toward him, close enough that he could easily reach out and touch me, if he wanted to, but I don't dare lay a finger on him, not when the slightest brush of our skin together is liable to set me off. "I touched myself, Beau. I made myself come remembering what you looked like when you did."

"Fuck, Brooke..." He squeezes his eyes closed and adjusts his hard cock in the gray sweatpants that can't conceal it. "Fuck..."

The frustration in his voice matches my own. A primal, pulsating thing that threatens to consume us both.

Even though there are a million reasons I shouldn't, I close the remaining distance between us, until my knee brushes his thigh. He opens his eyes slowly, tentatively, like he's afraid of what he'll find when he does, and dark burning orbs of lust stare straight into my soul.

Beau reaches out a hand and cups my cheek, brushing the rough, calloused pad of his thumb across it tenderly. "This is a bad idea, Brooke."

"I know."

"I can't give you what you want."

What I want...

Like that's so easy to explain. There are so many things I'll never have, *can* never have again. My entire future has changed, been altered to another unknown and frightening path, and I can never go back to the one I was on. I would never want to. Yet, sitting here with Beau, in this cabin, on this mountain, surrounded by nothing but trees and snow, I know what I want in this moment.

I drop my hand down to grasp his hard cock and squeeze it gently. "All I want is you."

"Fuck..." Beau closes his eyes again and inhales a deep breath through his nose, then lets it back out slowly through his mouth. Like he's searching for the control he lost this morning.

But I don't want him to find it. I don't want him to think about the reasons *not* to do what we both clearly want. I want this tension to break. I want it to shatter. I want everything I've been feeling since I left Seattle to melt away the way the snow does in the warm mid-day sun.

I gently caress him, relishing the feel of him growing even harder in my hand, and he grits his teeth. A muscle in his jaw tics. His fist tightens even more on the top of his leg closest to me.

"Please, Beau. We both want this—"

"Which is precisely the fucking problem, Brooke." His eyes flicker open and lock with mine, and I see the depth of the struggle there. Beau warring with himself over whether he should give in to what his body wants or pull back because his mind isn't ready to finally let me in, in any way.

I shift up onto my knees beside him and take his face between my palms. The rough whiskers of his beard scrape against my skin, and I lean in, stopping with my lips just short of brushing his. "Make me feel good, Beau. Make me forget why I have nightmares. Make me remember how good it can really be."

"Jesus fucking Christ..."

His lips meet mine, stealing my breath, and a satisfied groan rumbles through his chest and into mine.

I gasp into his mouth and swing my leg across his waist to straddle him, pressing his hard length between my legs exactly where I need it. Strong hands grip my hips, trying to hold me steady, but I roll them, needing the contact, seeking the friction. I grind down against his cock, and his hands tighten even more, his fingers sure to leave imprints on my skin in the best way possible.

He pulls his head back from me, his jaw tense, the muscles of his neck straining, and I rotate my hips again, shifting my angle slightly to hit the perfect spot, exactly where I so desperately need it. His hands tense again—impossibly tight—and his eyes widen slightly, as if he can see a train barreling down the track at him and can't move out of the way.

"Fuck, Brooke. You're going to make me come."

So close.

Heat builds low in my abdomen and spreads down into my core. I rotate my hips and grind down again, moving faster and harder against him. His lips find mine in another bruising kiss, and a gasp slips from his mouth into mine as his body stills and then jerks under me.

An inferno of ecstasy engulfs me, burning through my limbs, numbing all my pain and searing away all the things plaguing my mind, letting them float off like ash into the air surrounding us, like the snow that brought me to Beau in the first place. I tremble on his lap, my motions erratic and frantic, until I finally collapse, dropping my forehead against his and releasing a heavy, shaky breath.

* * *

BEAU

I thought I was embarrassed before, when I knew Brooke had seen me jerk off, but even the warm afterglow of an orgasm can't wash away the humiliation of coming in my pants like a goddamn teenager who gets dry-humped for the first time.

Real fucking smooth.

Brooke releases a contented sigh and drags back her

head, adjusting her position on my lap as she presses her mouth to mine, gliding her tongue across my lips.

At least she came.

The only thing that could have made this situation any more mortifying would have been if I blew my load like Old Faithful while she was left hanging. It's been a fucking long time since lust fogged my brain so badly that I lost control of my body. Far too long since I've had a woman like Brooke in my arms.

Fuck, I've never *had a woman like Brooke in my arms.*

She ends the kiss and leans back, locking her hooded gaze on me.

"I'm sorry I came like a horny kid dry humping for the first time."

A playful grin tugs at her kiss-swollen lips, and she angles her head down and captures my mouth again, this time undulating her hips against my semi-hard cock with clear intention. The wetness of both of our releases soaks the crotch of my sweat pants and the ones she's wearing, but she doesn't seem to care, just continues to work me up, making my dick as hard as granite again in mere seconds.

She runs her hands through my hair, tugging lightly at it. "I think it's hot...that you couldn't control it."

I bark out a laugh and shake my head. "Premature ejaculation is hot?"

That lazy grin returns as she glances down between us. "In this instance, very much so."

She clenches her legs together in a way that makes my cock ache to be inside her more than I even knew was physically possible. "I want you, Beau."

I tighten my grip on her hips, battling with my desire to flip her onto her back on this damn couch and pound her into oblivion when there are so many reasons not to. "Are you sure? I don't know how—"

"Yes."

She kisses me, silencing my ability to apologize again for the fact that I don't know how good I'll be or how long I'll last. Her soft fingers play along the waistband of my sweatpants. She slides backward slowly, and I lift my hips and let her tug them down and off, along with my boxer briefs. Her warm green eyes lock on my exposed cock, and it twitches under her assessment.

I've seen that look before, only it was on a coyote I caught stalking the chickens when they were out in the yard once the beautiful spring weather arrived.

Pure hunger.

Brooke isn't afraid to tell me, or show me, exactly what she wants, and I'm not in any position to deny her. She gives my dick one hard, long stroke and glides her thumb across the head.

Fuuuckkk.

I drop my head against the back of the couch.

Jesus, please let me last longer than thirty fucking seconds.

For the love of God...

There are countless reasons we shouldn't be doing this. My secrets. Hers. The fact she'll be leaving in a matter of days. The fact that I may blow my load again in five seconds...but right now, none of them seem to matter.

Not when Brooke's tongue glides along my lips and pushes for entry. Not when I open for her and tangle my tongue with hers. Not when I easily pull down the waistband of the pants already so loose at her hips and let them pool to the floor.

She steps out of them, the underwear she wore the day I

saved her life nowhere in sight, her pussy glistening in the fire light with her recent release.

My cock jumps, straining and begging to be buried hilt-deep inside her sweet heat. I reach down and grab it, stroking it slowly to ensure I'm ready for what's coming. Though, something tells me I could never fully be ready for this woman, for what she does to me, for what she's about to do to me.

She came to me lost, alone and freezing, running from something and needing my comfort and support, and now, she's coming to me all confident temptress. And I'm more than willing to let her devour me if that's what she needs right now.

I just hope neither of us regrets it.

Something tells me we *both* have enough regrets as it is, even though she won't open up and tell me what's really going on with her. But her motives for keeping her life private aren't my concern, especially not when I'm hiding so many major things from her. Things that would change everything between us in a fucking instant.

Brooke crawls back onto my lap and takes my cock in her hand, dragging the head through her wet pussy lips. I grit my teeth and grab her hips, digging my fingers into them, trying to find a way to locate some semblance of control to keep myself from embarrassment again.

Her lips find mine, and she wraps her arms around the back of my neck and slowly lowers down on me.

Sweet mother of God!

Hot, wet, tight walls clasp my hard flesh, sucking me in the same way her pain and beauty has the last few days.

She sinks, torturously slow, until I'm fully inside her, so deep, it feels like I'm reaching her fucking soul. Her mouth falls open on a gasp, and she drops her head back and clenches around me possessively. "Oh, God!"

Oh, God is fucking right.

I haven't believed in the man—or woman?—for ten damn years, but with her cunt wrapped around me, her body pressed to mine, I'm starting to have a religious awakening.

Still, it isn't enough. Not nearly enough.

I tug at the hem of my T-shirt that hangs down to her mid-thigh and pull it up and over her head, exposing her to me entirely. Perfect high, round breasts and a creamy expanse of smooth skin practically glow in the fire light.

As I drink her in, she squeezes herself around me, making me grit my teeth against the wash of pleasure. I flick my finger across her nipple, and she gasps and leans forward to kiss me, her tongue probing and rolling against mine as she starts to move on my lap.

She languidly rises up, letting my cock slip from inside her—all except the head, nestled just inside her pussy—and squeezes, then lowers herself down again in a way that's sure to milk another orgasm from me far faster than I'd like.

I groan into her mouth and pinch her nipple, which earns me another little gasp and a mewling sound as she grinds down against my pelvis, seeking friction against her clit.

Her frantic hands search for the hem of my shirt, and she pulls it up and over my head then sits back, her hands pressed against my chest as she moves up and down on my cock.

Small, soft fingers brush over the scar on my right pec then sink down over the two on my abdomen. I grab her wrist to pull her hand away, but when her green eyes widen in confusion, I drag it up to my lips to kiss her fingers to soften the blow of not wanting her touch there. Her eyes narrow on me slightly, but she keeps moving, bringing both of us barreling toward another release we both seem to need.

I lower my head and capture her nipple between my lips, pulling it in my mouth and sucking on it hard enough that her rhythm falters.

"Oh, God, Beau! Yes!"

Her words and the pleasure drenching them only drive me to suck harder and flick my tongue over the tightened nub. She jerks on my lap, her pussy tightening like a vise around me.

A warm tingle starts at the base of my spine, signaling another orgasm coming, but I refuse to give into it until she comes on my cock. I want to feel every damn *second* of her release, know that I was the one who brought her to it, who gave her not only a place to find refuge in the storm but safety from whatever sent her up here in the first place.

I brace my feet on the wood floor and shove up into her, meeting her every time she slams down, driving myself even deeper, the head of my cock dragging against the spot inside her that makes her breaths come out in hard, heavy pants.

Twisting and flicking her nipple between my fingers with one hand, I reach between us to find her clit with my other thumb and roll it there. She grinds down tighter against my hand, and I push up into her relentlessly until she finally freezes.

For one beautiful millisecond frozen in time, she's the picture of sheer bliss, a woman completely separated from her past and whatever torments her, a woman who got what she wanted...what she *needed*.

Her body jerks against mine. Her pussy rippling and clasping rhythmically as I continue to drive up into her. I grit my teeth through two more thrusts, then finally let her cunt milk my orgasm from me, spurt after hot spurt deep inside.

She collapses against me, burying her face in my neck, and I do the same, wrapping my arms around her and holding her steady, even though my entire world just got knocked off its axis.

What the fuck did we just do?

Chapter Thirteen

BROOKE

I roll over onto my back and reach toward the other side of the bed only to find it empty and the sheets cold.

No Beau?

Blinking awake, the harsh bright sunlight streaming in from the window makes me wince. That isn't the soft light of dawn—far from it.

Turning my head away from it, I stretch and yawn, my body aching in all the right places. All the places that remind me exactly what Beau and I did last night—multiple times. So, it shouldn't surprise me I slept so long.

My core clenches remembering how incredible it really was, and I squeeze my legs together and roll onto my stomach to spread out across the bed, inhaling Beau's woodsy, outdoor scent that now mingles with mine, clinging to the sheets and pillows.

He's probably been up for hours, doing whatever it is he

does around this place all day to keep it running all alone... while I'm in here being lazy.

Guilt creeps into my head, threatening to push away the afterglow of such a great night.

I should probably be helping with something.

No matter how many times Beau tells me I don't need to be doing anything, it doesn't feel right not to make some sort of effort to do something other than sit around the house and read books by the fire, while he's busting his ass to keep his place in good shape.

After a storm like that and after what we did last night, that feeling of obligation to him—and to this place—strikes at something deep inside me. The longer I'm here, the harder it's going to be to leave when the time comes. Walking away from the man who gave me exactly what I needed, exactly when I needed it, leaving this place where I found a moment to really breathe, will feel like losing the tiny piece of Heaven I managed to find in what was Hell on Earth when I drove that road out of Seattle.

But I have to leave—and soon—for both our sakes.

Until I can, I'm going to enjoy myself the way we did last night as long as Beau's on board with this change in our relationship. It certainly *seemed* like he was on board when he was driving into me last night like he couldn't get enough.

God knows I certainly couldn't...

And while I'd love to lie in bed and remember every moment in great detail, I need to get cleaned up and figure out if there's any way I can help around here to show Beau how much I appreciate what he's doing for me.

One final stretch and yawn draws a groan from deep in my chest, but I force myself to climb from the bed, tugging the blanket from the top of it to wrap around my naked body.

I never thought I'd be sleeping in the nude when it's this cold out, but Beau sure kept me warm last night. The only shudders and shivers running through my body were those of absolute pleasure.

No nightmares haunted my sleep. No horrible memories threatened to break me. The only dreams I had were of the handsome man with the ax who rescued me.

It won't last forever, Brooke.

I'm not stupid enough to believe that. Still, if the pleasant memories I now have from my time with Beau and dreams I've had here can last me forever, then any pain in leaving will be well worth it. I feel like I could survive anything as long as I have those.

And anything could be coming.

The truth catches up with you eventually.

I crack open the bedroom door and listen for Beau, but the typical silence of the cabin greets me. He's probably been working outside, taking care of the chickens and goats and whatever else he needs to, since before dawn. The reminder of how long ago that really was streams in the window and makes me hustle into the bathroom and crank on the water as hot as it goes.

Though, a cold shower might be more appropriate after Beau's scorching touch last night. Examining myself in the mirror, the proof stares right back at me—disheveled mess of hair, flush still apparent on my cheeks, kiss-swollen lips. But it's the soreness between my legs that truly speaks volumes.

After being alone here for so long, not touching a woman, barely touching himself, Beau let loose in a way that makes the steam filling the tight space feel even hotter.

I drop the blanket and step under the spray, letting the

hard water work away the tension in my body that all the unexpected physical activity has brought. It's been so long since I felt sore for the right reasons, I almost hate to lose it, but I force myself to grab the shampoo and lather my hair.

The scent I've come to associate with him envelops me. 'Til the day I die, the smell of winter air and the woods will bring the beautiful memories with it. But that's another reality I don't want to think about right now. I turn off the water and step from the shower, quickly dry, and make my way back to the bedroom to dress in my own clothes so I can go out and search for Beau.

But something makes me pause at the door and turn back. Something tugging at me, pulling me toward where my bag sits on top of the dresser—exactly where it has been since the moment Beau brought me here that first day.

It's the first time I've felt that itch to hold my camera in my hands again, to explore the beauty of this mountain and the man on it.

I pull it from the confines of the bag and the familiar weight brings a sense of peace. A peace I thought I might never feel when holding the camera again. Not with so many bad memories tied up with the good ones.

It's time to create something beautiful.

I tug on my jacket, boots, and far-too-thin gloves again, my gut twisting. The last time I put these on, I was leaving Seattle in the middle of the night in a frantic rush. Panicked and desperate to get away. To put as many miles between me and what that city held as possible. If my last-minute flight hadn't been canceled, I never would have ended up here. I never would have almost died. I never would have met Beau.

All the bad led to something so damn good.

My heart swells with the possibilities the day holds,

especially with the camera in my hand, and I tug open the door and step out onto the unfamiliar property for the first time.

Looking out the windows over the last few days hasn't done it justice. I pull the door closed behind me, and my breath catches at the beauty spread out before me now that all the snow has finally stopped and the wind has died down.

The Okanogan Mountain range stretches as far as the eye can see in either direction, snow-covered peaks jutting up into the high, wispy clouds, creating a stunning landscape no artist could top.

I snap a few pictures from the front door. This is a view I want to remember and hold in my heart when I'm long gone. Beau gets to wake up to this every day. Before I came here, I never saw the appeal of living this lifestyle, but this morning, it's crystal clear.

It's peaceful, and peace is something so few people find.

Whack.

The sound comes from the small barn building across the open front yard of the cabin and echoes through the small valley where the cabin sits.

Whack.

I set out across the snowy landscape toward it, stepping in Beau's footprints to try to avoid sinking too deeply into the snow.

Whack.

The closer I get, the louder the sound becomes. Rhythmic. Almost soothing, but I can't quite place it.

I approach the building slowly, not wanting to startle Beau or the animals he already warned me would be jumpy with someone they didn't know here. The wide barn-style doors stand flung open, exposing the interior of the space, and my steps falter.

Beau stands just inside, clad in only a pair of jeans and his boots, his chest bare, rhythmically swinging his ax at a piece of wood propped up on a stump, a lit cigar dangling from his lips.

Holy shit.

I knew Beau was beautiful, an Adonis really. His perfect muscles were on display when I saw him in the shower, but they were slightly hidden and distorted by the steam and the glass shower door. And then last night, I was concentrating on other things—other parts of his body—and we gave in to our desperation rather than spending time truly exploring each other's bodies. But now, I really have the opportunity to appreciate all his glory.

His rock-hard muscles ripple with each movement. Every swing of his ax makes his biceps and upper back muscles bulge and flex.

Good God!

I almost choke on my breath as I watch, and I slowly lift the camera and snap off half a dozen shots—mostly for myself—but if I ever do see Colleen again, she will absolutely die when she gets a load of him. He's every lumberjack fantasy I've ever had, and after seeing this, he will be every fantasy I ever have in the future.

Another step brings me closer to him, then another. My boots crunch in the snow, and he freezes and turns toward me, his ax propped over his shoulder.

His dark eyebrows rise as he takes me in and pulls the cigar from his lips. "You're awake."

"I bet you've been up for hours, haven't you?"

He offers me a little grin and nods, then turns back to the task at hand. "Yep." He sticks the cigar back in his mouth, props up another log, and swings. *Whack.* Smoke puffs up around him, and he offers a slight shrug. "I don't sleep much, and the internal clock wakes me up before dawn every morning."

Whack.

Whack.

I take a few more steps toward him but don't want to get too close to the weapon he wields with such precision since I'm not sure where it's safe to stand. "Do you need any help with anything? Getting the eggs or feeding the animals? I feel like I should be doing something."

He glances over his shoulder at me and pulls out the cigar again. "No, darling. I have everything taken care of."

Darling...

Under normal circumstances, a man I barely know calling me something like that would probably rankle me, but from Beau, the term of endearment is just that. Genuine, thoughtful. Not meant to be an insult to me or my intellect.

"I was thinking about taking some pictures today."

He freezes with the ax midway in the air and brings it down harder than I have seen him do it, lodging it into the stump he's using to chop the wood, before turning to face me properly. Slowly, he raises one hand to the cigar and takes a puff off it, his other hand at his hip. "Pictures?"

I hold up my camera. "Yeah, I'm a photographer. I thought I told you that?"

His jaw tightens, and the veins in his arms seem to pulse with anger. "No, you said you were self-employed."

"Well...I am. Photography is my job."

He nods slowly and examines the camera in my hand. "No pictures of me or the cabin. Got it?"

"Uh, sure, if that's what you want."

160

He turns back without another word, grabs the ax, shoves the cigar back between his lips, and sets another chunk of wood on the stump. His next swing seems to hold all his aggression, and he strikes it with enough force to send the two pieces flying outward.

What the hell is he so mad about?

* * *

BEAU

Brooke's boots crunch on the snow as she starts to walk away.

Dammit. I can't let her just wander off by herself.

Turning toward her retreating form, I pull my cigar from my lips and call back over my shoulder. "Don't go too far. You still don't have the right gear, and even though it's warmed up a lot and we aren't supposed to get any more snow, I don't need you getting lost and having to come save you again."

I don't bother waiting for her response, just grab another log, throw it up on the stump, and chop it in half. Muriel and Jezebel watch me from their pen, their black eyes locked on me with heavy judgment. Shifting my gaze to the chicken pen, I find them watching me with the same conviction. Almost like they understood exactly what I said to Brooke and why.

Okay, that was kind of a dick move talking to her like that.

Especially after what happened last night. Of course, the girls don't know about that, but the way they're looking at me, I wouldn't know that.

But a photographer?

Brooke definitely never told me that.

If I had known she had a camera with her this whole time, I definitely would have been more careful about what I said, more reluctant to let her know things than I already was. I would have kept an eye on that bag of hers more closely and ensured she wasn't photographing anything that could come back to bite me.

God dammit.

Whack.

I split the log, sending the pieces flying. Jezebel and Muriel jump back slightly from the front of the pen. They're used to seeing me do this, but not this aggressively. Not with so much anger and frustration.

"Sorry, girls."

It's not how the morning started out or how I wanted today to go. Not at all.

I woke to a warm, welcoming body pressed to mine, blond hair spread across the pillow in front of me. A gorgeous woman who gave me quite possibly the best night of my life despite my initial reluctance to give in to the attraction buzzing between us.

It was good.

Damn fucking good.

Better than I deserved, really. But now all those vivid memories are tainted by having to replay all the time we spent together in my head as I work my way through the wood and finish the cigar I *had* been enjoying before Brooke dropped that bombshell.

Did she ever have the camera out?

I can't even remember ever seeing her go *in* the bag, let alone holding a camera, but just because I didn't see her take a picture doesn't mean she didn't.

Stop, Beau.

Brooke hasn't given me any reason not to trust her. She has secrets, but I sure as shit do, too. Ones that seem to weigh more heavily on me the longer she's here. It feels like lying to her, even though all I'm really doing is withholding a few pieces of information.

Though, after last night, I was *this* close to telling her the truth.

Every time her fingers brushed over one of my scars and I moved her hand away. Every time I caught one of her moans and gasps with my lips. Every kiss we shared. Every time our eyes locked, I wondered how different it might be if she knew everything. How it would change things between us. How it would change the way she looked at me.

But I also didn't want to think about it *really*, didn't want to let the "what-ifs" interfere with what was turning into an incredible night. Didn't want to dwell on what might have been had we met under better circumstances, before we were both irreperably damaged by something or someone.

It's so easy to do that, to imagine how different things might have been, but one thing I've learned after all these years up here is that it only leads to further despair.

Lashing out at her like that was a product of my pent-up anger over what drove me up here in the first place and the fear that she will discover it all. A part of me *wants* her to.

I pause for a moment and stare up at the almost-clear sky, inhaling deeply from the cigar and watching the high, thin clouds float past. The familiar smell of tobacco and the nicotine racing through me help calm my tense body, but the effects won't last long.

As long as she's here, I'll be on edge. With her in my orbit, I can never get back to my regular existence.

She needs to go.

The longer this goes on, the harder it will be to stay detached, to return to what has become my normalcy.

I need to radio the sheriff again today to see where we're at. Given how warm it is today and the sun high in the sky, it won't be much longer before he should be able to get up to where her car stopped.

And in the meantime, there isn't any reason two consenting adults can't sleep together and find comfort and release in each other's arms, then walk away from each other. We both know that's what's going to have to happen. We both understand she has to leave. What happened last night doesn't change any of that.

It can't.

I wipe the sweat from my brow and take a second to assess the pile I've been working on for the last few hours. Keeping the house warmer than I normally would for Brooke's comfort has put a dent into the several cords of wood I usually keep in reserve, but hours of chopping have helped me work out some of my frustration over the whole situation and replenish my supply.

Rolling my shoulders to release some of the tension, curiosity over what Brooke is doing and a nagging sense of worry itch at the back of my head.

She shouldn't be out here alone.

It would be easy for her to get turned around and lost—or worse.

The memory of her blue lips and deathly-pale skin, how cold her body was when I held her that first day, slams into me hard enough for me to know I'm done with this for the day.

I lean my ax against the wood pile on the far side of the barn and grab my shirt from where it's draped over the chicken pen to shrug it on, then close the barn doors since I don't know how long I'll be gone and don't want to leave the animals exposed.

Theoretically, she hasn't been gone long enough to have gotten into any trouble, but then again, she seems like the type of woman who brings trouble with her. At least, she certainly has for me.

The kind of trouble that has me questioning every decision I've made since the day I came up here.

I snag my jacket and pull it on as I head out, following her footsteps in the snow to where they break off from mine. She went west toward the small ridge and nearest tree-line.

It would be a great place to snap some photos but also one of the most likely for her to run into one of the many predators out here. That camera won't do her much good against a bear that wakes from hibernation or a cougar on the hunt.

And it sure as shit can't protect her from me.

Chapter Fourteen

BEAU

My feet crunching in the snow should have alerted Brooke to my presence a long time ago, but either she isn't paying attention and is completely oblivious to what's going on around her or she's still pissed about how I snapped at her and is ignoring me.

Rightfully so.

She stands at the base of a massive fir, staring up at it and occasionally snapping a picture, though it looks like any other of the thousands of similar trees around us.

I stop a few feet behind her and watch her for a moment, trying to figure out what about *this* tree caught her attention. "What are you doing?"

She glances over her shoulder at me but almost immediately returns her focus to the tree. "Some sort of bird just flew in there, and I'm hoping to catch him as he flies out."

"There aren't many birds this high up the mountain this time of year. Most of them stay lower, where some of the waterways haven't frozen over. Do you know what it was?"

With a shrug, she lowers her camera, and finally turns toward me. "Not really. Ornithology isn't exactly my thing... but whatever. It was pretty. And right now, I just want to photograph some pretty things." She holds the camera delicately in her hands, like it's her most prized possession, and glances down at it. "I haven't really felt like I wanted to take photos until today. I want to make the most of it while my creative juices are flowing."

What happened last night definitely got my juices flowing...for her.

And seeing her so excited about shooting whatever flew into the tree gives me an idea of how to make up for my idiot move back at the barn.

"You want something really cool to photograph?"

The gold flecks in her eyes sparkle, her brows rising. "Yeah."

I glance down at the boots on her feet—definitely not ideal for where I'm going to take her, but they should be enough to keep her from getting frostbite. "Your feet cold?"

She peeks down and shakes her head. "No, I'm good. All this walking actually warmed me up. I'm sweating."

Chuckling, I approach her, my boots crunching in the snow again. "Yeah, it can be a little deceptive out here at times. It's cold, but if you're really working and sweat, then that freezes when you slow down and you're back to being cold."

"Oh..." Her lips turned down. "I hadn't really thought about that."

"You'll be fine. We're not going far, and the sun will be up for at least a few more hours."

"Where are we going?"

I motion toward the trees behind her. "Through there."

167

Brooke gulps and stares into the darkness of the forest. "Is that safe? I mean, aren't there like...predators up here?"

"Yes."

"Yet you want to go into the dark woods."

I lean in and brush my lips against the back of her ear. A shiver rolls through her—though, I doubt it has anything to do with the weather. Even though her gear isn't really made for this type of weather, it's unusually warm today, warm enough that as long as we stay in the sun, she shouldn't be too cold. "Don't worry, Brooke. I'll protect you."

She turns her head, until her mouth brushes mine. "With what? Your bare hands?"

I grin at her. "I have a few tricks up my sleeve."

"Oh, I have no doubt you do."

The same heat that blistered between us last night returns as we stare at each other out here in the snow, but this is definitely not the place or time to get distracted by the possibility of a repeat performance. Not when she was so excited about snapping some pictures and I know just where to take her.

I step backward, breaking the hold she has on me, and take her free hand in mine. "Come on. Let's go." I tug her toward the tree line, her steps reluctant. "I promise it'll be okay. It'll be worth it."

"If you say so."

We step between the tall firs and into the woods, where walking becomes much easier—a lot of the snow that otherwise covers the ground blocked here by the canopy.

Other than the sounds of our footsteps snapping small twigs and crunching through the snow where it did reach the ground, the typical silence of the mountain helps me dispel any remaining tension I felt from earlier.

It starts to open up in front of us, the sunlight breaking through the thinning trees.

Brooke hurries her steps, moving beside me instead of lagging behind. "What's up there?"

I squeeze her hand. "That's where we're going."

And she'll love it.

It's always been one of my favorite places on the mountain, especially in the spring and summer, but even in the dead of winter, the beauty of this spot is unmatched—and coupled with what I know we'll find here, it's something she *has* to see before she leaves.

We step out from the trees to a large, flat clearing covered in pristine snow. Ancient trees surround it, towering up like sentinels guarding some epic secret, the mountains rising high behind them, a second layer of protection for this spot.

"Wow..." Brooke tugs her hand from mine and turns to take it all in. "This is beautiful."

She pulls up her camera and tries to take a step forward, but I place a hand on her arm to stop her.

"Don't walk into the clearing. That's a frozen lake, and this time of year, the ice can be a little iffy."

"Oh, God." She presses her free hand to her chest. "I could have fallen in."

I grin at her again. "I said I wouldn't let anything happen to you, didn't I?"

She releases a little puff of breath that's just barely visible in the chilly air. "Yes."

"So...trust me. I didn't bring you here to show you the lake. I brought you here to show you that."

A large shadow crosses over us then shoots across the white expanse of the lake, and I point up.

Brooke jerks her head skyward, her jaw dropping open. "Oh, my God. Is that a bald eagle?"

It soars above us, circling lazily in the almost perfectly clear blue sky.

"Yep. There's a nest in one of the trees on the far side of the lake. The male and the female have lived up here for years, and occasionally, I'll see a couple of new ones coming back that I think might be their offspring from years past returning to their nesting site."

"Oh, my God. That's *incredible.*" Brooke takes another step forward, carefully eyeing the lake, though it's almost impossible to tell exactly where the shoreline is.

She lifts her camera and begins snapping away rapidly, a huge grin spreading across her lips, lighting up her face in a way I haven't seen since she's been here.

Damn. She really loves this.

That makes me feel like even more of a dick for how I reacted to the camera earlier. But after years of hiding, of protecting my privacy as much as humanly possible, the thought that it could be gone with one push of a button shook me more than I want to admit.

The eagle floats to the right and disappears behind some trees before it re-emerges.

Brooke motions toward the lake, still a few feet in front of us. "How far out can I go?"

"Only a couple more feet. We can walk around it near the tree line if you want to get different angles. We can head over to where the nest is. Though, I don't know if you'll be able to see it from the ground."

"Let's try."

Her quick, excited answer makes me chuckle.

"Okay."

I never thought I'd be playing tour guide to a beautiful woman up here on this land that was meant to be my refuge from the human race, yet something about it feels right. Her excitement. Her pure joy over the beauty of nature. Her seeing things and experiencing a world she probably never would have had a chance to. Being the one who gives that to her makes my heart swell, almost painfully, in my chest.

I step around her and put myself between her and the edge of the lake.

She lifts an eyebrow. "What are you doing?"

"Making sure you're safe." I point down toward the hidden water. "It can be hard to see the shoreline, but if either of us is going to go in, I'd much rather it be me."

Her eyes widen. "Don't say that. I wouldn't be strong enough to pull you out."

I snort and shake my head. "True. But now you know how to warm me up."

A hot pink flush spreads across her pale skin. "Yeah, I guess I do."

"Come on." I incline my head indicating for her to go first, and I trail slightly behind her and to the left, keeping myself between her and where the danger lies beneath the blanket of snow.

We pause several times, waiting for the bird to circle overhead again, and after a few minutes, it reappears across the lake. Brooke stops again and snaps off a series of pictures as fast as she can while it swirls and descends into a huge fir tree.

"That's where the nest is."

She examines it from where we stand, still a good fifty or sixty yards from it. "Would they have eggs this time of year?"

171

"Yes, and they also bring their small prey there to eat."

"Don't you ever worry they'll try to eat your chickens?"

"I have to be careful in the summer, for sure. I let them graze in the yard in a secured pen. Eagles and hawks definitely try, and there have been bear and mountain lion tracks on my property before. Though"—I reach out and rap my knuckles on a tree trunk—"knock on wood, I've been lucky and haven't lost any animals yet."

"Wow." She gapes. "It really is just about survival out here, isn't it? I mean..." She trails off and takes in the area around us. "This is beautiful. Stunning, really. But it seems like you're always working, constantly struggling just to keep the place going by yourself. Do you ever do anything... for fun? Or is it all just about work to survive?"

Even a few days ago, I would have completely agreed with her assessment, but so much has changed. I fought it every step of the way, but it did, anyway.

I take a step toward Brooke and pull her into my arms. "Last night was the first fun I've had in a very long time."

She grins at me, whatever anger or annoyance she had over my attitude earlier forgotten. "Me, too."

Thank fuck.

I press my lips to hers and pull her against me fully, enough that she can feel my cock stirring to life again. "I definitely think we should have some more fun when we get back to the cabin."

Her lips curl into a smile against mine. "Oh, yeah, most definitely."

* * *

BROOKE

The setting sun streaks through the tree tops, casting an ethereal orange-pink glow across the stunning winter land-scape, so stark in contrast to the pristine white of the snow untouched by anything but the occasional animal scampering across it.

Firing off as many shots as I can, I attempt to capture every single detail. Not just because it's beautiful enough to make any atheist believe in a higher power, but because I want to remember it exactly like this forever. I want to relive my time here with Beau anyway I can—the only time I can actually remember being happy in the last few years. Looking at these photos will do that, will give me an escape from an unknown future once I leave here and face whatever is coming for me.

Something tangible I can hold in my hand. Something *real* when I know there will be some nights and days I question whether this ever was.

"Hey, Brooke..."

I jerk my head to the side and find Beau standing where I left him several yards away—and I have no idea how long ago—leaning against a tree, casually watching me.

He inclines his head toward where we came out of the trees. "We need to get going."

"But I'm not done." I motion toward the sky. "I don't want to miss any of this lighting."

Beau glances up at the tops of the trees and out over the lake and smirks at me. "The lighting is exactly the problem. As soon as the sun sets, it's going to be pitch black in those trees, the kind of pitch black you can't even imagine, being from the city. It will be so dark you can't even see your hand in front of your face. Especially tonight when there won't be any moon."

"Shit."

I glance around the lake again. The long shadows continue to stretch out across the landscape, like fingers reaching out for something only they can see. And they are getting dangerously long. It makes for stunning photos, but we are out here without a flashlight or any other means of navigation.

"Plus, the temperature is going to start dropping like my fucking ax soon. We need to get inside before hypothermia or frostbite set in."

I take one last long, lingering look at the beautiful sunset and snap my final picture as Beau pushes off the tree and approaches.

"Don't look so sad. We can always come back tomorrow night if you really want more photos, or I can take you to a couple other places that would probably be incredible."

"Oh, that would be amazing. I want to get as much as I can. I haven't been this inspired by location in a really long time."

He heaves out a long, heavy breath and scans the frozen lake. "Yeah. It is definitely inspiring."

"Is that why you chose it?"

Beau turns back to me, his brow drawn low over his dark eyes. "Chose what? To bring you here?"

I shake my head. "No, chose here to build your cabin and as where you wanted to go to get away from whatever it was you wanted to get away from."

His shoulders stiffen as he contemplates my question. I truly can't blame him for his refusal to open up to me or tell me more of his secrets, more about what brought him up here in the first place, about those scars, but I guess I had thought maybe last night changed something.

Maybe.

And maybe he'll never reveal anything. It might be just as well. It might hurt a tiny bit less when I have to leave if I don't let things between us get even more personal.

Who the fuck am I kidding?

They already *are* too personal. Too close. Too involved. Too complicated.

If he learns the truth about why I'm here, he'll be devastated. Even if I wasn't leaving soon, all of this would come crumbling down faster than the gingerbread houses I always tried to build as a kid at Christmas.

Beau glances at the sky again and motions over his shoulder. "We need to go." He holds out his hand to take mine, but my attention is drawn back to the way the sunlight strikes the side of his face. I want to snap a picture of it so badly. I want to remember him looking like *this* in *this* light. But he said no photos, and I can't disrespect him by taking one just because I want to be able to look at it forever.

Instead, I turn and take a few more images of the last rays of the dying sun, but before I even know what's happening, I'm lifted from the ground and release a squeal. "What the hell, Beau?"

He throws me over his shoulder like I weigh nothing, letting me dangle with my face right near his perfect, hard ass while his strong arm tightens around my thighs, holding me in place. "I told you we had to go. You weren't moving. So, I'm moving you."

I smack him on the ass with my free hand. "Knock it off! I was going to leave. I just wanted a couple more photos."

Beau offers a snort and shakes his head.

"Let me down."

"I don't think so."

"You're going to carry me all the way back through the woods and across the property to the cabin like this?"

"Apparently so. You don't leave me much choice."

I growl at him and his laughter only confirms how ridiculous it sounds. His muscular body easily moves through the snow around the frozen lake, making our way back toward where we originally exited from the woods. I pull my head up and take one last look at the most beautiful place I've ever seen before he steps into the darkness of the tree cover.

The temperature drops fast and hard now that we're completely out of the sun, and a shiver runs through me despite the heat of Beau's body radiating up through his shoulder under me.

He squeezes his arm wrapped around my legs. "You cold?"

"No."

I refuse to admit he was right, that we probably should have left a half an hour ago to ensure we utilized the last lingering vestiges of daylight.

He snorts again and smacks my ass hard enough to make me yelp and almost drop my camera. "Maybe you should listen to me."

Annoyance burns through me, and I scoff and smack him again on the ass, so hard my palm actually stings this time.

Dammit.

I shake it out and glare even though he can't see it. "I don't appreciate you telling me what to do, *Beau.*"

"Yeah, I kind of gathered that, *Brooke.*"

"Grrrr!" I growl again, the only way I can express my frustration since there's no way I am getting out of his hold.

He just chuckles, shaking me gently. "You need to stop making that noise, darling, or you're going to have one very big problem when we walk into that cabin."

"Oh, really?"

"Uh huh."

Despite my annoyance at his Neanderthal behavior, only one response seems appropriate. "Well, you know I'm perfectly capable of handling big wood."

Chapter Fifteen

BROOKE

Beau kicks the door to the cabin closed behind us, stalks over to the couch—apparently not caring that he's tracking the snow from his boots all over his floor—and flips me off his shoulder and onto the leather.

I bounce lightly and let my jaw drop open incredulously. "I can't believe you just did that."

The man has the audacity to appear confused, his brow furrowing. "Did what?"

He can't seriously think I wouldn't have an issue with his performance out there.

Even after living without a woman around for a decade, surely Beau knows that type of behavior is going to lead to some sort of confrontation. Men don't just throw women over their shoulders and march through the woods with them anymore—at least, not where I'm from.

I jump to my feet and set my camera down on the end table so it doesn't accidentally get caught in the crossfire.

"You just threw me over your shoulder like a caveman and dragged me back to your 'cave.'"

Beau barks out a laugh and rubs a hand over his beard. "Well, doesn't that create a lovely mental picture..."

Crossing my arms over my chest, I issue a little *harrumph* noise, but all it manages to do is make Beau fight a smile. "I don't like it, Beau, not one bit."

He holds up his hands and retreats a step, but the slight curl of his lips tells me he still thinks this is funny. "Okay, okay. I get it."

I press a finger into his chest. "I could have walked."

"Yes, you *could* have but you didn't."

"Why do men always have to act like they control everything and they're the ones with all the answers so women should just fall in line and do whatever they're told?"

He recoils slightly, and regret over saying it settles on my chest the moment the words are out of my mouth and I witness his reaction.

Beau has definitely been a little bit bossy and short-tempered, but this is his house and I'm not even really a guest. I'm an intruder, one he rescued from certain death. So, he has every right to want things done a certain way and to want his privacy in certain regards.

Now I'm just projecting my own issues on him, when really, he has been a *relatively* good host and didn't mean anything negative by what he just did. He was being protective and playful—nothing more.

His gaze softens. "I'm sorry, Brooke. I didn't mean it like that. I was just trying to make sure we got back here before it got dark. You know when the most dangerous times of day are to be outside?"

Of course not.

I have zero wilderness skills and almost died the last

time I attempted to spend any time with Mother Nature. "I assume night because it gets so cold during the winter?"

"Dusk and nighttime. There are a lot of things that hunt once the sun goes down."

"Hunt?" The word sends another chill through me even though the cabin is relatively warm despite the fire dying down while we were away. "Aren't all the bears hibernating?"

"Yes, and it is rare for one of them to leave their den during this time, but when they do, it's usually because they're hungry. And you don't want to run into a hungry bear. But the bigger concern is cougars."

"Cougars? I'm going to assume you mean mountain lions and not older women on the prowl."

He grins before seriousness tightens his features. "They hunt at night, and they don't differentiate between a deer and human. If it has blood flowing through its veins and it's moving, they're going to go after it. I didn't have my gun with me"—he motions toward where it leans against the wall near the fire—"so, I didn't want to get stuck out by the lake."

"I'm sorry. I didn't mean to put us in a dangerous situation."

Seems to be the story of my fucking life.

"It's okay. You didn't know."

Apparently, I suck at avoiding dangerous situations. I suck at protecting myself from all different kinds of predators.

But I was *with* Beau, and if anyone knows this land and the dangers of it, it's him.

I prop my hands on my hips. "Still, you didn't have to throw me over your shoulder."

"You didn't like the view back there?" The corner of his

lips curls into a smile and any tension I created with my earlier comment melts away with it.

"It left a little to be desired."

One of his dark eyebrows slowly rises. "Oh, really?"

I chuckle and shake my head. "No. One thing you definitely do *not* have to worry about is how good your ass looks in a pair of jeans. Like I said...cover of GQ and all that."

He tenses again and his smile falters slightly, but he manages to hold it in place this time even though it now looks fake. Beau really doesn't like compliments or accept them well, and here I thought I was the one with issues.

The man saved my life. More than once.

Burying my own pride, I bite out the words. "And...you were right."

His brow furrows. "About what?"

"It did get really cold, and it was pretty damn dark out there."

"Dark enough that you probably would have gotten lost without me?" He raises an eyebrow at me, waiting for confirmation of what he already knows to be true.

There isn't any use denying it. When it comes to surviving up on the side of a damn mountain in the middle of winter, I don't have a fucking clue.

"Yes, okay, fine. Are you happy now? Happy that I'm admitting that you were right?"

He fights a grin at my incredulous tone. "It really pisses you off, doesn't it? That I was right."

I huff out a breath that flutters the hair on my forehead. "Yes."

Here I go projecting my own shit onto him again, but at least I realize it now. And he deserves an explanation for why it rankled me so badly.

Locking my gaze with his, I unleash a simple truth that

has been plaguing me for years and has only gotten worse in the recent past. "I feel like all my decisions have been wrong lately."

* * *

BEAU

The seriousness of her confession zaps all lingering humor from me in an instant. This entire situation just seems to be getting more and more complicated, and I never intended to make it more difficult for her. All I wanted was to keep her safe.

"Shit, I'm sorry. I wasn't—"

She holds up a hand to stop me. "I know you weren't. Really. It's okay. It's my issue, not yours. And I didn't mean I regret this"—she motions between us—"at all. I'm just...I don't know..."

Tell me about it...

My own head has been such a jumble since she stumbled into my life. *I don't know* seems about as apt a description for how I feel as any.

I reach out and drag her up against me. "I didn't mean to upset you. I just wanted to get you back here safe and sound in one piece, with all your fingers and toes intact and no more bouts of hypothermia."

A genuine smile pulls at her lips, and she wraps her arms around my neck. "You know...that night after I woke up, you told me that you had to strip me out of my wet clothes. I vividly remember when I asked you if you were naked, too, you kind of clammed up and just said 'body heat.'"

"I remember that, too."

All too vividly.

The first time I touched a woman in a decade or got mostly naked with one, it was purely to warm her up and save her life. That's not something one forgets easily.

"So..." She watches me expectantly with humor dancing in her green eyes. "Are you going to tell me now?"

I drag her even closer—impossibly close—so that our chests press against each other hard enough that I can feel her heartbeat against mine even through our jackets. Yet, somehow it isn't close enough.

"I stripped you down to just your underwear right here."

Though then, she was helpless, and now, she's anything but. This woman isn't afraid of me, isn't put off by my inability to engage with her like a normal human being all the time. She isn't scared of what a man who has lived alone for so long, isolated from humanity, might be capable of. Instead, she looks at me with expectant eyes, warm with affection and need.

I grab the zipper of her jacket and slowly lower it, then push it off her arms and let it fall to the floor. "Then, I got down to mine and pulled you in my arms on that bear skin rug in front of the fire..."

My fingers play at the hem of her shirt, making her suck in a sharp breath. I tug up the fabric gently, and she raises her arms to let me pull it off, exposing her black bra holding her absolutely perfect breasts.

"I wrapped a blanket around us..." I trail my finger from her collarbone down that flawless valley of porcelain skin, sending a shudder through her. "And I held you...for hours, until your lips lost that blue tint and you stopped shaking so violently, until I thought you had reached the point where your life was no longer in danger."

Though somehow, those hours seemed to last an entire lifetime. The longer I spent with her in my arms that day, the more the memories bombarded me—the good and the bad. The harder it became to push away the past and keep it, and my secrets, long buried.

She squeezes her eyes closed for a moment. "I remember it a little bit..." When she reopens them, true affection burns back at me. "I remember feeling warm and safe, like I could relax and stop running."

"I don't want you to have to run, Brooke. I did it a long time ago. Look where it got me."

"This place is beautiful, Beau. I can't believe how beautiful it is."

"It definitely has its perks. But..." I trail off because there isn't any way to say it without telling her something I shouldn't. "Never mind. I think we had discussed having some fun when we got back."

I waggle my eyebrows playfully, hoping to distract her from the direction the conversation was heading in. She eyes me warily for a second, looking like she's about to redirect me exactly where I don't want to go, but instead, she pushes up on her tiptoes and presses a kiss to my lips.

Her hands snake down between us and cup my hard cock through my jeans. "I can definitely think of something fun I want to do."

"Oh, yeah?" I ask against her lips. "What's that?"

"You'll see..." The playfulness returns to her eyes and her words, and she sets to work pulling off my jacket and shirt. Her hands play at the waistband of my jeans, and I grab her wrist to stop her. She just grins at me and pulls her hand from my grip to unbutton and unzip them, letting my aching cock spring free.

Fuck.

Brooke bends down to untie her boots and kicks them toward the front door, then backs up until she's directly in front of the fireplace, the bear skin rug under her feet. She motions for me to come over to her with a crooked finger.

Good God, she's beautiful.

Honey-blond hair flowing around her shoulders, evergreen eyes flashing with mischief and lust, her breasts heaving in their lacy confines.

I can't get to her fast enough and tug off my boots and jeans while she throws a few more logs on the fire to get it roaring again. Though, I doubt we'll need its heat this time. An inferno already rages through my body. More than a desire for this woman: an inherent need that terrifies me more than any predator out there in the darkness.

Her eyes lock on me as I approach, and her tongue darts out to wet her lips.

Oh, fuck. She's serious.

I haven't had a woman's mouth around my cock in a decade. If I thought last night was embarrassing, this will be even worse. Just thinking about her wrapping her mouth around me makes my dick jump in anticipation.

She reaches out and takes my hand, dragging me the final step to the rug, and sinks to her knees. The fire builds beside us, the flames catching on the newly added logs and creating an orange-red glow that covers her face as she wraps her hand around the base of my cock and sucks my length into her mouth.

"Oh, good God."

I dig my fingers into her thick hair and tangle them in the silky tresses. Her tongue glides along my flesh and flicks at the head, making my hips buck and driving me even deeper down her throat.

"Fuck."

She moans her approval and swallows, the motion cocooning my cock even more in the heat and wetness of her mouth.

"Jesus, Brooke, I can't—"

Her hand around my length tightens and strokes me harder, in time with her sucking vise-like lips. Instinctively I push even deeper, driving my cock into her mouth over and over, fucking it with a reckless abandon while she moans around my flesh.

It only takes a second for me to lose complete control. "Fuck, Brooke."

I come down her throat, my body jerking, my fingers twisting into her hair to hold me steady and keep me upright on legs that want to give out with the sheer power of my release.

Last night, I thought I had found Heaven on Earth for a few hours, but this was truly ethereal, like I was lifted from my body and left behind all the rage and pain that have consumed me for so damn long.

I finally stop my hips, and she pulls her mouth from around me, licks her swollen lips, and grins up at me with pride glowing in her gaze.

She's far more dangerous than I ever could have known.

Chapter Sixteen

BEAU

Even after I've spent a decade alone up here, waking up without Brooke beside me in the bed immediately feels wrong. I push myself up onto my elbow and scan the still-dark room for her, but the cool sheets beside me mean she's been up for a while—definitely not the routine she's had since she got here.

I glance toward the window to find only the faintest hint of light coming through it—that strange time just before dawn, when the world is just starting to wake up but hasn't fully yet.

Did she have trouble sleeping?

I sure as hell didn't. Not after the hour we spent out on the rug before we ate and then came in here for the rest of the night and wrapped up in each other. That, coupled with all the chopping I did yesterday, left my body achy and sore. Stretching my arms above my head, I lean side to side, my lower back twinging from all the recent activity.

Some days, this body really feels fucking old and broken.

I'd much rather be working out some tension another way and had even planned to spend a little extra time in bed this morning with Brooke instead of getting up at the ass-crack of dawn, but it seems that woman has other plans.

And she's certainly changed mine.

If she hadn't wandered into my life, I would have spent the storm holed up next to the fire, reading, and probably drinking far too much good booze that I won't be able to replenish for a while. But that blizzard brought more with it than just snow, it brought something I never wanted, never thought I could have.

Something that I'm going to lose in a day or two.

Which means I shouldn't be wasting what little time I have left with her.

I climb from the bed, tug on a pair of jeans and a T-shirt, and open the bedroom door. A familiar caramelized, nutty scent hits me immediately. Not only is she up, but she's already made coffee.

A man could get used to this...

Exactly the problem.

It's better that she's leaving so soon. In the long run, staying here for even a few extra days would only make it so much harder for me to return to how I was living before and for her to go find whatever it is she's ultimately looking for.

I run a hand over my face and make my way into the kitchen only to find it empty, save for the pot of brewed coffee.

There aren't many other places she could be. I glance toward the office door, but it's closed—just as it should be. She wouldn't go in there again, anyway. Not when she promised not to. My eyes are drawn to the roaring fire she must have tended when she woke, and I start to turn away from it and toward the front door, but stop and whirl back toward the fireplace.

Oh, my God.

Mom's vase occupies a place of honor on the mantle, cracked and a bit worse for wear, but standing together in one piece, nonetheless. I approach it slowly, my throat tightening.

Brooke...

She must have dug the broken pieces out of the trash can and glued it back together. Tears burn my eyes, and I brush them away and reach out to touch the vase, then jerk my hand back, afraid it might still be too fragile for handling.

Massive cracks run through it, marring what was once a flawless glazed surface. The irony of her piecing it back together isn't lost on me, and the enormity of her gesture simultaneously crushes any hope I had of remaining ambivalent to her leaving and also buoys my need to find her.

I glance at the front door, my heart willing me outside where she must be. After our conversation yesterday, hopefully she's not stupid enough to go out to take photos alone, but there isn't anywhere else she could be except outside.

That woman deserves a huge thank you.

And then some...

I tug on my boots and jacket, pour myself a cup of coffee, and step out into the chilly morning air. Though still surrounded by the dark of pre-dawn, I can just make out that one of the barn doors stands open, a sliver of artificial light coming from it, spilling out onto the packed down snow.

Maybe she went to try to get the eggs?

I chuckle and take a sip of my coffee as I make my way

toward the barn. Brooke better be up for a fight with the girls. My guess is she'll receive a few pecks for her efforts.

Just picturing her wrestling with the angered hens makes me grin. It wasn't easy for me, either, when I first came up here, and I have my fair share of stories about how I learned my lessons with the animals.

I approach the open barn door and find Brooke squatting in front of the chicken pen toward the back corner, whispering something to Betty Sue and Joanne. Her brow furrowed, she gestures with her hands as if she's talking to another human—which doesn't make me doing it seem so crazy anymore.

At least, comparatively.

Leaning against one of the posts just inside the door, I watch her for a minute and sip my coffee.

Her words float over to me. "So, don't worry. I'm not trying to steal your man or anything like that."

I can't fight the laugh that bursts from my lips, and Brooke jerks to her feet and spins toward me, her hand pressed to her chest.

"Oh, my God, you scared the crap out of me. I thought I heard something earlier and have been jumpy as hell ever since."

I grin at her and take a sip of my coffee. "Sorry. I was surprised you were already gone from bed this morning."

She sighs and runs her hands back through her slightly disheveled hair. "Yeah, I woke up about two hours ago and just couldn't fall back to sleep."

I approach her slowly. "You could have woken me up. I can think of a few ways we could have passed the time this morning."

A pink flush creeps up her neck and across her cheeks, and she dips her head and averts her gaze. "Yeah, I can, too, but you looked so peaceful. And I figured after all the work you did yesterday, you could use the sleep."

I finish the rest of my coffee and set the cup on the edge of the fence post so that I can pull her into my arms and kiss her properly, pouring all my confusion and appreciation for what she did into it. When we finally come back up for air, I cradle her face between my palms, and she grins up at me.

"I saw what you did. The vase..."

"Oh, yeah, I'm sorry it doesn't look very good. I did my best but—"

"But nothing." I kiss her again, softly, barely brushing my lips to hers. "Thank you. You have no idea how much that means to me that you did that."

Or how much it has confused everything.

She offers me a tiny smile. "It's the least I could do after bashing you over the head with it."

I press my lips to hers again, in a lazy kiss that suggests we have all the time in the world, but a series of frantic clucks behind me breaks the spell. I pull away and turn toward the pen, eying the hens with my arm wrapped around Brooke's shoulder. "Are the girls being nice to you?"

Brooke glances at the chickens and shrugs. "I haven't gone in yet. Almost as soon as I tried to open the gate, they both started squawking and charging at me and running around all crazy."

I chuckle and shake my head, watching Joanne and Betty Sue scurry around, all out of sorts. "I'm not surprised. I told you they can be a little demanding."

She glances over at the goat pen. "What about the goats? Should I try to milk them?"

I bark out a laugh and watch them nervously move around their pen. "Only if you want to get kicked or bitten."

Her brows rise. "Wow, your animals are violent."

"No, they just don't know you."

They were the same way with me when I first got them, and it would take a while for them to be comfortable enough with her to allow her to do these things.

And she's not going to be here long enough for that.

A vise tightens around my chest at that thought, and to avoid thinking about it any further in this moment, I pull away from her and open the chicken pen. "I'll grab the eggs so we can make breakfast."

"Okay." Brooke shoves her hands in the pockets of her jacket and stands watching me as I greet the girls and make my way to the coop to get their eggs, despite unusual protests on their part.

Brooke's presence really got them riled up. It's been a long time since I've seen them like this.

I shoo away Joanne and grab the eggs, then turn back toward Brooke and freeze. The eggs fall from my hands and shatter on the hard ground with a sickening splat.

Her eyes widen. "What's wrong?"

Jesus Christ...

All the time I've been up here, all the mornings I've come out and milked the goats and gotten eggs from the chickens, and not once have I seen a cougar.

Now one stands just behind the stack of wood I store on the other side of the barn. It must have slipped in behind Brooke this morning without her even noticing it.

I thought I heard something earlier and have been jumpy as hell ever since...

It was the cougar moving around in the darkness, stalking its prey.

"Don't move. There's a cougar on the other side of the barn."

Had I not caught that brief glimpse of its eyes reflecting

the light from the overhead bulb in the center of the building, it might have launched an attack without us ever seeing it coming.

It explains why the chickens and goats are so jumpy. Caged animals always seem to know when a predator is lurking and they have no way to get away from it.

"What?" Brooke whips her head to the side to look for it, her eyes widening even more, her entire body shaking. "Where?"

"Behind the wood pile. Turn to face it, then don't move."

"Oh, my God..." Panic makes her voice waver. "But what do I do?"

"Don't move."

The cat takes a step forward, keeping to the shadows on the other side of the barn, far away from the ring of light the bulb provides. It's stalking Brooke as it would any other prey, likely because she stands between it and the easier kills of the chickens and goats.

I cautiously take a step forward, then another, but the cat's focus appears to be on Brooke.

Goddamnit.

My shotgun is still inside the cabin, and there's no way I could sneak out and get it and make it back in here without triggering an attack from that thing.

One thing I learned very early on living up here is that when encountering a cougar, you have to make yourself seem bigger and unafraid. Face it down, remain calm, never give it your back, and *never ever* run because you *will* lose that race.

I need to get this fucker out of here.

Our only hope is my ax resting against the woodpile, only a few feet from the threat itself. I can try to get to it, but it will mean moving away from Brooke. If the cat attacks, I won't be able to protect her from it, won't be able to get in the way or make any attempts to fight it off.

It's a chance I have to take.

Otherwise, we're just sitting ducks.

Keeping my eyes locked on what I can see of the cat in the shadows—really, little more than a faint pale outline of its pointed ears and reflecting eyes—I slip from inside the pen and inch my way into the darkness of the wall closest to me.

Only a few yards separate me from the woodpile, the cougar, and our salvation.

Please God, let this work. If anything happens to Brooke...

My breath catches in my chest as the possibilities race through my head. I thought what happened ten years ago killed any will I had left inside me to live, but if Brooke gets hurt, I know that will truly be the end.

* * *

BROOKE

My legs shake so badly that it feels like they might give out from under me, like I might drop to the cold, hard earthen ground in this barn and never get back up. It's what my body wants to do. It wants to submit. It wants to give up. But I lock my knees and keep my eyes focused dead ahead, toward the shadows on the far side of the barn, where the big cat stalks me.

I know fear. I've felt the worst of its hold, experienced thinking I would lose my life to the worst kind of animal there is, and its familiar grip takes me now, threatening to drop me to my knees.

Only Beau's words keep me standing.

Face it.

Don't move.

Standing here, waiting to be attacked, my entire life flashes before my eyes. Mom working double-shifts at the diner to put a roof over our heads. High school. Discovering my love for photography. Falling in love.

Every mistake.

Every triumph.

Every friend.

Every foe.

Every damn choice I've made that brought me to this exact moment.

I might die here today, in this small barn, on this vast property up a desolate mountain, miles and miles and miles from civilization, but I'm not sure I can regret anything that got me here. Not when I've had the best few days of my life.

Please don't be my last...

A flash of movement out of the corner of my eye makes me turn my head slightly, and Beau presses his back to the wall at the far side of the barn and starts inching his way around toward the pile of wood he added to just yesterday.

God...

Things seemed so simple then, when I woke up yesterday morning. Yes, they were still damn complicated, but we managed to push that aside long enough to have another brilliant night.

Now...I'd give anything to go back, to stay in bed with him this morning rather than come out here. To think I was actually doing something to help. All I've done is put our lives in danger.

I'm not cut out for this place. Not meant for this type of life. It's a nice dream, a fantasy I can cling to when I need to escape the anguish of reality. But that's all it is—a fantasy. Beau's life and world, not mine.

It can never be real.

Beau motions for me to keep my eyes on the cat, and I return my gaze to where I last saw it, but the darkness of that corner of the barn makes it impossible for me to tell if it's moved.

These cats are expert stalkers and hunters. I don't know much but I know that. And I was so oblivious to the potential danger this morning that I let it slip right in behind me.

It's the only time it could have gotten in here. There's no way Beau wouldn't have spotted it or heard it if it came in after him. It was already inside, hiding behind the wood when Beau arrived, waiting for an opportunity to strike at me or the animals Beau depends on so much.

My fault. All my fault.

One more reason I don't belong here. I didn't just bring danger to myself; I brought it to Beau and the animals he loves.

And there's a very real chance Beau is going to get hurt with what he's attempting. Dread sits like a rock in my stomach, getting heavier with each step Beau takes.

He makes it to within three feet of the ax, but a low hiss from the darkness just to the left of the weapon sends him skittering back a step. I try to track him in my peripheral vision without taking my eyes off the cougar, but I'm not so sure what good it will do even if I do see it coming for me.

I have no way to stop it, no weapon or innate strength that might help me fight it off. The most I can hope for is that it would be a quick death, that the cat would go for my jugular and end things fast.

Beau lunges forward and grabs the ax, his fast motion bringing a snarl from our adversary.

It knows he's here now, but I don't know enough about cats or wild animals at all to know whether that's a good thing or a bad thing. My guess is bad given the noise it's making. It hisses and snarls again and takes a step further toward the lit part of the barn until I can finally see its pointy ears sticking up and its bared teeth.

Oh, my God.

Beau approaches me slowly, walking sideways, never taking his eyes off the threat.

I peek at him. "What are you going to do?"

He keeps his focus across the barn. "I'm going to try to get it the hell out of here."

"And if you can't?"

He casts a furtive glance my way. "Then I'll deal with it any way I have to."

Placing himself between me and the cat, Beau leaps forward and swings the ax in a huge arc through the air. "Out. Go."

The cat hisses and retreats a step but doesn't move toward the door.

Beau swings again, spinning the blade wider, making himself seem even bigger. "I said go! Get the fuck out of here!"

He wields the ax expertly, swirling it high and wide, but all it does is seem to piss off the animal. The cougar charges at us so fast that all I see is a blur of pale fur and Beau swinging the ax.

It barely misses the cat but sends it scurrying back a few steps. Its haunches raised, it bares its teeth and snarls again —pissed but unwilling to give up a potential meal of either me or the poor animals in here.

Beau maneuvers the weapon again, sweeping it high and low, advancing on the cat fast and without hesitation, the blade barely missing each time. The cougar scampers backward, then finally darts toward the open barn door, and slinks out into the pale morning light.

My legs give out, and I collapse on my knees in the dirt. Beau rushes toward the door and secures it before racing back over to me and dropping the ax to the ground. He pulls me onto his lap, his warm arms enveloping me, his chest heaving, heart racing against mine.

His lips pressed to my temple, he squeezes me tightly. "Are you okay?"

"Oh, my God...it-it was going to kill me."

He releases a deep breath and glances around the barn. "It probably smelled the chickens and the goats when you opened the barn and followed the scent. You were just between it and its original target."

"Is it going to wait out there for us?" The image of the cat lingering in the shadows and pouncing as soon as we step out that door makes me flinch.

"No." Beau pulls me in even tighter and buries his face against my hair. "Now the sun's coming up. They don't like to be out in daylight very much. Especially not hunting."

"Did you hit him with the ax?"

He shakes his head and assesses the weapon. "No, with cougars, it's all about appearing big and unafraid. Letting them know that you're the alpha and that this is your territory."

I pull away and stare up at him, his eyes glistening with unshed tears. "Will it come back, though?"

His jaw hardens. "It might now that it knows there's prey here, but this building is secure. The only way in is that door, and I always keep it barricaded unless I'm in here.

And I always have a weapon—either my gun or my ax —near me."

A sob rips from my chest, and I bury my face against his strong one. "I was going to die. I was going to die."

Flashes of a not-so-distant memory mingle with this new one. The terror the same. The adversary so different.

"Shh." Beau pushes to his feet with me cradled in his arms. "It's okay, I've got you."

His words barely register. The fear in my chest tightens it so badly that I can barely draw in a breath.

"Just breathe, Brooke." He presses a kiss to my temple and carries me toward the door, pausing for only a moment before he slowly eases it open and glances out.

The sun crests over the trees to the east, and warm morning sunlight spills out across the white pristine space between the barn and the cabin.

"It's safe. That cat probably ran away as fast as its feet would carry it."

"It's not safe. It's never going to be safe." Another sob rips from my lips, shattering the silent stillness of the morning. "I'm never going to be safe."

"I got you, Brooke. I won't let anything happen to you. I promise."

That's a promise I know he can't keep.

Chapter Seventeen

BEAU

Night fully descends on the mountain before Brooke finally stops trembling. The pitch blackness outside never scared me, never made me fearful of living up here alone, it never kept me lying awake in bed, but tonight, it's different—so different that I barely recognize it.

It conceals a danger now, one I always knew was lurking, one I had seen evidence of, but now that I've stared it down, face-to-face, can hear the threatening hiss and growl every time I close my eyes, everything looks so different.

Staring out the bedroom window into the utter darkness surrounding the cabin, a sense of dread settles heavily on my chest, and I reach up and rub at it, right on the spot one of the scars has occupied the last ten years.

Every rattle of the blowing wind. Every creak the cabin makes. Every flash of movement of the shadows in the shadows only makes it worse.

I turn toward the bed where Brooke sits against the headboard watching me carefully.

Though she's finally stopped shaking, her foot still bounces up and down nervously. "See anything?"

I shake my head, running my hands over my face, and squeezing my tired eyes closed. "No, but even if it did come back, it can't get in here and we have the gun."

They're the same words I've spent the entire day saying to her, but they don't seem to make any more of an impact now than they have the other times I've said them.

The claws of fear have dug themselves into her so tightly that the terror won't let her go. It won't let her relax despite me trying everything from warm tea, to liquor, to a long hot shower, to just holding her and telling her everything will be all right.

This is about more than the confrontation with the big cat. This is the same kind of fear she had with the nightmare; a soul-crushing type of fear that no amount of rational thinking can eliminate.

I stand next to the bed and stare down at her, so fragile and small, not the other woman I've seen over the last few days who stands up for herself and calls me out on my bullshit.

The words she kept repeating float through my head.

It's not safe. It's never going to be safe. I'm never going to be safe.

Brooke truly believes that. Even though I've promised her nothing can get to us in here, that nothing will touch her, she still believes those words she uttered at the height of her terror.

She pulls her knees up against her chest and rests her chin on them, staring at some unknown spot on the comforter that has suddenly become very interesting.

"Brooke, look at me."

It's a simple request, but she doesn't comply right away. She squeezes her eyes closed for a moment, like she's gathering strength or trying to prevent herself from breaking down again, before she turns her head and rests her cheek on her knee facing me.

"What?"

"I'm not going to let anything happen to you. You're safe here. Do you believe that?"

She pulls her lip between her teeth and considers my words. Tears re-form in her eyes.

"Please don't cry, Brooke. It's over. You're okay. I'm okay. The goddamn goats and chickens are okay."

They were still shaken up when I checked on them later in the morning, but they'll be fine. Brooke, I'm not so sure about.

A sob bubbles up her throat, and her body resumes the trembling we only managed to get under control an hour ago. "I know." She holds up a hand almost as if in apology. "I know that. I just...can't seem to make it stop."

"Make what stop?" I slide onto the bed next to her, wrap my arm around her shoulder, and pull her up against me.

"The fear. The shaking. The tears. Any of it."

I press my palm against her cheek and turn her face toward me. "It's okay to be scared, but you can't let it consume you. It's my fault..."

"What?" She shakes her head. "No."

"It is. I should have prepared you better for being up here, for what you might face. For how to handle yourself if you were on your own and something happened. I should have warned you what to look for, to always be alert. It was my mistake, not yours. And now, it's left you like this."

Exactly why she doesn't belong here.

This is no place for a woman like Brooke. No place for anyone, really.

It's too rugged.

Too raw.

Too untamed.

To just throw someone into this life isn't realistic.

"No, Beau." She wipes away the tears and takes a deep breath in and out, which seems to calm her a little bit. "It isn't your fault. I should have just stayed in bed with you. I should have lain here and let you hold me, left the world outside, all the people and the dangerous animals, to their own devices."

The corners of my mouth turn up. "There's always tomorrow."

"That sounds like a good plan." The tiniest of grins finally breaks across her lips.

"Yeah, it does sound like a good plan, and I have an even better one for right now."

Her eyebrows arch up. "Oh, yeah?"

"Yeah."

"What is it?"

I lean in and press my lips to hers, then pull away and kiss across her damp cheek to her ear. Brushing my lips against the lobe, I inhale her scent and think about what I've been dying to do for days.

"I was thinking of a way to distract you. From everything plaguing your mind."

Brooke shifts against me slightly, her hand sliding over my shoulder and up the back of my neck. "Distraction is good."

Her heart pounds against my chest, and I pull her ear lobe between my lips and nip gently. She groans and jerks under me, clinging to my shoulders as I move over her and press her down into the mattress, covering her with my body.

My mouth finds hers, and she smiles against my lips.

"I like this distraction idea."

"Mmm...me, too." I settle between her legs, the T-shirt she wears giving me access to push my hardening cock to the apex of her thighs.

She reaches down to grab me, but I catch her wrist before her hand reaches my waistband. I kiss her again, sliding my tongue into her mouth, tasting a hint of the bourbon she drank earlier. Then I press a kiss to her palm and slowly reach for the hem of her shirt.

"Not yet, Sleeping Beauty."

Her mouth opens like she wants to ask me a question or object to me stopping her, but I silence it with another kiss and lift the shirt over her head, exposing her flawless pale skin.

I kiss my way down her long, elegant neck and over both of her breasts, stopping to swirl my tongue around each stiff peak. The attention makes her squirm beneath me, raising her hips up, seeking something I intend to give her—just not yet.

Every flick and swirl of my tongue over her nipples makes her tense under me and clench her thighs. I work my way lower, relishing the heat of her skin and how responsive she is to my touch.

By the time I've settled between her legs, with her sprawled out on the bed open for me, she's a panting wet mess. I drag my finger through the glistening arousal coating her pussy lips and up around her clit, and she bucks her hips off the bed.

I press my palm flat against her stomach and ease her

back down, then drop my head and slowly drag my tongue through her cunt to finally taste the most exquisite thing I've ever experienced in my life.

* * *

BROOKE

Beau glides his tongue across my pussy and up around my clit, sending a wave of pleasure coursing through me strong enough to make my vision blur. His beard rubbing against my inner thighs, abrading the sensitive skin there so beautifully, creates the greatest sensation of pleasure and pain. One I'll always remember.

I bury my hands in his thick, dark hair and cling to it as he probes me with his tongue deep inside, trying to devour me whole.

Even though we were almost just eaten by a wild animal, this isn't like that. This feels like more of a branding, of Beau somehow staking his claim that my pussy belongs to him and him alone. It's Beau wanting to drink me in the same way I did him in front of the fire last night.

He slips a thick finger inside me, curling it up to find that magical place inside that always sends my head spinning. I moan and drag my nails along his scalp, earning a contented groan against my wet flesh as he pumps that finger in and out of me and lashes at my clit.

If this is Beau's idea of a distraction, then I'm perfectly happy to let him distract me forever, or at least until we can't be distracted anymore, until the real world finds our little isolated spot and finally knocks on that door and tells me it's time to leave.

I cling to him like my life depends on it. Now, as much

as the day he found me, or this morning, Beau is a lifeline, a safe place to land. Where I can find true bliss and contentment. A one-in-a-million kind of guy who literally gets down on his knees to worship me.

And worship me, he does.

He prays at the altar of my pussy, licking and sucking and probing me in a steady rhythm that builds me up quickly and sends my orgasm crashing down over me violently. I tense at the overwhelming sensations wracking my body, and my hips buck up, driving my pussy against his face even harder. Far from deterred, Beau holds me steady with one hand while using the other to continue to drag on my orgasm, never stopping, even for a breath, before he sets to work, trying to force me into a second release—one I'm not sure I'm capable of.

"Oh, oh, God. It's-it's too much. I can't. I—"

Beau flicks the tip of his tongue across my clit, and my entire body jerks. He drags his head back and looks up at me with lust-soaked whiskey eyes. "We aren't done with our diversion yet, Brooke. We're far from it."

Oh, God.

And here I thought Beau was the one protecting me. When really, he might be the one who ends me.

He drops his head again and sets to work building me up again until he sucks my clit between his lips and pulses it hard, sending me skyrocketing off to the stars again. I thrash under him, simultaneously wanting more and wanting to push him away to avoid the overwhelming sensation.

When I finally start coming back down, he shifts up the bed, pushing his sweat pants down and freeing his hard cock. His eyes locked with mine, he settles between my legs and eases into me slowly.

Not like the other night.

Not like last night.

Not hard and fast.

Not animalistic and basic.

Not two people fucking away the tension and stress.

This is something else. Something so much worse for us.

He draws his hips back and slowly plunges into me again, capturing my mewl with a languid kiss and holding my face in his palm as he braces himself up on his other arm. "You are so beautiful when you come, Brooke. I could do that all day, every day, and die a happy man."

Oh, God.

He can't say things like that to me. He can't make me consider the possibility that it could be real, that there's any chance of this ever happening again anytime in the future.

He can't.

But I can't get the words out, can't bring myself to shatter this illusion we've built. Only a strangled groan rips from my lips as he rolls his hips and grinds his pelvis against my hypersensitive, overworked clit.

"Fuck...Beau, I—"

"Shh." He silences me with another kiss and shifts his hips to alter the angle and change the friction, hitting me in a way that makes my head drop back on a gasp.

"Oh, God. Right there."

The head of his cock drags against just the right spot for those stars to dance against my closed lids.

My body starts to coil again, building to something I'm not sure I'm ready for or that I'll ever survive.

I cling to his shoulders, my nails digging into the hard muscle there. "Please, Beau. *Please!*"

He brushes his lips over mine and kisses me deeply, pressing his body tightly against mine as he continues to move in cresting rhythm. "Tell me. Tell me what."

"I want you..."

They're the same words I said to him the other night, but they mean something completely different this time. Something more. Something I know I can never have.

A tear leaks from my eye and trickles down my temple, and he increases his pace and starts driving me closer to the edge. I dangle off the precipice, fighting both to jump over it and to stay here, knowing that either way, I'm going to lose. Either way, I have to.

Dropping his lips against my ear, Beau's heavy, hot breaths tickle the hair against my neck. "That's it, Brooke. You're right there. Come for me again. I want to feel you clenching around my cock and hear you say my name."

"Oh, God. Oh, God."

He rolls his hips and tilts the angle slightly, and I arch my hips up to meet his.

It's all it takes to finally push me over. Bowing up against him, my body jerking and spasming, I fight to keep my eyes open, to watch him find his release through my own. He grits his teeth, his neck muscles straining, and plunges into me one more time before he gasps and sags against me, pressing his face into my neck.

We lie together for a moment, each of us trying to catch our breaths, and Beau slowly pushes up onto one elbow and locks his gaze on me.

"Stay..."

"What?"

My orgasm-fogged brain must be hearing things and having a hard time processing words.

"Stay, Brooke." He shakes his head. "Shit. I know this is terrible timing. Especially given what happened today. And there are things we obviously need to talk about, things we need to work out, but..."

He trails off and stares into my eyes, searching for an answer that I'm not sure I can give him. Instead, I lean up and press my lips to his, the only answer I'm capable of in the moment because no matter how much I want to stay, it might not be up to me.

Chapter Eighteen

BEAU

A pulsating noise shatters the silence of the bedroom, jerking me awake to a room far brighter than it typically is when I get up. I blink rapidly, tilting my head, trying to place the sound from outside.

Soft at first, the longer I sit and listen, the louder it becomes, moving closer to the cabin. Something oddly familiar about it tickles at the back of my mind.

It takes a minute for my sleepy brain to process it, and Brooke shifts in the bed next to me and sits up, squinting and looking toward the window.

"What is that noise?"

Shit. Something I know all too well.

My spine stiffens, and I roll away from her and out of bed to dress quickly. "A helicopter."

Her eyebrows fly up. "A helicopter? What would it be up here for?"

I nod and move for the door, ignoring the second half of her question.

There are only two possibilities—either Nate finally got sick of my refusals to come to speak to the board and decided to come up himself to drag me back, kicking and screaming, or Sheriff Roberts borrowed it from Brewster to get up here because the roads still aren't passable.

Since there isn't any emergency to bring law enforcement up the mountain, I can't imagine he would occupy such a precious resource, which means it's likely Nate bringing a problem I don't need or want.

I could try to keep Brooke inside, away from him, away from the inevitable questions he will bring—the things I intend to tell her eventually—but she's too stubborn to do that, to do what she's told and stay in bed. It's better if I have some control over the situation, if she's there with me.

Stepping into the hall, I call over my shoulder to her. "Get dressed. We'll meet it outside."

The chopper only grows louder with its approach, until it must be almost directly over the house, the sound of my old favored mode of transportation making my ears ring.

I tug on my jacket and boots, and Brooke emerges from the bedroom in her clothes, her eyes watery and unfocused. She twists her hands together in front of her, shifting nervously and glancing toward the windows at the front of the cabin.

Pausing, I turn back to her. "You okay?"

She gives me a sharp nod even though she looks far from okay.

It's been a traumatic and emotional twenty-four hours for her, from the cougar attack to what happened between us last night, so throwing another surprise in the mix is sure to unsettle her a little.

"I'm sure everything is fine, Brooke."

It's the only thing I can think to say when I have no clue

211

why Nate would show up unannounced. The situation with the board and the new environmental bill shouldn't require a personal visit, and even if it *did* and he couldn't get through to me because the cell towers are down, he knows to radio the sheriff's department to relay any messages.

I grab the door handle and open it, letting in the sound that's almost deafening after so long without the typical noises of the outside world permeating these walls. "Throw on your boots and coat."

Shielding my eyes from the morning sun, I squint at the helicopter as it comes down to land in the clearing to the left of the cabin. Only, it isn't Nate. That isn't one of the company choppers, which means it must be the sheriff.

What the hell is going on?

Brooke steps out of the cabin, stands next to me, and shivers—maybe from the chill in the air made worse from the wind kicked up by the rotating blades, or maybe from the lingering trauma of what happened yesterday.

The door on the helicopter slides open, and Sheriff Jim Roberts climbs from inside, followed by one of his deputies. Two more stay in the chopper, watching us with hard, accusatory eyes.

Jim ducks and holds his hat, hustling as fast as he can through the snow toward us. He offers me a tight smile and stops a few feet away from me, eyeing Brooke, as does the deputy beside him.

"I wasn't expecting to see you today, Sheriff."

"Hey, Beau." He inclines his head toward me in greeting. "I hadn't expected to be up here today. The roads are still pretty much blocked once you get out of town. We only managed to get to where her vehicle died, but under the circumstances, this couldn't really wait until we could get all the way up here."

"Under the circumstances?" I raise an eyebrow at him, a deep sense of foreboding tightening my chest. "What the hell are you talking about?"

He glances at Brooke before refocusing on me again. "Let's just say I'm happy to find you in one piece."

"In one piece? I'm a little lost here."

The sheriff compresses his lips together into a thin line and motions with his head for his deputy to move next to Brooke. "You'll understand in a minute."

The dutiful deputy pulls Brooke's hands behind her, while Jim steps directly in front of her.

"Brookelynn Ann Neal, I'm placing you under arrest for the murder of Tommy Baker. You have the right to remain silent. Anything you say can and will be used against you in a court of law. You have a right to an attorney—"

Arrest?

Murder?

His words finally register, and I shake my head. "Whoa! Wait a minute...murder? What the hell are you talking about?"

The deputy continues to cuff Brooke, despite my protestation, tightening one side then the other around her wrists.

Tears roll down her cheeks to her quivering lips. "I'm so sorry, Beau." She pleads at me with sorrowful green eyes but doesn't protest or make any attempt to interfere with the deputy. "It isn't what it looks like."

Sheriff Roberts offers me an apologetic look. "I ran the plates on her vehicle and discovered a BOLO for it and a warrant out of Seattle for *her*. She apparently shot her boyfriend and then fled immediately after and came up here to avoid capture."

"No." Brooke shakes her head, a sob escaping her. "Beau, that isn't what happened. I—"

"Stop!" I hold up a hand to stop both her and the sheriff from continuing.

A sharp pain stabs at the base of my skull, and I rub at it and squeeze my eyes closed, trying to get some grasp on what's going on around me.

Murder.

This can't be fucking happening.

This can't be right.

I force my eyes open and turn to Jim. "There has to be some mistake. I know Brooke. She wouldn't do something like this."

Jim narrows his eyes at me, the blue sharp as ice. "She's been up here a week and you know her well enough to know if she would commit murder or not?" He offers me an incredulous but almost sympathetic look. "I'm sorry, Mr. Beaumont, but I think this might be a situation in which you need to reassess your beliefs about what you think you know about her."

"Oh, my God..." Brooke's eyes widen at his words, her tears continuing to fall. "Mr. *Beaumont?* As in...*the* Beaumonts? Beaumont Lumber?"

Fuck.

I didn't even notice he used my full name. Brooke being arrested for murder has apparently eliminated my ability to comprehend what's happening and being said around me.

"Oh, shit." Sheriff Roberts holds up his hands. "I'm sorry, Beau. I didn't mean to—"

I cast a glare at him that shuts him up instantly. His deputy assesses me with wide eyes. It's only a matter of time before this information gets spread around faster than herpes.

Keeping things quiet and remaining anonymous has been at the top of my priority list since I came up here, and now, it's all gone to hell because of Brooke—who has been *lying* to me since the moment she got here.

Even about her damn *name.*

I point at the deputy, hoping I can at least make an *attempt* to stop the spread of the information. "You keep that shit to yourself." Then I turn to Brooke, who still gawks at me as if she's seeing me for the first time. "You've been keeping some pretty important information from me."

Her mouth opens and closes, like she's searching for any form of response she can make to my statement, any way to defend herself. Tears flow down her cheeks again. "It seems we both have a few secrets, doesn't it?"

* * *

BROOKE

Beau.

> *Luke freaking Beaumont.*
> *God, I am so stupid!*

The cabin that felt just a little too luxurious for such a remote location. The beautiful kitchen. The expensive solar system. The antique desk and book collection. The goddamn vase he told me was priceless—which probably is. A family company. People thinking he wasn't fulfilling his obligations to it...

> *Oh, my God.*
> *The scars...*

It explains so much. It explains *everything.* Yet, leaves

so many damn questions I'll never get the answer to now. The Beaumonts are the Kennedys of the West Coast. They built an empire while most of the country was still in its infancy.

Why did he come here *when he could have gone anywhere in the world?*

I swallow down my shock and questions and stare at the man I thought I really knew despite spending such a short amount of time together. "A lot of people think you're dead."

His jaw tightens beneath his beard, and his entire body tenses as he glances at the deputy behind me. "I know. I'd like to keep it that way."

The sheriff holds up his hands again and shakes his head. "I'm sorry, Beau. It won't happen again, and I promise Deputy Neilsen will keep his mouth shut, too." He glares at his deputy and tips his head back toward the helicopter. "Finish reading her rights and get her loaded up so we can get out of here. Don't want to waste any more fuel and we need to get this back to Brewster as soon as we can."

Bile climbs up my throat, and trying to swallow it down only threatens to make me choke on it.

This can't be it. This can't be how it ends.

Last night, he asked me to *stay*. He told me he needed me to. He told me things had changed, that seeing that cougar almost attack me forced him to see what was right in front of him that he was trying so hard to deny.

All of that only hours ago.

But now, Beau watches me with accusation and fury in his gaze as the deputy tugs at my cuffed hands to get me walking. "Beau, p-please believe me. You *have* to believe me."

His hard eyes darken to an almost black, and he takes a step toward me, then moves back, shaking his head. "I don't even know who you are. How can I believe anything?"

He thinks it's a lie. He thinks all of this has been some grand, extravagant scheme, that I was using him and faked it all.

The deputy leads me through the snow, away from the cabin and Beau and toward the waiting helicopter. Whatever he's saying floats away on the wind, and Beau's words drag a wail from deep inside my chest—an anguished cry I didn't even know I was capable of that sounds almost inhuman, like something one of the animals out here would make. But it's the only sound that comes out. The only thing that can encompass the agony tearing up my soul right now.

They have it all wrong.

All wrong.

And now, I'll never get to explain it to Beau.

I'm never going to get the chance to tell him that it's all a lie, that everything they say is so damn wrong. I'm never going to get to tell him everything I've been afraid to reveal, all the truths that cursed my dreams until I slept in his arms. All the things I held close to my chest to protect him.

He's going to believe the worst, and there's nothing I can do about it.

Each step the deputy pulls me toward the waiting helicopter feels like being dragged further and further away from home, from where I'm supposed to be.

Somewhere I only spent a week somehow became the only place where I felt *right*.

The crunch of the snow under my boots, the very thing that almost killed me only days ago, becomes the true sound

217

of death. The death of everything I thought I could have with Beau. Death to that dream I held for a few hours. The only good thing I ever had. Dead.

Wind from the spinning blades whips around me, drowning out the sobs I can't stop from coming. The deputy climbs in, and I turn and watch the sheriff say something to Beau before he follows after us.

He helps me up into the helicopter and buckles a seat belt around me with my hands cuffed uncomfortably behind my back.

It's only the start of all the pain I'll endure.

I gaze out the still-open door at Beau standing outside the cabin, the place where I may have only spent seven days but where I feel like I lived a lifetime. The place I found a way to forgive myself and feel safe again. Where I managed to forget what had happened for a few moments.

And now, I have to leave it all behind and fight for my life while Beau remains here thinking I'm a murderer—and there's nothing I can do about it.

We both had secrets. Big ones. But he was wrong when he said he didn't know me. He does. And despite what he held back from me, I know him.

He won't give me a chance to explain.

He won't leave the cabin to come to Seattle.

He won't expose himself to come learn the truth.

I understand why now.

After what happened to him, to his family, of course he doesn't want to interact with the world outside his safe haven on the mountain.

And I can't blame him at all for it. If I were in his shoes, I would likely do the same. After seeing this place, I wouldn't want to leave either, not knowing what I do about how awful people are in the world. About how much hate and violence and just *bad* permeates everything and even people who once were good.

This is the last time I'll see him. The surety of that wraps around my throat, threatening to strangle me.

Beau reaches up and scrubs a hand over his beard. The sheriff gives a curt wave to Beau, then pulls the door closed, leaving me to try to see him through the window.

He stares at the helicopter stoically, watching it rise up off the snow, kicking it up like the storm that brought me here as we ascend.

That storm saved me and doomed me at the same time, and we take off across a bright blue sky to face my fate.

Chapter Nineteen

BROOKE

"Miss Neal, I really need you to pay attention and answer my questions."

"What?" I shake my head and try to focus on the old man in the ill-fitting suit sitting across the small table in the tiny room where attorneys meet with clients in the King County Jail.

How long has he been talking?

"I said, I need you to pay attention and to answer my questions; otherwise, this meeting is pointless."

"I'm sorry. I guess I'm a little distracted, for obvious reasons."

He sighs and sets his puffy hands on the table over the legal pad he's barely written anything on. "I understand this is a very stressful situation for you, Miss Neal, but if we don't have an open line of communication, then there's very little I can do for you."

"I'm sorry. I'll try to concentrate."

Try to push away the memory of that look on Beau's face as we flew away on the helicopter.

Betrayal.

Pain.

Disbelief.

He looked at me like I was a completely different person. Like I was someone he didn't even know. When, really, over the last week, I feel like he's come to know me better than anyone ever could.

I square my shoulders and offer half a smile to the man in front of me. "What did you say your name was again?"

"Dick Buting. Your public defender. I'll be representing you at the initial appearance tomorrow morning. Now, as I was saying, all we're doing is going in and entering a plea of not guilty. Then, we'll be arguing bail."

"I might get out on bail?"

He chuckles and sits back. "Not unless you have millions of dollars available that I don't know about."

"Millions?"

He raises a bushy eyebrow at me. "Miss Neal, you've been charged with murder in the first degree. Literally the most serious crime the State of Washington has, carrying the most strict penalties, and from what I can see in this criminal complaint, they have a very solid case against you. That isn't going to make the commissioner or the judge that we're in front of any more likely to let you go for any amount of money that's actually going to make it possible."

"What do you mean they have a lot of evidence? I didn't murder anyone."

His red-rimmed eyes drop down to his papers again, and he flips a stapled stack back to the first page. "This part right here is the affidavit of one of the officers on the case.

Gwyn McNamee

They have to submit it as evidence that there's probable cause to charge you when they file the complaint."

"Okay?"

What the hell is probable cause?

"Well, it says here that Tommy Baker was found deceased in his apartment a week ago after his sister arrived and couldn't get in so the super used his keys to enter via the locked door. It also says that he shared the apartment with one Brookelynn Neal. Both names were listed on the rental agreement and neighbors confirmed they had resided there together for several years. It also indicates that your fingerprints were all over the place, including in his blood, indicating you had been there either when or after he was shot. There were also women's size six shoe prints in the blood. Your fingerprints were also on the gun. They also have surveillance video from the CCTV cameras inside the apartment building lobby showing you rushing out of there carrying a small bag at ten p.m. on that same date, looking very frazzled. It also indicates that the coroner gave the time of death as between eight p.m. and twelve a.m. on the same date." His gaze darts up to meet mine. "You can see where I'm going with this."

I suck in a deep breath and close my eyes.

Don't break down now. Don't break down. You have to remain calm.

Explain it to him.

"You're my attorney, right? Anything I tell you, you can't tell anyone else?"

"Right."

"I did kill him. I'm the one who shot him. I pulled the trigger, but I *didn't* murder him. It was self-defense."

He narrows his old blue eyes on me. "Miss Neal. People who kill someone in self-defense don't flee. They don't drive

222

off into the mountains and hide out at remote cabins. Innocent people don't run."

"But I'm *innocent*. I swear, I didn't murder him." The tears stream down my face and fall to the table, and I suck in a shaky breath. "You have to believe me."

"No, I don't, ma'am. I have to represent you. It doesn't matter what I believe." He releases a heavy sigh. "I hate to say it, ma'am, but this is a very strong case for the prosecution. No jury is going to believe this was self-defense when you fled. Period."

I open my mouth to say something else, to try to offer some sort of defense and explanation for what I did, but the door to the room swings open and a tall, dark-haired man in an immaculate suit steps in.

"Brookelynn Neal?"

"Uh..." I wipe my nose on the back of my hand that's not cuffed to the table. "Yeah. I'm Brookelynn Neal."

He offers me a kind smile that shows off a perfect set of teeth. "I'm Allen Daws, your attorney."

Dick turns back toward him and raises an eyebrow. "*I'm* her attorney."

The new arrival sneers at him and motions toward the door. "Not anymore. The public defender's office is no longer needed. I've been retained to represent Miss Neal in this matter."

Retained?

That doesn't make any sense. No one I know has that kind of money.

"Retained by whom?"

Allen glances at me and returns his focus to Dick without answering my question. "We'll discuss that later. Once your former attorney has left the room."

Dick shoves his legal pad into his battered, old briefcase

and pushes to his feet with some concerted effort. "If you want to take on this loser of a case, you go right ahead, by all means." He grabs the complaint off the table, steps over to Allen, and pushes it against his chest. "A copy of the complaint, in case you don't have it."

Allen grins at him. "I have it, but thank you."

My former attorney casts me one last annoyed look, then shuffles out the door down the hallway, letting it slam back into place behind him with a finality that makes me flinch.

I shift on the hard seat while Allen Daws slowly lowers himself into the chair Dick just vacated and offers me a smile that's far kinder than I anticipated.

"Brooke...may I call you Brooke?"

"Uh, sure..."

"Don't worry. I'm going to help you. But first, I need you to tell me exactly what happened. Every single detail. Don't leave anything out."

"I don't understand. I don't have any money. Did Colleen hire you?"

His dark eyebrows furrow. "I was hired by someone who wants to ensure you don't get fucked over by the system. And that's what I intend to do." He leans back casually in the chair and twirls his pen between two fingers. "I don't care *if* you killed your boyfriend. I don't care *why* you killed your boyfriend. It's my job to make sure you don't go down for it, regardless."

It's not that different than what Dick told me, but for some reason, the way Allen puts it eases a little bit of the vise around my chest.

He pulls out a legal pad and slaps it down on the table. "Now, start from the beginning..."

* * *

BEAU

I pace in front of the fireplace, on the rug where I spent that wonderful night with Brooke—back and forth, back and forth—likely leaving a wear pattern in the fur and floor around it after spending so much time here over the last two days.

Ever since Jim arrived and took Brooke, I haven't been able to concentrate on anything. Every moment we spent together—from that awful beginning to the night I asked her to stay—replays in my head on a constant loop. Haunting me. Torturing me. Threatening to break me as much as the accusation against her does.

Murder.

The word blazes in my head, seared into my brain like a brand. All I see when I close my eyes is her and that word. It's one I know well, one I try to avoid using because if I do, it usually means I'm talking about the one thing I try to forget, the one thing I ran away from.

I pause in front of the fireplace and stare into the leaping flames. They twist and swirl together, fighting to consume the oxygen in the air the same way I've been fighting to find breath since Brooke left.

No matter how many different scenarios I concoct, I can't come up with one that explains all of this.

I want to believe she didn't do it. I want to believe there's no way she could. But really, I know nothing about her. I didn't even know her real name until Jim said it.

Brookelynn Ann Neal. Not Brooke Beck.

So many things clicked into place in that instant. Why

she wasn't prepared when she came up here to her friend's cabin. Why she never wanted to talk about her past. Why she was having nightmares.

Killing someone would do that.

All of it was because she was running. Because she had just *killed* someone and needed to get out of town fast.

She grabbed the basics, what she could, and she left without looking back. She was going to hide out at the cabin as long as she needed to in order to figure out her next move, which was probably going to be to try to cross the border into Canada, to try to hide out.

Because that's what murderers do.

They run.

They hide.

They lock themselves away.

Hoping that no one will ever discover their true identities or make them pay for their crimes.

I know that all too well.

Only, instead of finding a friend's cabin, she found me and fucked up my entire life.

My cell phone rings, and I practically launch myself at the end table. Allen's name flashes on the screen, and I jab my finger on the "Accept" button. "Did you see her?"

"Hello to you, too."

"Fuck the pleasantries, Daws. Did you see Brooke?"

"I saw her and met the useless attorney they had assigned her. The guy had her all worked up and upset before I got there."

I wince and squeeze my eyes closed, needing to ask but also dreading the answer. "Is she okay?"

"She's sitting in a jail cell charged with murder. How do you think she is?"

"Can you get her out?"

He chuckles low. "Beau, this is a murder in the first degree charge with some very aggravating facts that do not play in her favor."

"Aggravating facts like what? Are you saying she did it?"

"Wow..." He pauses for a moment. "She really didn't tell you anything. Did she?"

I grab my drink off the table and down half of it. "No, she didn't."

"Well, it isn't my place to go into any specifics with you about anything that she told me in confidence."

"Oh, fuck you, Allen. We've known each other since we were fifteen. I know where all your skeletons are buried. The least you can do is tell me about hers."

He releases a heavy sigh. "Beau, you know I can't divulge anything that she told me. But I'll tell you what's in the complaint. None of it is good."

Every word of the laundry list of evidence against Brooke he rattles off tightens my gut. Shared apartment. Fingerprints in blood. Video of her running. I grip my glass so hard, my fingers actually hurt.

"They're probably going to ask for two million."

"Two million?"

"Yes, fairly standard in this type of case and these facts. They have to consider the need to protect the public which means a high bail they don't think she can meet."

"I'll pay it." The response comes out before I even consider it. "Whatever it is, I'll pay it."

"Beau, wait a minute. Let's think about this for a second. That's a lot of fucking money and you barely know the girl."

"It's nothing. A drop in the fucking bucket. I don't want her sitting in jail any longer than she needs to be. Just tell me where to have the money wired and I'll do it."

"Once she makes her initial appearance tomorrow morning and the bail is actually set, I'll let you know how much it is. My hope is that I can have a conversation with the DA and potentially get these charges dismissed before we even have to worry about any sort of trial."

"How the hell are you going to do that? I know you're a miracle worker, but you just said yourself that things don't look good."

"They don't." He pauses for a moment, like he's considering something. "But I think we have a strong self-defense argument."

Self-defense?

Brooke flinching away from me when I raised my voice. The nightmare she had that was bad enough to cause that panic. Her comment about reading about a bad boy rather than experiencing it on your own. Saying she would never be safe.

It all comes rushing back to me.

I had suspected that she had suffered at the hands of someone who did something awful to her; I just never realized how bad it was or what it led to.

"Did that bastard lay a hand on her?"

"I can't tell you anything she told me. I'm sorry. But rest assured, I'm going to do whatever I can to get these charges thrown out. And if I can't do it quickly, we'll get you to post the bond and get her out. But they're probably going to need you to come to court."

My shoulders tense and the bourbon in my stomach burns. "What? Why?"

"Because you're the one posting the bond. They need your signature because you're agreeing to ensure that she complies with the terms and conditions, which are pretty standard. Don't commit any further crimes. No drugs or alcohol. Make all your court appearances. The judge may even order her placed on house arrest for the protection of the public. In which case, she would have to have an ankle monitor and stay wherever she's living."

"Does she even have anywhere to live?"

"That's a good point. She mentioned a friend named Colleen. If she's in town and agrees Brooke can stay there, we can use her place, but the court would probably prefer if she actually stayed with you since you're the surety for the bond."

"Shit. Allen, you know I can't do that. You know I can't come there."

"I understand it would be difficult under the circumstances, but you're going to have to make a decision and pretty soon."

"Fuck."

"I'll keep you updated if I learn anything new. In the meantime, you might want to start planning your flight out of there if you're going to do this bond thing."

"Thanks." I end the call and down the rest of my drink, replaying his words, each one ratcheting up my anger and the tension in my body.

If he can't get these charges dismissed and the bond is that high, Brooke could sit in jail until there's a trial, and then there's no guarantee she wouldn't go to prison for the rest of her life.

For the week Brooke was here, I knew I wouldn't see her again after she left. It was a given we had both accepted well before that chopper showed up. But that all changed that night. When I asked her to stay. When I realized I needed her to.

The thought of knowing she's rotting away in some jail cell, especially if what Allen said is true, is completely unfucking-acceptable. I chuck my tumbler into the fire. The flames explode with the fuel thrown on them and the glass shatters on the stone, bursting glass out across the floor.

This puts me in an impossible situation.

One I can't win.

Chapter Twenty

BROOKE

"**D**o you understand the charges as they have been read here today, Miss Neal.

"She does, Your Honor."

Allen reaches over and squeezes my leg, trying to get me to refocus on what's happening.

"I do, Your Honor."

Am I really sitting here in front of a judge charged with murder?

The entire situation is so surreal, like I'm watching someone else's life on television, not my own spiraling out of control.

How the hell did this happen?

Because of Tommy.

Because of me.

Because I didn't do what I should have a long time ago.

"And now on to the issue of bail...Mr. Reyes?"

The prosecutor motions toward me from the table

beside us. "The state is asking for a cash bail of three million dollars with additional conditions."

Three million?

I turn toward Allen who just pats my hand and lets the prosecutor continue.

"Miss Neal is charged with the brutal murder of her boyfriend and then fleeing the county in an attempt to avoid capture. Therefore, she's already proven to be a flight risk and a danger to the community. As conditions of bail, if she were to be released, the state requests electronic monitoring and house arrest, save for meetings with her counsel or medical appointments."

"Mr. Daws?" The judge motions to my attorney, who appears unaffected by the request of the state.

"Your Honor, the state's request for bond is absolutely absurd. Miss Neal has zero record, not so much as a single arrest or even a parking ticket. They only had her prints for comparison because of an incident when she was in high school and the store she worked at was robbed. They took all employee prints for exclusion." He glares at the prosecutor. "There's also no evidence that she was trying to flee or that she intended to remain out of contact with authorities. She was literally trapped on the side of a mountain for a week with no way to return or get in touch with anyone. She's been cooperative with me as her counsel, and she has somewhere that she can reside here in town and a co-signer willing to ensure she complies with the conditions of bond. We would request that an amount of $500,000 would be reasonable."

$500,000 is reasonable?

I almost choke on my own breath.

He can't be serious.

Even though it's much less than the three million the

prosecution is seeking, I don't have that kind of money. At this point, I don't even have five hundred dollars to my name. And Colleen must have spent every cent she has to hire Allen to represent me, so she can't help with posting bond.

I'm going to spend the rest of my life in jail...

"Where would Miss Neal be residing and who would be the co-signer on her bond?"

"She will be residing at 7195 Fairhaven Avenue, which is the residence of her friend Colleen Reynolds, who is here in court today, Your Honor."

I turn back in my seat and spot Colleen sitting on one of the hard benches in the courtroom. She offers me a sympathetic smile, and I return it. Then my gaze drifts to less friendly faces. Tommy's dad and Jeanine watch me from the other side of the courtroom, a sneer on her lips, her eyes red and puffy from tears.

Don't cry for him.

Tommy was an asshole to her as much as he was to me. She made that very clear over the years when telling me stories about them growing up. He may have been her brother, but he was also her tormentor.

I don't understand the tears for him. Maybe I never will. The same way I don't understand the guilt I feel over killing him.

Logically, I know I had to. If I hadn't, he would have killed me. But it's still there. Gnawing away at me, attacking me in my dreams every night since I've been in this Godforsaken place, away from Beau and the safety of his embrace.

Red. The blood. It's all I see in my dreams. Covering everything...

The judge studies some paperback on his desk. "Would

Miss Reynolds be posting the cash bond on her behalf, as well?"

Allen clears his throat and glances around the courtroom while I refocus my attention on the judge. "No, Your Honor. Another friend would be."

What?

The judge raises his white eyebrows. "This person also resides in the county and understands that they will be accepting responsibility for any violations Miss Neal makes of the bond and that they could potentially lose any money posted if she violates it?"

"I'm aware, Your Honor." Beau's voice from the back of the courtroom freezes me stock still.

I turn slowly to look over my shoulder. His hard, dark eyes meet mine, every bit as wild and unsettled as they were that day I stumbled into the clearing and his life.

The judge examines Beau. "And you are, sir?"

Beau takes several steps forward, glancing at the people in the courtroom who are watching him expectantly.

In a clearly custom-tailored suit, even with the beard, he looks every bit the successful businessman. Gone is the wild, unkempt man I fell in love with on that mountain.

He swallows thickly, unease likely only I can spot making his hand twitch at his side. "Luke Beaumont, sir."

Several gasps echo in the courtroom, and the judge's eyes widen. A rush of voices talking excitedly at once fills the air, and he slams down the gavel.

"I'll have silence in the courtroom. Did you say Luke Beaumont?"

Beau clears his throat and inclines his head toward the judge. "Yes, Your Honor."

"Well, Mr. Beaumont, this might be the first time I've

ever had a co-signer of a bond be someone half the world speculates is actually dead."

Offering the judge a tight smile, Beau nods. "I can assure you, Your Honor, I'm very much alive and very willing to post the bond on behalf of Miss Neal while she resides with her friend, Colleen."

The judge leans back in his chair and steeples his hands in front of his mouth as he contemplates the situation. "As both counselors are well aware, the goal of bond is to ensure the defendant complies with the terms and makes their court appearances. However, it should also be used as a means to protect the public from any potential dangers the accused may pose. Now, while Miss Neal has the benefit of the presumption of innocence at this point, I have to say that the evidence that's been presented in the criminal complaint is certainly concerning and demonstrates a risk to the general public. Because of that, I'm going to do this...I'm going to place a two-million-dollar cash bond on Miss Neal to secure her appearance in court. I'm also going to order house arrest to be monitored via ankle monitor to ensure protection of the public. I will allow Mr. Beaumont to post a cash bond on her behalf. However"—he holds up a hand —"I'm not going to allow her to live with Colleen Reynolds. Mr. Beaumont, if you're going to take the responsibility of paying for her bond, I want her residing with you."

"Excuse me, Your Honor?" Beau's incredulous tone drives through my heart like a sharpened stake.

He doesn't even want to see me again, let alone have me in his personal space.

"Your Honor, I don't live in the city anymore. It would be an incredible inconvenience for me to have to remain here while this case pends."

The judge shrugs. "Then Miss Neal will remain in

custody. I feel this is the only way to adequately protect the members of the public and to ensure that she's in compliance with the terms of the bond."

Oh, my God, I'm never getting out.

All the rest of the words exchanged between the court and the attorneys become an indistinguishable jumble until Allen finally touches my shoulder to get my attention. The deputies come over and take my arm to lead me from the courtroom.

I cast one final glance toward the benches to see Colleen with a tear streaming down her face offer me a wave, but there isn't any sign of Beau.

The man couldn't run out of here fast enough.

Who can blame him?

It's the first time he showed his face in public in a decade, and he was just told that he would have to move back to Seattle and live with me if he wants to post my bond.

That's the last thing he's going to do—which means I'm going to be stuck in custody.

Maybe forever.

BEAU

My knee bounces up and down uncontrollably, and I tap my fingers on the steering wheel in a rhythm that might put me to sleep if I weren't so amped up. Even though night has descended over Seattle and the darkness surrounding the SUV is heavy enough that no one can see in, I still feel exposed. The hair on the back of my neck stands on end, and I can't stop fidgeting while I wait for the jail to release Brooke.

It was a no fucking brainer that I was going to sign that bond. There's no way I would have let her rot in a jail cell while this case goes on if I had any way to avoid it. Only now, what I've been avoiding are all the pings on my phone notifying me of my name coming up on Internet articles.

I knew what would happen the moment I showed my face in that courtroom—or at least the moment I said my name—and like clockwork, the Internet alerts started and my phone won't stop ringing.

Nate is going to kill me.

After months of telling him I wouldn't come back to meet with the board on the environmental issues, after years of refusing to set foot in the company headquarters, here I am waltzing into court and announcing my name publicly and tying myself to someone accused of a brutal murder.

I scrub my hands over my face. "Jesus Christ, what am I doing?"

Part of me wishes I could drive away. Just leave. Go back to the mountain and my cabin and forget any of this ever happened. It would save a lot of people a lot of trouble. Except I wouldn't be able to forget anything. Not when that cabin reminds me of Brooke and her time there, of our time there together.

Her scent still lingers on the sheets. The couch feels empty without her sitting beside me. The whole place is somehow cold, despite how many logs I throw on the fire.

I would never be able to walk away and leave her alone like this. Not even when the very real sense of betrayal still flows through my blood.

She didn't tell me...

Somehow, that feels so much worse than me not telling her who I really was. I wasn't hiding anything except my family name. She was hiding a damn crime and running from the law.

All the hours we spent in bed together, she never came clean. Not even on that last night when I asked her not to leave. She was going to stay with that lie between us, knowing the police were going to be looking for her.

How am I ever supposed to forgive that?

I'll do what I can for her, pay for Allen and give her somewhere to stay until this gets resolved, then I'll go back to living my life the way I want to—alone.

Without the complications of the outside world. Without the complications of a woman. Without emotions.

As it should be.

The side door to the jail opens, and Brooke steps out wearing the clothes I had Allen bring to her—soft sweatpants and an off-white Henley just big enough for her to feel cozy, exactly what I know she needs after being in that place.

She glances up and down the street, and I suck in a deep breath and step from the SUV. The door slamming behind me makes her jump, and she turns toward me.

"Beau...I-I wasn't expecting you to—"

"Stop." I hold up a hand. This isn't the time or place to have the conversation we need to. I've made enough public displays today. "Get in."

I tilt my head toward the passenger side of the SUV, and she opens her mouth to say something but bites it back.

"Okay." Her response is soft, barely audible, almost like she's afraid to even speak to me.

Maybe she should be.

I return to the driver's side and climb in as she settles into the passenger seat. With a little more force than necessary, I throw the vehicle into drive and peel away from the curb—probably faster than I should, considering where we are.

We fly through the streets, the speed of the car matching my racing heart.

The streetlights whiz past us—everything so damn bright that it hurts my eyes. One day here and the lights and sounds are enough to drive me right back up the mountain again.

"Where are we going?" Her question breaks the silence.

"My condo."

"You have a condo here?"

I keep my eyes straight ahead on the road. "It's where I lived before. I never sold it. Just have someone go in and clean it once a month and keep it maintained. Occasionally, a friend comes in from out of town and uses it."

"Oh..." She settles back in her seat and returns to silence.

I peek at her out of the corner of my eye to find her staring out at the city, watching it fly by as we make our way toward the place I once called home, the place I never thought I'd set foot in again.

We pull into the underground garage, and I turn off the car and climb out without a word to her. She does the same and follows me to the elevator. I slide my ID card into it and press the button for the penthouse, feeling her eyes on me the entire time.

She stands rigid in the center of the elevator car, staring straight ahead at her reflection while I stay to her left doing the same. Our eyes meet on the polished steel before I force myself to look away, force myself to ignore the tension building in the tiny confined space.

I thought it had been bad in the cabin, but this...this is pure torture.

We reach the top floor and the elevator dings as the doors slide open. Brooke waits for me to step out, then follows behind me slowly, into the vast modern living room with low, sleek metal furniture and high white walls and ceilings.

"Wow, this place is so..." she trails off as I head straight for the bar.

"Sterile?"

"I was going to say *different* from your cabin."

Facing the bar, my back to Brooke, I pause with my hand over the bottle, contemplating the last time I was here. "It *is* different, because I'm different. I'm not the same twenty-eight-year-old man I was when I lived here."

Riding high on life. Everything and anything I wanted at my fingertips. Going through the motions as if that would never change. Totally oblivious to what was coming.

Not by a long shot.

I pour myself a scotch—a nice, smoky Islay. One of Dad's favorites. "I'd offer you a drink, but that would be violating a term of your release. And if it's all the same to you"—I turn back to face her and take a sip—"I'd rather not lose two million dollars."

"Jesus..." She shakes her head and drops her face in her hands. "I'm so sorry—"

"We're not doing that. I didn't want to hear your apologies up there, and I don't want to hear them now. I want you to tell me the truth. I want you to tell me everything. Now."

Chapter Twenty-One

BEAU

Brooke wanders past me over to the floor-to-ceiling windows that offer an expansive view of the water and wraps her arms around herself tightly, the same way she used to at the cabin whenever she was feeling exposed and vulnerable.

I have to fight the urge to walk over there and pull her into my arms. That wouldn't do any good right now. Not when I'm this worked up, this angry with the situation. Not when I have no idea how I even feel about this stranger standing in this strange place that used to be mine.

She releases a heavy sigh. "I was with Tommy for three years. It didn't start out bad, but I don't think most relationships do. Then, he started drinking more and even started using some drugs recreationally. At least, 'til it wasn't recreational anymore. He just kind of..." She shakes her head. "I don't know...became a different person. I don't really blame him for it. He wasn't in control of himself. But when he lost control, he lost his ability to think rationally and he would come at me, accusing me of stealing money from him because he used it on drugs and couldn't remember."

My free hand at my side curls into a fist, and I tighten the other around the glass to keep myself from tossing it at the wall. I thought I needed to hear the truth, every dirty and bloody detail, but now, I'm not so sure.

"He used to yell at me about how I didn't work and mooched off him because he didn't think selling my photography and doing weddings and portraits and things like that was a real job."

She pauses for a moment and swallows through her tears, and I take a long drink of my scotch to fight back my own.

I really don't want to hear this. I don't want to hear all the gory details about what she suffered, but I need to. If I don't know everything, all that we're dealing with, it will put me at a tremendous disadvantage in trying to help her defend herself in court and wherever else we need to.

More importantly, I need to know why she lied to me.

Why?

She had so many opportunities. So many times she could have asked for my help.

Did she think I wouldn't help her? That I would turn her over to the police as soon as we could get down the mountain?

Brooke takes a steadying breath and wipes the tears from her cheeks, still staring out the windows. "He started to hit me about a year ago. The first time, it was more like a slap, almost a warning shot across the bow that he wasn't happy with me and that I needed to watch myself. So, I did. I walked around on pins and needles with him. Always trying to avoid an argument. Always looking for ways to try to make him happy. Because if he wasn't happy, he was angry. And you didn't want him angry."

All the times I lost my cool with Brooke at the cabin flash through my head like daggers stabbing at my brain.

No wonder she was afraid of me.

She sniffles and swipes under her eyes again. "He beat me bad a couple of times. Put me in the hospital."

I finally manage to swallow another drink through the rock of emotion lodged in my throat while all I see is red. "Why didn't the police arrest him?"

Brooke turns toward me, her eyes wet and red. "Because I lied about what happened. I made up a story. I thought they either wouldn't believe me or he would walk on the charges and come at me even worse. I'm sure some of those officers knew I was lying, but there was nothing they could do about it when I didn't cooperate."

"How many times?" I tighten my hand on my glass. "How many times did that bastard put you in the hospital?"

She shrugs almost nonchalantly, as if we're discussing a shopping list and not the man who brutalized her. The woman spent so long downplaying what was happening to her that even now, she can't see the truth of it. "I don't know, three or four? The last time was just too much. I couldn't take it anymore. So, I left. I went to Colleen's. Of course, she knew, or at the very least suspected, what was going on, though, I never admitted it to her before then. I finally told her everything, and she told me I could stay as long as I wanted. Only, Tommy knew where she lived and I knew it would only be a matter of time before he sobered up enough to come looking for me, or worse—he would come looking for me when he was high and out of his fucking mind."

She inhales deeply and closes her eyes.

"So, I moved around, slept on a few different friends'

couches for a while. I managed to stay away from him for about a month. I saved up enough to book a flight and take a little vacation by myself, to celebrate, and I had done enough jobs and was finally ready to rent my own place. But I realized almost everything I needed to do that was still in our apartment. My birth certificate, my social security card; the things I didn't think about grabbing when I left. They were in a safe where he also kept his gun and his drugs."

Oh, hell...

I can already see where this is going, and the bile climbs up my throat, burning it harder than the liquor did when I drank it.

"I went back when he should have been at work, shouldn't have been anywhere near the place. It should have been safe. But"—she chokes back a sob as a fresh round of tears fall, slapping her hand over her mouth.

"But it wasn't?"

"No. It wasn't. He came home while I had the safe open, while I was going through everything to make sure that I took anything that was mine. He flew off the handle the moment he saw me and immediately knocked me to the floor. Told me he always knew I was a thief and now he had proof. Called me a lying whore and said that he wasn't going to let me get away with it." She wraps her arms around herself tighter. "He grabbed me by my hair and dragged me off the floor. I kicked him hard enough to get him to release me and scrambled to try to get away from him and ended up back in front of the safe."

"Where the gun was..."

She nods. "I didn't even think. I just reached for it and pointed it at him. I didn't even know if he kept it loaded or not. But he had pulled it on me once and threatened to use it, so I knew it worked. I figured it would be enough to stop him. Only he just laughed and said I didn't have the balls to do it. He said that he was going to fucking kill me, and when he lunged at me again, I fired."

"How many times did you hit him?"

The details mean everything in this case. She has no idea how important they really are.

Brooke shakes her head. "I don't know. I think twice. Maybe three times. I just kept firing until he stopped."

She stands in front of me. Her body vibrating, her tears choking her as she relays the story to me. I had anticipated most of it based on Allen telling me she had a self-defense claim, but it was far worse than I ever could have imagined.

A year. A damn fucking year.

While I was up at the cabin, locked away from the world, pretending no one else and nothing else existed, she was suffering at the hands of this monster. She was too afraid of what he would do if she left him, and then when she did, he tried to fucking kill her.

I swallow back my rage so that I can try to speak. "Why did you run? With your medical records and the evidence at the scene, you could have told the police it was self-defense. They might have arrested you, but if they had looked into it, they would have seen that."

She shakes her head and sobs. "I don't know. I just panicked. I thought about how bad it would look with the open safe, like he walked in on me robbing him or something. And Tommy's dad is a retired cop. Even though they were kind of on the outs and didn't talk much, I know his father would have stepped in and ensured I was prosecuted. All I could think about was getting away from all of it. Away from him. Away from Seattle." She glances back at the water. "I had been planning on heading to the airport after I grabbed my stuff, to go on my little vacation. The flight was supposed to be that night, late, but my flight was cancelled due to the weather. Then I remembered Colleen's cabin and how she'd told me I could use it whenever I wanted. She told me where they hid the key so I could get in at any time. When she told me, she had thought I'd be using it for a romantic trip with Tommy. She had no idea when I texted and told her I was heading up there for a week that anything had happened."

"Jesus, Brooke..."

* * *

BROOKE

Beau shakes his head, his jaw clenched, free hand fisted at his side as he grips the glass with the other one hard enough to whiten his knuckles.

"I know this looks bad."

His eyes widen and his mouth opens slightly in disbelief. "That's what you think? I'm upset because this *looks* bad."

"Well...yeah. You just walked into the courthouse and gave over two million dollars bond for me and I might get convicted of murder. This won't look good for you or your company."

"I don't give a flying fuck!" His harsh tone makes me shrink back even though half the room still separates us.

He holds up his free hand. "I'm sorry. I'm just..." He runs it through his hair. "I'm not mad because this looks bad, Brooke. I'm mad because of what he *did* to you. I'm mad that any man would think, *could* think that it was ever okay to do any of that. On drugs or not, it never should have happened." He sucks in a heavy breath, like he's trying to find his control again but failing. "I'm upset because you got hurt."

"I let him hurt me. I stayed with him and let him control my life. Control me. It's all my fault. I—"

"Stop." Beau downs the rest of his drink and sets the glass on the low table behind the couch before he makes his way over to me and stops only a foot away, close enough that his familiar scent fills my lungs. He may look different dressed like this, but he's still Beau, still the same man he was up at that cabin. "Stop blaming yourself. None of this is your fault."

"I should have left."

"No." He shakes his head. "You can't look back on it now and say that. It's easy in retrospect, but in the moment, we do things and say things we shouldn't. Sometimes, we accept things as part of our lives that shouldn't be because we want love and companionship and need that connection. That's just being human."

Deep down, I know what he's saying is true, but this is the man who suffered tremendously and then became a recluse. He shut himself away from people, wanted anything *but* a connection.

"You didn't."

He freezes, his body stiffening. "We aren't talking about me right now, Brooke. I'm trying to figure out how to get you out of these charges. Everything you've said should be easy to prove based on the evidence. Have you already told all of this to Allen?"

I nod, remembering how awful having to tell all that to a complete stranger was while sitting in an orange jumpsuit. Little did I know how much worse it was going to be telling it to Beau. "Yes. He asked me to tell him everything. And I did."

"Good. He has unlimited resources at his disposal. I've already told him that. A private investigator...whatever he needs. He'll get everything together and present it to the DA, and we're going to make this go away."

Hope swells in my chest, but it's quickly replaced by harsh reality.

"You can't say that. It's a murder case. And like I said, his dad was a cop. They stick together. They make sure people pay when their loved ones get hurt."

Beau closes the distance between us and takes my face between his large palms. It's the first time he's touched me in days, and the warm, comforting heat of those familiar rough calluses make me sag against him.

"He may have a lot of friends on the police force or even in the district attorney's office, but it's nothing compared to what I have. Don't underestimate what the name Beaumont means around here, the power it holds."

I stare into his whiskey eyes, watching turmoil swirl in them. "I don't understand why, Beau. Why were you up there? Why are you living like that when"—I wave a hand around—"you literally have billions?"

He tenses again, and this time, with my chest pressed to his, I can almost feel his physical agony radiating into me.

"Do you know what happened?" He says the words carefully and slowly, like they're painful for him to even speak, but I know exactly what he's referring to.

"Yes, I mean, I think I do. I remember someone shot at you and your parents and they were killed."

He squeezes his eyes closed for a moment, like he's reliving that day while standing here in front of me, and when he reopens them, they shimmer with unshed tears. "It was a disgruntled employee. Someone I had pissed off. Someone who probably wouldn't have even thought about doing something like that if I hadn't set him off by cutting his hours and paycheck over something stupid. My parents just got caught in the crossfire. I was the person he was aiming for. If they hadn't been with me that night, if I hadn't invited them to the symphony, if they hadn't gone with me, they would still be alive, and I'd be the one buried in the ground."

"You can't think like that."

"Can't I? How am I supposed to think, Brooke? The man was waiting for us outside because he knew I would be there. I always went. He ambushed us and unloaded an entire magazine into us. My father died instantly, which was a blessing. My mother..."

I press my hand against his chest and feel his heart racing at having to relive the memory.

"She wasn't so lucky. Somehow, I managed to crawl over to her despite being shot three times myself. I pulled her into my arms and held her for what felt like hours before an ambulance arrived when, really, it was only a handful of minutes. But it was too late. She was dead, too."

"But *you* survived."

Beau drops his gaze to meet mine again, a single tear trailing down his cheek. "I wish I hadn't."

"Is that why you went up there? So, you could just wither away and die, choking on your own guilt?"

He clenches his teeth together, his jaw tightening. "As soon as I got to the hospital, I knew. I knew I didn't want to keep living after what had happened. I couldn't imagine my life without them. I was very close with them, especially my mother, and when they put me under to operate, I prayed to not wake up."

I press my hand harder over his heart, wanting so badly to tell him I've been there and felt the same things, but I haven't experienced the kind of loss he has, not like that. Not in such a violent way. But I do know guilt, and I can see now that he's been drowning in it for years.

He swallows thickly and shakes his head. "But then I did." His shoulders rise and fall casually, as if the fact that he survived means nothing to him. "And I ordered my best friend, Nate, to get me out of that fucking hospital and to make sure no one leaked any of my medical information. Anyone who operated on me or who worked for the hospital was required to sign an NDA and were threatened if they told anyone, anything, we'd come after them, on top of any HIPAA issues. The attorney for the company released a statement that confirmed the death of my parents and left what happened to me up in the air, saying that my injuries were life-threatening and they weren't sure if I was going to make it."

Tears sting my eyes, and before I can stop them, they fall. Beau watches them with great interest and uses his thumbs to brush them away.

"It wasn't a lie. Even after the doctors repaired the damage the bullets had done, I had lost my will to go on. I wanted to die, and then the man who shot my parents committed suicide in his jail cell. I never got to see him pay for his crimes, and I spent weeks recuperating at a friend's house and realized God wasn't going to answer my prayer. Right then and there, I vowed to never go back to that life of excess, with everything being handed to me on a silver platter. I didn't want everything that Mother and Father worked so hard to give me. I just wanted to be left alone in my misery."

"So, you went to the cabin?"

"The Beaumonts own that entire mountain, Brooke. We've been logging it for generations. That building you drove past on your way up the mountain is one of our old locations. I shut it down when I moved up there because I didn't want there to be any chance of anyone seeing me and recognizing me. And even though I wasn't strong enough, even though there was no way I should have been doing it, I went up there alone and I built that place by fucking hand. I did it all the way my father's ancestors did when they came out west, with the help of a few men from town who knew better than to ask questions. I worked for everything I had up there and tried very hard not to give myself the luxuries that I abused so badly down here and took for granted."

"Except for the good booze…"

The corner of his lips twitches up despite the heaviness of the topic. "I allowed myself a few indulgences. That happens to be one of them. And I had to stay connected to the world—at least, somewhat—because technically, I'm the CEO of the company, even though the board runs it. In ten years, those board members are basically the only people who have true confirmation that I'm still alive. Aside from Sheriff Roberts who only found out because he got suspicious of me up there when I was building my place, and I had to tell him so that he could keep an eye out in case any media showed up."

"So, that's why there's been so much speculation about whether you're actually dead or not. People think the company would keep up pretenses if you had died?"

He nods and glances toward the windows. "Apparently. I am the last Beaumont, and even though we're a publicly traded company, with a board of directors now, and a number of people who could step up to my position, the stock prices would tank if my death was confirmed. I think that's what makes everyone so suspicious. And now, we have a new environmental law trying to get passed that could affect some of our business." He sighs and returns his focus to me. "They've been wanting me to come out to address it. But I've refused."

"But you came out for me. You showed up in open court for me."

His calloused thumb brushes over my cheek. "I did, Brooke."

"What does that mean?"

"I don't have a fucking clue."

He presses his lips to mine in a kiss filled with a hundred promises he can't make. Ones I can't return. But I still allow myself to get lost in the possibility of Beau, the fantasy that things will turn out okay, and that one day, we might be back on that mountain again.

Chapter Twenty-Two

BEAU

Chaos. That's what coming back has meant. Utter, complete, total, unending *chaos*.

Between the media camped out in front of the condo building and the way they've latched on to the charges against Brooke as much as the story about my miraculous return from the maybe dead, the last week has been a nauseating whirlwind. And on top of all that, I've had to deal with Nate and the demands from the board that I come down to headquarters to address the on-going issues.

I stare out the window and down at the media vans occupying the street as far as I can see, phone pressed to my ear, waiting for Nate's response to yet another refusal on my part.

"You need to come."

Tightening my hand around the cell, I grit my teeth to keep from lashing out at Nate. It isn't his fault the board is being so damn demanding.

"They cut you some slack before because you hadn't left the damn cabin in a decade. But now that you've publicly announced your return and done so to support an accused *murderer,* we can't make that excuse anymore. They want to see you immediately. They've scheduled a board meeting for tomorrow morning."

"I'm not coming, Nate. I have other matters to deal with at the moment."

He chuckles low. "Like the blond Black Widow you're sleeping with?"

If anyone else but Nate had said that, it probably would have earned them a punch in the gut and face, but my lips curl up into an almost smile because he knows she's far from that.

After everything I've told him, after explaining what happened between us at the cabin and in the time since I came back to Seattle, he truly understands how important she's become to me.

"How's she doing, anyway?"

I run a hand over my freshly shaven face, the feeling of the smooth, exposed skin so foreign that I jerk my hand back. "I guess she's as okay as she can be when she's cooped up in here, just waiting for her fate to be determined."

The only thing that has even remotely kept her or me sane has been falling into each other's arms at night and spending our days catching up on all the mindless television I've missed out on over the years.

"What does Allen have to say about his negotiations with the DA?"

"I talked to him this morning. He was on his way to a meeting with the DA to discuss her case."

It's what we've been waiting for. He and his team have

been working non-stop for a week, conducting interviews, collecting their own evidence, doing everything they could to build a case to help Brooke.

"Allen said he had a lot of confidence in the potential that this meeting would result in a dismissal. Really, between her medical records, the affidavits our private investigator got from witnesses who had seen her injuries or witnessed their arguments and him get violent with her, he doesn't think the prosecutor is going to want to risk embarrassment in front of a jury or the media by prosecuting a battered woman, especially one romantically involved with a Beaumont."

"That's good, isn't it?"

I glance over my shoulder toward the stairs to ensure Brooke isn't within earshot. "Of course it is, but it's also very hard to know this information is going to likely end up becoming public. The DA is going to have to justify his dismissal, and with the media attention this has already had, he is going to want to use this to save face and show how compassionate the District Attorney's office is toward true crime victims."

Nate releases a sigh. "Yeah, I can see that. It's better than the alternative, though."

"I'm not so sure either of us would survive a trial."

"Well, I'm not so sure you're going to survive as CEO if you don't show up at this meeting tomorrow, sir."

When Nate slips into "sir" mode with me, it means he's no longer speaking to me as a friend but as an employee. It means he's being dead serious.

I growl and bang my fist against the glass. "You tell the board that they waited for ten years so they can wait a few more days."

"You know I'll do my best."

"You always do."

That familiar guilt settles in my chest, and I look out at the water—one of the few things I actually missed about this place when I was up the mountain.

"Hey, Nate. What happened when I left...I just want you to know that I appreciate everything you did for me. What you tried to do for me. I'm sorry if I didn't show you that back then."

"I understood, Beau. I loved them, too. You know that."

"I know."

Which is what made it all that much harder.

Seeing Nate's own anguish over Mom and Dad's death only drove me deeper into blaming myself and wanting a way to escape it all. They were like second parents to him and it was my actions that got them killed.

"Do you love her?"

Shit.

It's the question that's weighed heavily on my mind since the first time she touched me in the cabin, where the answer has only become more convoluted and twisted as time has gone on and harder to answer.

"I care a lot about her."

"Really? That's all you're gonna say?"

"What's that supposed to mean?"

"I've known you a long time, and I've spent years trying to get you to leave that damn cabin. And you did it within two days for that woman. If you don't think you love her, you're fooling yourself."

Hell...

Nate chuckles again and sighs. "I'll talk to the board for you tomorrow. You better pray you still have a job."

"My prayers are tied up with other things at the moment."

And it's the first time I've spoken to the supposed big man upstairs since Mom and Dad's death. After He didn't answer my prayer to take me from all the pain I was in, I gave up on Him as much as I did myself. Just another thing Mom and Dad would have been horrified to learn about how I've acted since they've been gone.

"Let me know what happens with the DA."

"I will."

I end the call and slip my phone back in my pocket, then turn to find Brooke standing at the bottom of the stairs, her hands twisting in front of her nervously.

"Was that Allen?"

"No. Nate."

"Oh..."

She approaches me slowly, almost cautiously, the same way we've been dancing around each other for days. The only place we seem to not have a problem communicating is the bedroom, holding each other so neither of our nightmares will return while we share the same one—that she might actually get convicted for this.

I wrap my arms around her shoulders and pull her to me. She buries her face against my chest, and I press a kiss to the top of her head.

"The meeting should be over soon. Then, we'll hear something."

She drags her head back and looks up at me, familiar tears pooling in her eyes. "What if it's bad news? What if the DA isn't going to dismiss the charges?"

I cup her cheek and tilt her face up toward mine even more. "Then we fight it with everything I fucking have. We get the best experts in the fucking world. We track down every person who ever knew Tommy since his birth to say what a violent asshole he was. We put on the best defense money can buy. I have plenty of it, but none of it means anything if I don't have you."

* * *

BROOKE

Staring up into his dark eyes, I know the anger in his tone isn't directed at me. That first night here, when I told him everything, when I finally came clean and bared my soul to him, I thought it was. I thought he was mad I could have been so weak and stupid, but now, I realize it's because I hid the truth from him, especially that last night before they came for me.

I had every opportunity to come clean, to tell him what was happening, to explain *why* I was really up that mountain, to ask for his help and support, and I just couldn't do it. Every time I tried, the words froze on my lips, and instead of having that horrible conversation with him, I lost myself in him again.

That created a wound, a rift between us that sometimes feels bigger than the Grand Canyon, one I'm terrified we will never fully close. But at least I know he doesn't blame me for *this*. He believes in me completely and will do anything to help me.

"No one's ever done anything like this for me before, Beau. I don't know how to thank you."

He presses a kiss to my lips that's tender and soft and all-too-brief. "I'm not about to live my life without you, Brooke. We may have only had a week together in that cabin, but that week showed me something extraordinary."

"What's that?"

"That I can still love someone. That taking the risk of opening up and exposing all my pain to someone else, laying all my weaknesses on the table, only invites the opportunity to heal and find something better. That I don't have to hide in my own grief and wallow in it alone anymore."

"What are you saying, Beau? You don't want to go back to the cabin?"

His chuckle makes his chest vibrate against mine. "Of course, I do. This place"—he waves a hand around the condo—"it's so lifeless—so *not me* anymore. The cabin is where I belong. But it doesn't mean I have to cut myself off from the world so much. Doesn't mean that I have to cut *you* out of my life. I love you, Brooke, and when all this is over, I want you to come back with me to that cabin that never had any life in it before you came. I spent all my time building a world where I didn't have to deal with anything or anyone and I could work out my frustrations by chopping down tree after tree after tree, where an ax was my goddamn best friend and the only conversations I had were with goats and chickens. How fucked up is that?"

I chuckle slightly but his words, the ones he so casually tossed in there, make my chest tighten. "And you love me?"

His eyes warm, and he lowers his forehead to mine. "Do you really think I would have come down here and done all this if I didn't?"

"I don't know. I thought maybe you felt obligated for some reason after what we said that night. I saw how you reacted when the sheriff showed up."

"I was hurt that day when the sheriff arrived. Hurt that you didn't tell me the truth from the beginning. I could have protected you. I would have made sure things were done right from the beginning. And it would have saved both of us a lot of pain." He pulls back and kisses me softly. "But I also understand why you did it. You fled up into those mountains for the same reason I did, and then, we found each other, almost like it was fate."

"You believe in fate?"

He shrugs slightly. "Not necessarily, but I believe in what we have. If you do..."

"Oh, God, Beau. Of course, I do." My tears fall now in earnest. "You saved me from more than just that damn storm. You showed me kindness I didn't know still existed in the world; that I had forgotten about after all the years I spent with Tommy. You understood me in a way no one else ever has. I want to go back up to the cabin with you. There's nowhere else I'd rather be."

The shrill ring of his phone in his pocket jerks him back from me—the sound ominous when we've been waiting for it for so long.

"I should get that. It could be Allen."

I nod and step back from him slightly, but he wraps his arm around my waist and pulls me close again as he tugs his phone from his pocket and answers. "Hey, Allen. I'm going to put you on speaker with Brooke."

He presses the speakerphone button and a soft static sound fills the condo. I hold my breath and wait for my fate to be told to me.

"I had a long meeting with the DA. I laid out everything our private investigator found—those old videos from the apartment complex that showed several of the older assaults or the immediate aftermath, the affidavits of the neighbors who heard arguments and violence, her medical records, and—"

Beau growls. "Get to the fucking point, Allen."

"And the DA has agreed to dismiss the charges without prejudice. He doesn't want to go up against a defense paid for by a Beaumont where we would paint him as attacking the victim of abuse by pursuing the charges."

I suck in a sharp breath. "Wh-what what does that mean?"

"It means you're free, but if they ever get any additional evidence that supports their original theory or that contradicts anything that we've suggested, he still has a right to reissue the charges. I don't think that'll happen though because there's nothing out there for him to find, right?"

"No, of course not. So, it's really over, then?"

"It's really over."

Beau presses a kiss to my temple. "Thank you, Allen."

"You owe me one."

"I owe you more than one." Beau ends the call, drops his phone back into his pocket, and drags my lips to his for a heated, heavy kiss, while pressing his hard body against mine.

His cock stiffens between us, and I run my hands over his freshly shaved cheeks. I once told him he could be on the cover of GQ, and at the time, I had no idea why he reacted so badly. Now I know it's because he was on it, not even six months before his parents were killed and he was shot. I don't know that I would have recognized him though, even if I were holding that cover in my hand and staring at the man who lived in that cabin. They are two different people, and with his face soft and smooth like this, it feels so foreign, yet also Beau.

Pulling back, I grin at him and try to think of anything I can possibly ever say to explain how I feel. "Thank you, Beau, for saving me."

"You're very welcome. Thank you for saving *me*."

I chuckle, then bite my lip. "Anytime, but hey, I do have a request."

He raises a dark eyebrow at me, his lips curling into a half-grin. "What's that?"

"Please grow back the beard."

Epilogue

BEAU

The hot summer sun beats down on my exposed shoulders, and sweat drips down my back and chest. I heave the beam onto my shoulder and carry it from my workspace in front of the barn to the side of the cabin, then lower it down to the ground with the others.

Wiping the sweat from my brow with my hand, I examine the partially completed addition to the cabin I've been working on for the last several weeks.

It's coming together. Not as fast as I'd like, or as fast as I could have done it six months ago, but having Brooke here with me gives me a distraction I won't ever complain about.

Instead of working myself to the bone, to the point of exhaustion and pain because I believed I needed to do it, I get to snuggle in with Brooke every night and plan a future I finally want.

"Hey, babe?" Brooke's voice floats through the quiet summer air.

I turn toward the front of the cabin and swipe at

another bead of sweat dripping down my temple. "Back here!"

She appears around the corner of the cabin, alabaster skin glowing in the warm sunshine and blond hair flowing around her like a damn halo, her hand on the swell of her expanding belly. "Oh, there you are. I need your help."

"With what?"

A familiar scowl turns her lips, her frustration with some of the limitations of being pregnant and getting bigger becoming more and more evident each day. "With every-thing lately..."

I chuckle and make my way over to her, pulling her into my arms and pressing a kiss on her lips even though I'm all sweaty and disgusting from working out here all day.

Brooke pulls away and wrinkles her nose. "You stink."

"You like it."

She can't fight her grin, and she reaches down and smacks my ass, then takes my hand and pulls me toward the front door. "Maybe, but really, I need your help...again."

"With what?"

I was really hoping to get another section up before the sun goes down tonight, but I haven't been able to deny this woman anything, so if she needs me, that means setting the project aside until she's done with me.

"I'll show you."

"Okay..."

Something's up.

She's usually a lot more direct than this, and since she started her new life up here with me, she definitely hasn't been afraid to tell me exactly like it is—even when it's something I don't want to hear.

What is she up to?

I never know these days.

But after the shock of finding out Brooke was pregnant not long after we returned to the cabin, there isn't much she can do that will surprise me.

She pulls me in the front door and toward the office I now share with her. I scan the room, looking for what she might need help with.

"Do you need a book?"

The top shelves are high enough that she couldn't reach them even before her belly started growing, but now that she's almost seven months along, there are even more she needs my help to grab.

Brooke glances at the shelves but shakes her head and points to a framed photo laid out on my desk, next to the one of me with Mom and Dad.

I freeze, and she squeezes my hand.

"What's this?"

Grinning, she tugs her hand from mine, picks up the frame, and turns it toward me. "It's a picture I want to hang in the baby's room."

I accept it from her, my throat tightening as I take in every detail and try to find my voice. "When did you take this?"

Brooke chews on her bottom lip—a sure sign that she's nervous about something—and holds up a hand. "Don't be mad."

"Do I ever get mad?"

She scowls at my joke. "Don't make me answer that, Beau. You won't like it."

I grin at her and return my focus to the picture. "Seriously, when did you take this?"

"That morning we went up to the lake, but it was before you asked me not to take pictures of you or the cabin. I swear, I had kind of forgotten it was even on there, but when we got up here and got everything settled, I went back through my camera and found these. And that one was just...too good not to frame."

It's strange looking at yourself in a photograph and finally seeing what you really look like. No matter how long I looked at my reflection in the mirror up here, I never recognized the man staring back at me. When this picture was taken, I didn't even know who he was.

But now, only six months later, I know exactly who this man is.

The shirtless man, swinging an ax, with snow around him and the sun casting a shadow on the side of his face—he was a man living half a life. A man barely living at all.

And all that changed because of this woman. Because she stumbled into my isolated world and opened it up to so many things, opened *me* up to so many things.

Love. Happiness. A future. A *family*.

All the things I thought I could never have.

BROOKE

Beau stares at the photo for so long, his hands clenching the frame firmly, that a tiny bit of fear starts to turn my stomach worse than the morning sickness did.

"Beau, are you mad?"

I've learned to read him well over the last six months, become good at gauging his moods and knowing what he needs—whether that be time alone out in the barn or in the forest hacking away at a tree to rid himself of whatever memory or guilt or annoyance is bothering him, some quality time snuggling on the couch with a good book, or a little TLC in the bedroom.

But with his head angled down, his face not visible, it's impossible for me to tell what he's thinking. Right now, I feel like that girl who woke up in Beau's bed not knowing where she was or what was going on.

Something wet falls to the glass on the frame, and Beau wipes it away with his thumb and lifts his head to finally look at me again. Another tear trickles from his eye. "Hell no, I'm not mad. I'm the happiest I've ever been."

A giant weight lifts off my shoulders, and I release a heavy sigh of relief.

When I found those pictures buried behind the hundreds of others I took up at the lake that day, I had completely forgotten about them. My first reaction was to delete them, to delete the evidence that I had not done what Beau asked, that I had not obeyed his wishes. But then I looked at them and saw how beautiful they were. How beautiful *he* is. How perfectly the pictures capture the man I fell in love with then, and who I love even more now.

"Really?"

One corner of his lips quirks up. "You certainly know how to capture a good photo."

I grin at him and blink away the tears starting to fall from my own eyes. "I had a very handsome subject who made my job easy."

He chuckles and sets down the photo on the desk to pull me against him, my belly separating us.

"Thank you." He presses a kiss to my lips. "I think it would be the perfect addition to the baby's room."

"You do?"

For some reason, I thought he would put up more of a fight about this.

Beau nods and brushes hair back from my face. "I do."

"So...we're going to do a lumberjack theme?"

He barks out a laugh and shakes his head. "I guess it would be appropriate. My parents would love it."

"I'm sure they would. Following in the family tradition, huh?"

"What do you bet Nate sends him an ax for his first birthday?"

I raise an eyebrow. "First? No, that's definitely a birth gift."

Our combined laughter fills the small room where we once had a confrontation that sent me running from him, and Beau drops his hand to my belly to rub it gently.

"That might be a little young to get him started, but I'll have him swinging one in no time."

"I'm sure you will."

His smile falters slightly. "Are you still nervous about having a baby up here? Because I told you, we can always go back to Seattle. I would understand if you'd rather raise a child there than here, with all the inherent dangers and—"

"Stop." I press a finger over his lips. "Yes, I am nervous about it. The weather, and the bears, and the cougars..."

He sighs, no doubt remembering our close encounter just as vividly as I do.

"But this is home, Beau. This is where you and I belong. And where *he*"—I place my hand on top of Beau's on my stomach— "belongs, too."

"You're sure? Because it would save me a lot of work if I didn't have to finish the addition."

Laughing, I playfully shove at his shoulder. He captures my face between his palms and kisses me deeply, just like he always does, pouring all of his emotions into it.

"I love you, Brooke Beaumont."

"I love you, Luke Beaumont."

I raise my hand and hold it against his beard. "And thank you so much for growing this back. That whole baby face thing just wasn't working for me."

He grins. "Anything for your lumberjack fantasies, darling. Anything."

* * *

I hope you enjoyed *Billionaire Lumberjack*.

More lumberjack goodness is coming in 2023 with an all new reclusive billionaire in Billionaire Lumberjack's Baby!

A wounded billionaire in hiding. A surprise baby. One woman trapped on the mountain with them...

I fled to the mountains to escape the pain of my past.

Anguish ruled my days and haunted my nights.

It became my constant companion.

An ax in my hands became the outlet for my agony.

It was the way I liked it.

The way it *needed* to be.

No amount of money would ever bring back what I lost.

Nothing could ever heal the scars.

Until a knock at my cabin door brings a feisty new lawyer from my company...

Carrying a tiny, crying surprise she says is mine.

It was one night of solace in the arms of a stranger.

A stranger who claims I'm the father of this child.

I can't handle a baby.

Or the feelings brought up by the woman assigned to deliver him to me.

I tried to escape my life, but now it's forcing me to face it—whether I like it or not.

Grab this steamy stand-alone about a damaged billionaire, a surprise baby, the attorney stuck in the middle of it all, and discover what happens when they're forced together in his cabin with building tension, old wounds...and a tiny human!

PREORDER NOW: books2read.com/ BillionaireLumberjacksBaby

Until then, keep reading for a sneak peek at *Savage Collision* (available now).

To stay up to date on news, releases, and sales from Gwyn, sign up for her newsletter here: www.gwynmc namee.com/newsletter

SNEAK PEEK AT SAVAGE COLLISION

one

SAVAGE

Naked women gyrate on stages—asses, tits, flesh on display —their images covering three-quarters of my computer screen, but they are merely blurs in my peripheral vision.

My focus is on the top right corner, where one of my vendors is unloading his truck on the loading dock, and taking his sweet-ass time doing it. He's no doubt using it as an excuse to gawk at the girls. Byron is in heated discussion with him about something. Hopefully, my club manager is reaming him out for taking up so much of our damn time with an unload that should take only minutes.

Why are people so fucking lazy these days? What happened to work ethic?

Mom and Dad made damn well sure all their children understood the importance of a hard-day's work and always giving it one hundred percent. I guess that kind of thing just isn't instilled in people anymore. It shouldn't surprise me really, the degradation of society, not when I see the degenerates who always manage to find their way in here, despite my best efforts to keep the club clientele upscale.

Byron and the vendor move to the back of the truck and start unloading several handcarts-full of cases of beer at a time. At least I can always rely on Byron to get the job done.

I return to the paperwork on my desk but barely have time to regain my train of thought before my office door flies open, slamming against the wall.

Instinctively, I reach under my desk, wrapping my hand around the grip of the Sig Sauer 1911 Scorpion I keep mounted there. I look up, expecting to find one of Domenico Abello's thugs, because, surely, that would be the only person capable of making it past both Gabe and Byron to end up in my office unannounced.

My breath catches in my throat when, instead of a burly threat, my eyes land on what I can only describe as a Victoria's Secret model. An enraged one.

She is furious—the fire in her stormy blue eyes and her scowling red lips are a dead giveaway. With a toss of her long, wavy blonde hair behind her shoulder, she thunders into my office as if she owns the place.

I track her progress across the room, taking in her polished appearance—from her French-manicured nails, thousand-dollar bag, and Burberry trench down to the four-inch Louboutin stilettos that make her long, elegant legs extend beyond comprehension as she clicks across the wood floor with purpose.

My cock hardens instantly and, despite my surprise at my body's reaction to her, I steel my expression and shift uncomfortably in my chair.

Damn. This woman is livid, and hot as fucking hell.

I doubt she's a threat, though—to anything but my libido —so, I remove my hand from the gun and surreptitiously slide it to my crotch to adjust my erection before reclining and watching her speculatively. Despite this being my office, my domain, I wait patiently for her to say something. A hint of uncertainty and maybe discomfort surface from beneath her diamond-hard demeanor.

"Are you the owner?"

She stops several feet short of my desk, props her hands on her shapely hips, and huffs in defiance. Her voice is level and steady when she asks the question, but her eyes give her away. They roam over me with blatant interest, and the slight flush on her neck and cheeks only confirm my suspicion—she's checking me out.

I relax in my chair and school my features, trying to hide my amusement. I answer her question with a nod. "I am, and you might be?"

"Danika Eriksson." She tosses her name at me like a poison dart, and her bravado impresses me despite my uncertainty about her purpose here.

Do I know her? Should I be recognizing her name? No, I would remember a woman like her.

Movement in the open door catches my attention. Gabe eyes Ms. Eriksson with concern. I wave off my best friend, right-hand man, and business partner with a look, and he nods his understanding before disappearing down the hall.

"What can I do for you, Ms. Eriksson?"

She crosses her arms over her chest in a huff, which only succeeds in pushing her abundant breasts higher.

Not helping the raging hard-on situation, lady.

"You can tell me where the hell you get off tricking young, innocent girls into selling themselves like slabs of beef in your disgusting club." She spits the words at me, completely, unabashedly unafraid to insult me and my business, while standing right in front of me and looking me in the eye.

I struggle to withhold a grin at her audacity as I lean forward, resting my elbows on the edge of the desk.

"I can assure you, Ms. Eriksson, that none of my employees are 'tricked' into doing anything."

She scoffs and shifts her weight, drawing my attention back to her impossibly long, shapely legs. The woman must be at least five foot seven without those heels on. With them, she towers over me in all her elegant glory.

"Bullshit..." She searches my desk for a nameplate, then looks at me again when she doesn't find one.

The corner of my mouth quirks up before I can stop it. "Savage, Savage Hawke. But please, call me Savage, and just what is it you think you know about my employees?"

"Savage?" Her eyes narrow, and then, she rolls them. "Your parents honestly named you Savage Hawke?"

This isn't the first time someone has questioned my name, or that my name has left me the butt of some joke. "Yes, they did. It's a family name."

My gaze naturally drifts to the framed photo on the corner of my desk. It was my father's second-to-last fight. He's standing in the center of the ring in Madison Square Garden, the WBA heavy-weight championship belt around his waist, and I'm hoisted above his head, both of us smiling in his victory. I was ten.

She follows my stare and when she sees the photo, her eyebrows pop up in recognition. "Wait, your father is Sam 'The Savage' Hawke?"

Stunned doesn't even begin to describe how I feel, hearing my dad's name from her. It takes me a moment to shake off my surprise, but eventually, I manage a smile and nod. "I'm surprised you recognize him." I lean forward to grab the photo and turn it around so she can see it more clearly.

In my thirty years on this planet, I don't think I've ever met a single woman who knew who my father was. Men, on the other hand, gape in awe when they find out my lineage. I guess it just goes with the territory of being the son of a heavy-weight champ, and one who died the way he did.

She takes a step closer to me, bending down slightly to get a closer look at the photo. "Holy shit! I can't believe you are 'The Savage's' son! Of course I know who he is. My dad was a huge boxing fan. I grew up watching your dad's fights from my old man's lap."

"That's great." And very unexpected. I'm not quite sure what to say. Talking about my father is always bittersweet.

Her smile and astonishment fade, and she glances at me apologetically. "Shit, I'm sorry..." Before she finishes her thought, she seems to realize she's been sidetracked from her intended purpose. She straightens herself, squares her shoulders, and I can tell she's ready to get back to business.

"Well, Savage," she says my name like it's a four-letter word, "I would very much appreciate it if you kept your sleazy hands off my baby sister."

Bingo!

She isn't the first, and she certainly won't be the last, person to find their way into my office on their high horse, accusing me of taking advantage of some innocent little sister, cousin, or friend.

"And who is your baby sister?"

Her face scrunches in disgust at my inability to immediately make the familial connection.

"Nora Eriksson, she started shaking her ass and tits for you almost three weeks ago."

The way she throws the words "ass and tits" at me, I have to cover my mouth with my hand to hide my grin. This woman is all attitude, and it is sexy as fuck, although I have no idea why. She definitely isn't my usual type, although, I'm not sure if I even know what my type is anymore. Certainly, she's about as far from Becca as one can get, yet my cock is still straining against my pants.

I clear my throat before responding, hoping to give myself a second to regain my composure. "Ah, yes, Nora. My manager, Byron, hired her. I've only had the pleasure of meeting her on one occasion, but I can assure you, Ms. Eriksson, she was in no way 'tricked' into taking her position here."

She glowers at me, and her hands ball into tight fists at her sides. "I know my sister, *Savage*, and there is no way in hell she just up and decided she wanted to be a fucking stripper. She was tricked, or forced..."

I barely manage to contain an eye-roll. "If I didn't have such thick skin, I might be insulted by the way you throw your words at me like daggers." I sit back and enjoy watching her distress at my ability to maintain my cool. The color in her cheeks flares, and her blue eyes flash at me.

Who knew angry could be such a fucking turn on?

* * *

DANIKA

My blood is boiling and this man—Savage Hawke—has grated my last nerve. I can barely contain my desire to climb across his desk and smack him across his handsome, smug face for acting so high and mighty. He is a pussy peddler. A goddamn sleazebag who preys on young, impressionable, desperate girls in order to make a quick buck.

Savage Hawke.

He even has a porn star name. It wouldn't surprise me if he was shooting them in some back room.

It's too bad he's so fucking gorgeous. He runs a hand back through his thick, wavy black hair and focuses his Caribbean-blue eyes on me with a calm that makes me want to throw my purse at him.

My traitorous body reacted to him instantly, heat churning deep in my belly the moment I walked into his office and saw him dominating the space behind his large, wooden desk.

The longer we talk, the worse it gets, and I have to press my thighs together to stop the dull ache there.

Damn, it has been way too long since I had a good fuck. What? Twelve days?

I'm so busy fuming and trying to rein in my runaway sex drive, I completely forget to respond to him.

"Ms. Eriksson," he continues, giving me a smug smile, "I have a very rigorous interview process established to ensure none of my employees begin work here under any duress..."

I lift my brow in speculation and to ensure he's aware of my disbelief. *Bullshit!* I bet their "interview process" involves lap dances and blowjobs in the champagne room.

"...Byron conducts a very thorough interview with each girl, including a complete background check to determine if they are under any serious financial strains. If I find they are, I typically offer them a personal loan, to be repaid at standard interest rates, to ensure they aren't tempted to engage in pursuits some of the other clubs are often known for. We also do weekly drug testing and nightly breathalyzers, as our girls are forbidden from engaging in any illicit drug use and cannot perform while under the influence of any alcoholic beverages."

I don't believe him for a second. No damn strip club operates like that. He must think I'm some dumb, naïve, bimbo blonde to believe I'll fall for his line of horseshit.

He reclines back in his chair and waits for me to say something.

What does he expect me to believe? That he's a pussy peddler with a heart of gold?

"Surprised I'm not a total scumbag?" His amusement is evident in the slight turn at the corner of his luscious mouth. "There are a hundred trashy strip clubs in New Orleans a man can go to if that's what he's looking for—drugs and easy women. I wanted to offer something different. People are always a bit shocked to learn how I run my business. But when I built The Hawkeye Club, I wanted it to be an upscale and supremely classy gentleman's club and established a very strict set of rules and regulations to ensure that both my reputation, and the reputation of my girls, remains pristine."

I huff and take a step closer to his desk. "My sister was the goddamn valedictorian of her high school class and had a full ride to Tulane for pre-med. Then, this morning, out of the blue, I find out from one of her roommates that she has dropped out of school and started working here. She's twenty years old, for Christ's sake! Clearly, you can see why I'm concerned. I mean, why the hell would she do that?"

He offers me a small, understanding smile and leans over his desk, toward me. The fabric of his dress shirt stretches across his broad shoulders and strains against his massive biceps. My mouth salivates, and I fight the flush I'm sure is creeping up my neck. The worst thing about being fair-skinned is the complete inability to hide my reactions, especially to men like Savage Hawke.

"I do understand, Ms. Eriksson, but I don't have the answer for you. Have you tried asking your sister?"

Shit. I should have seen that question coming.

I shift uncomfortably and twist my hands in front of my body. "No, she's been avoiding my calls. That's why I finally went to her apartment today, to make sure she's okay."

He almost looks sympathetic.

I wonder how long it took him to perfect this nice-guy act.

"Well, I think you need to talk to her. I don't think she's on the schedule tonight, but you can ask Byron downstairs, and, if she's here, he will gladly show you to the changing rooms in the back so you can speak with her."

Casting an uncomfortable glance toward him, I move my purse from one shoulder to the other and turn to leave without a word. Absolutely no good will come from me spending any more time in this room with this man.

Savage Hawke is precisely the type of man I always end up getting myself into trouble with: dark, strong, passionate...

I almost stumble when a vision of him slamming me back against the wall and yanking up my skirt to gain access floods my mind.

Jesus—I bet he takes absolute control in the bedroom, and I bet he fucks like a complete animal. Men like that don't do things slow and sweet.

"I don't even get a 'thank you' or a 'goodbye?'"

His sultry, deep voice stops me halfway to the door. I look over my shoulder at him.

Deep breaths, Dani. Keep it together.

Don't let him see how he affects you. Don't let him see you rattled.

"I don't have anything to thank you for." I raise my head high and strut out the door, not bothering to close it behind me. I punch the button on the elevator and tap my foot impatiently.

I need to get out of here.

I need to get as far away as possible.

I need to find Nora.

I need to find something to prevent me from racing home, grabbing my Rabbit, and spending the rest of the day fantasizing about that man.

I need to find something to prevent me from racing straight back to his office, climbing over his desk, and straddling his lap.

An angry fuck can be supremely hot—ripped clothing, hair pulling, strong, groping hands—but having an angry fuck with my stripper sister's deviant boss would be an epically bad life choice.

Savage Collision is available now at all retailers:

books2read.com/SavageCollision

About the Author

Gwyn McNamee is an attorney, writer, wife, and mother (to one human baby and two fur babies). Originally from the Midwest, Gwyn relocated to her husband's home town of Las Vegas in 2015 and is enjoying her respite from the cold and snow. Gwyn has been writing down her crazy stories and ideas for years and finally decided to share them with the world. She loves to write stories with a bit of suspense and action mingled with romance and heat.

When she isn't either writing or voraciously devouring any books she can get her hands on, Gwyn is busy adding to her tattoo collection, golfing, and stirring up trouble with her perfect mix of sweetness and sarcasm (usually while wearing heels).

Gwyn loves to hear from her readers. Here is where you can find her:

FB Reader Group: https://www.facebook.com/groups/1667380963540655/

Facebook: https://www.facebook.com/AuthorGwynMcNamee/

Newsletter: www.gwynmcnamee.com/newsletter

Website: http://www.gwynmcnamee.com/ Twitter: https://twitter.com/GwynMcNamee

Instagram: https://www.instagram.com/gwynmcnamee

Bookbub: https://www.bookbub.com/authors/gwynmcnamee

OTHER WORKS BY GWYN MCNAMEE

The Inland Seas Series (Romantic Suspense)

Squall Line (Book One)

WAR

Out on the water, I'm in control.

I don't make mistakes.

But the fiery redhead destroyed my plans and

left me no choice.

I had to take her.

Now I'm fighting for my life while battling my growing attraction
for my hostage.

Grace may have started my downfall, but she could also be my
salvation.

GRACE

The moment he stepped foot on my ship, I knew he was trouble.

He took me, and now, my life is in his hands.

But things aren't what they seem, and Warwick isn't

who he appears.

The man who holds me hostage is slowly working his way into my
heart even as greater dangers loom on the horizon.

War and Grace.

Dark and light.

Love and hate.

This storm may destroy them both...

AVAILABLE AT ALL RETAILERS:

books2read.com/SquallLine

Rogue Wave (Book Two)

CUTTER

Complete the mission.

It's what I was trained to do—no matter what.

But when things go to shit right in front of me, my objective gets compromised by a set of fathomless amber eyes.

This isn't a woman's world.

Yet, Valentina refuses to see how dangerous the course she's plotted really is.

How dangerous I am.

VALENTINA

The man who saved my life is just as lethal as the one trying to take it.

Maybe even more.

While he may have rescued me, in the end,

Cutter is my enemy.

The one intent on destroying everything I've striven for.

But the scars of his past draw me closer even though I know I should move away.

Cutter and Valentina.

Anger and desire.

Fight and surrender.

This wave may drag them both under...

AVAILABLE AT ALL RETAILERS:

books2read.com/RogueWave

Safe Harbor (Book Three)

PREACHER

When it comes to firewalls, no one gets

through my defenses.

For the past five years, protecting this band of f-ed up brothers has been my mission.

But Everly pulls me from my cave and does the one thing no one else ever has...

She makes me believe there's a life outside the world

on my screens.

Too bad actions have consequences, ones that threaten everything and everyone around me.

Including the beautiful tattoo artist who has managed to etch herself onto my heart.

EVERLY

The emotional upheaval of the last six months would be enough to break anyone.

And I can already feel myself cracking.

A tall, sexy, tattooed bad boy is the last thing I need thrown into the mix.

All I want is to keep my head down and pour my pain

into my art.

But Preacher walks into my life and offers me safety in a world
where I thought there was none.

Until our pasts finally catch up with us...

Preacher and Everly.

Fear and loss.

Hope and heartbreak.

This harbor may be their salvation.

AVAILABLE AT ALL RETAILERS:

books2read.com/SafeHarbor

Anchor Point (Book Four)

ELIJAH

Life outside the walls of my prison cell is far harder than the time
I did inside.

There, I had my misery to keep me company.

Out here, I'm forced to face the reality of

everything I've lost.

Nothing can repair the gaping hole in my chest.

Yet, a broken woman wrapped in chains threatens to unravel the
tangle of excuses I use to keep everyone

at arm's length.

But letting Evangeline into my world means exposing her to the
real threat.

Me.

And all the terrible things that come along with that.

EVANGELINE

Taken.

Enslaved.

To be sold to the highest bidder.

The monsters who stole me away from my life

have no conscience.

I'm not so sure the man who rescues me is any different.

He's an ex-con and a pirate— not to be trusted.

But the dark veil of anguish that shrouds him can't hide the truth
of who he is at his core.

Elijah isn't the enemy.

He may be broken and tormented...

And exactly what I need.

Elijah and Evangeline.

Agony and regret.

Faith and acceptance.

This anchor may pull them both down...

AVAILABLE AT ALL RETAILERS:

books2read.com/AnchorPoint

Dark Tide (Book Five)

RION

There is no black and white in this life.

The line between right and wrong blurs.

I'm constantly crossing it.

Saving a life is just as easy as taking one.

And I'm damn good at both.

Finding a woman who can survive in this world was never on the radar.

But Gabriella pulls me from the bottom of a bottle and touches me in a way no one else can.

Too bad secrets and lies have a way of catching up with everyone.

GABRIELLA

How did I end up here, slinging drinks at a dive bar in the middle of nowhere?

The choices that brought me to this were never even a glimmer of possibility only a few years ago.

How things can change so fast...

And now, my path puts me on a collision course

with Orion Gates.

His bigger-than-life size and personality should

be a warning.

The profession he's chosen should be the ultimate

final straw.

But instead, I find myself unable to resist his pull.

A decision that could lead to the end of all of us.

Rion and Gabriella.

Lust and lies.

Betrayal and ruin.

This tide may drown everyone...

AVAILABLE AT ALL RETAILERS:

books2read.com/DarkTide

* * *

The Hawke Family Series

***Savage Collision* (The Hawke Family - Book One)**

He's everything she didn't know she wanted. She's everything he thought he could never have.

The last thing I expect when I walk into The Hawkeye Club is to fall head over heels in lust. It's supposed to be a rescue mission. I have to get my baby sister off the pole, into some clothes, and out of the grasp of the pussy peddler who somehow manipulated her into stripping. But the moment I see Savage Hawke and verbally spar with him, my ability to remain rational flies out the window and my libido takes center stage. I've never wanted a relationship —my time is better spent focusing on taking down the scum running this city—but what I want and what I need are apparently two different things.

Danika Eriksson storms into my office in her high heels and on her high horse. Her holier-than-thou attitude and accusations should offend me, but instead, I can't get her out of my head or my heart. Her incomparable drive, take-no prisoners attitude, and blatant honesty captivate me and hold me prisoner. I should steer clear, but my self-preservation instinct is apparently dead—which is exactly what our relationship will be once she knows everything. It's only a matter of time.

The truth doesn't always set you free. Sometimes, it just royally screws you.

Tortured Skye (**The Hawke Family - Book Two**)

She's always been off-limits. He's always just out of reach.

Falling in love with Gabe Anderson was as easy as breathing. Fighting my feelings for my brother's best friend was agonizingly hard. I never imagined giving in to my desire for him would cause such a destructive ripple effect. That kiss was my grasp at a lifeline—something, anything to hold me steady in my crumbling life. Now, I have to suffer with the fallout while trying to convince him it's all worth the consequences.

Guilt overwhelms me—over what I've done, the lives I've taken, and more than anything, over my feelings for Skye Hawke. Craving my best friend's little sister is insanely self-destructive. It never should have happened, but since the moment she kissed me, I haven't been able to get her out of my mind. If I take what I want, I risk losing everything. If I don't, I'll lose her and a piece of myself. The raging storm threatening to rain down on the city is nothing compared to the one that will come from my decision.

Love can be torture, but sometimes, love is the only thing that can save you.

Books2read.com/Tortured-Skye

Stone Sober (The Hawke Family - Book Three)

She's innocent and sweet. He's dark and depraved.

Stone Hawke is precisely the kind of man women are warned about— handsome, intelligent, arrogant, and intricately entangled with some dangerous people. I should stay away, but he manages to strip my soul bare with just a look and dominates my thoughts. Bad decisions are in my past. My life is (mostly) on track, even if it is no longer the one to medical school. I can't allow myself to cave to the fierce pull and ardent attraction I feel toward the youngest Hawke.

Nora Eriksson is off-limits, and not just because she's my brother's employee and sister-in-law. Despite the fact she's stripping at The Hawkeye Club, she has an innocent and pure heart. Normally, the only thing that appeals to me about innocence is the opportunity to taint it. But not when it comes to Nora. I can't expose her to the filth permeating my life. There are too many things I can't control, things completely out of my hands. She doesn't deserve any of it, but the power she holds over me is stronger than any addiction.

The hardest battles we fight are often with ourselves, but only through defeating our own demons can we find true peace.

AVAILABLE AT ALL RETAILERS:

books2read.com/StoneSober

Building Storm (The Hawke Family - Book Four)

She hasn't been living. He's looking for a way to forget it all.

My life went up in flames. All I'm left with is my daughter and ashes. The simple act of breathing is so excruciating, there are days I wish I could stop altogether. So I have no business being at the party, and I definitely shouldn't be in the arms of the handsome stranger. When his lips meet mine, he breathes life into me for the first time since the day the inferno disintegrated my world. But loving again isn't in the cards, and there are even greater dangers to face than trying to keep Landon McCabe out of my heart.

Running is my only option. I have to get away from Chicago and the betrayal that shattered my world. I need a new life-one without attachments. The vibrancy of New Orleans convinces me it's possible to start over. Yet in all the excitement of a new city, it's Storm Hawke's dark, sad beauty that draws me in. She isn't looking for love, and we both need a hot, sweaty release without feelings getting involved. But even the best laid plans fail, and life can leave you burned.

Love can build, and love can destroy. But in the end, love is what raises you from the ashes.

AVAILABLE AT ALL RETAILERS:

books2read.com/BuildingStorm

Tainted Saint (The Hawke Family - Book Five)

He's searching for absolution. She wants her happily ever after.

Solomon Clarke goes by Saint, though he's anything but. After lusting for him from afar, the masquerade party affords me the anonymity to pursue that attraction without worrying about the fall-out of hooking-up with the bouncer from the Hawkeye Club. From the second he lays his eyes and hands on me, I'm helpless to resist him. Even burying myself in a dangerous investigation can't erase the memory of our combustible connection and one night together. The only problem... he has no idea who I am.

Caroline Brooks thinks I don't see her watching me, the way her eyes rake over me with appreciation. But I've noticed, and the party is the perfect opportunity to unleash the desire I've kept reined in for so damn long. It also sets off a series of events no one sees coming. Events that leave those I love hurting because of my failures. While the guilt eats away at my soul, Caroline continues to weigh on my heart. That woman may be the death of me, but oh, what a way to go.

Life isn't always clean, and sometimes, it takes a saint to do the dirty work.

AVAILABLE AT ALL RETAILERS:

books2read.com/TaintedSaint

Steele Resolve (The Hawke Family - Book Six)

For one man, power is king. For the other, loyalty reigns.

Mob boss Luca "Steele" Abello isn't just dangerous—he's lethal. A master manipulator, liar, and user, no one should trust a word that comes out of his mouth. Yet, I can't get him out of my head. The time we spent together before I knew his true identity is seared into my brain. His touch. His voice. They haunt my every waking hour and occupy my dreams. So does my guilt. I'm literally sleeping with the enemy and betraying the only family I've ever had. When I come clean, it will be the end of me.

Byron Harris is a distraction I can't afford. I never should have let it go beyond that first night, but I couldn't stay away. Even when I learned who he was, when the *only* option was to end things, I kept going back, risking his life and mine to continue our indiscretion. The truth of what I am could get us both killed, but being with the man who's such an integral part of the Hawke family is even more terrifying. The only people I've ever cared about are on opposing sides, and I'm the rift that could end their friendship forever.

Love is a battlefield isn't just a saying. For some, it's a reality.

AVAILABLE AT ALL RETAILERS:

books2read.com/SteeleResolve

Find all of Gwyn's works at www.gwynmcnamee.com